CASTIEL SKULL

The

Vampire's

Drudge

For my aunt, Crystel Hamilton, who unknowingly inspired me to keep writing, even when I was blinded by my own clouds of darkness.

CONTENTS

CHAPTER 1
YEAR 1842 - RED

The moon gazed down at me, and I blankly stared back at it. I used to love looking at the moon night after night. It always brought a smile to my face. However, tonight was different. I did not find comfort in the moon as its light fell upon my face; rather, it made me feel as if I was alone in the world. Tears began to fall from my face, wetting the hard and dirty floor on which I slept. I continued to watch the moon for hours from a hole in the roof until it drifted out of sight. Moments later I heard a man hollering for us all to wake up. There were many people lying in the room beside me, on the floor. The hard earth, where my body laid without rest, did not bother me. I was used to it.

"Get up! We have work to do," the man yelled as the door of the small room burst open. Startled, I jumped up off of the floor, unsure of what I was supposed to do. The unfamiliar face of the bald, lanky, black man, looked around the room until his eyes met mine and he bowed his head toward me.

"What's your name?" he asked.

I was a shy child, never wanting to speak to people, especially strange men. I reached to grab my hair to hide my face, a habit I had done since I can remember, but it was gone. I forgot, they cut my hair off. I was bald, just like everyone else in the room with me.

The man stepped closer to me and squatted down to my height, which was very short because after all, I just turned four years old a few days prior.

"It's alright, I'm not going to hurt you. What's your name, little girl?"

"Sass... Sassandra," I whimpered.

"Sassandra? That's a beautiful name. Did you sleep, Sassandra? No? Well, I'm sure you will tonight. Come with me, the master will want to see you first thing."

"Where are we? Where is Mama and Papa?" I asked the man.

"We're in Savannah, Georgia," the man answered, ignoring the question about my parents.

We left together, leaving the huts and the others behind us, following a small trail as it climbed up a slight incline. The moon followed us as we walked, and in its light, I saw these beautiful things growing from the ground. Their colors were magnificent to gaze upon. I reached out, touching as many as I could. Their texture was unique, but unfamiliar, soft and smooth. I could not decide which ones I loved most. I was captivated by them all.

"What are these?" I asked.

"Those things are flowers. Haven't you ever seen flowers before?" the man grunted.

"No, what do they do?"

"Well, I guess people just look at them. We grow them to sell for profit, not that we get any of it. This here is the biggest floral plantation in the South. Now come along and stop asking questions."

The walk was very long but the flowers kept my mind from noticing. I actually had to run part of the way to catch back up because I was mesmerized by their bright colors. There were thousands of them, all different types. It was difficult for me to keep up, plus I was short compared to the man I was following. He reminded me of my papa. Once we got past the fields of flowers, the path turned from being narrow and just dirt to a bit wider and laid with small pebbles that led us to a white house with a large tree on the side of it. This house was nothing I had ever seen before. It was very large. Nothing like my village had.

The man veered to the left and turned to look at me. He waved his hands for me to follow him and put a finger over his lips to tell me to stay quiet. I quickly caught up with him and he grabbed my hand, pulling me around the corner of the house.

"Now, Sassandra," he said, "before you go into this house,

I need you to understand some things. First, do not ask the master any questions. He doesn't like questions, ya hear? If you ask him anything he will punish you. Do you understand?"

"Why can't I ask any questions?" I asked.

"Because you can't. If you have questions, ask one of us."

One of them? I was confused. I didn't understand. I squished my eyebrows together and was going to ask another question but the man interrupted me.

"Make sure you stay busy. If you are unsure of what to do, just watch the other ladies around you and do as they do. Do not make eye contact with the master. Keep your eyes to the ground when he is around you, ok?"

"Um... I don't really know what's happening. I just want to go home." I began to cry again. I missed Mama and Papa.

"Sassandra, I'm sorr..." the man began to choke up and cry himself. He cleared his throat and started again as he wiped the tears from my cheeks. "I'm sorry, but we are slaves. This is your life now. You have to do what the master tells you to do. We all do. Otherwise, he'll kill us... or worse. Now, when you go inside, just remember what I told you. I will try to find you later to check on you. Whatever you do, don't try to run away. As long as you listen and stay busy, you should be alright."

I just nodded. I was young. I didn't understand half the words he was saying to me. I didn't know what master and slave even meant. All I could think about was seeing Mama and Papa again. I wanted to go back to my home. Instead, the man took me back around the house and gently knocked on the door. The door creaked

4

open and there stood a lady. She beckoned me inside but I was afraid. I did not want to go through this door. She gave me a kind smile and grabbed my hand, pulling me inside the house. Like the man outside and myself, she too did not have any hair. I entered the home and was about to ask a question but then I stopped myself, remembering what I was just told. I followed the lady into a long narrow room. She opened another door and we went into a much larger room where we sat down and quietly waited. I felt like I was going to suffocate. All the windows within the room were covered by thick draperies, shutting out the outside world. A few other women, also with no hair on their heads, entered the room and they sat down beside us. No one said anything to me. They just smiled and nodded their bald heads toward me. I tried to smile back but I didn't recognize any of them. None of these women was my mama.

The room was quiet for several minutes until we all heard it. *Tap, tap, tap.* Someone was coming. *Tap, tap, tap.* The door swung open and a man entered the room. Once again, I found myself to be confused. This man did not look like other people did. He was different. His skin was not dark like all of ours, but exceedingly white. His eyes were — I gasped. I forgot to not look at his eyes! I quickly looked to the wooden floor. I listened as the pale man continued to pace the room. His feet were covered, unlike all of ours. He had, what I found out later were called, shoes on his feet. I looked at my own bare feet. They only had dirt on them.

Tap, tap, tap, was all I could hear. He walked across the room, turned around, *tap, tap, tap,* and walked across the room again. The entire time no one said anything and the entire time I stared at

5

my own dirty feet, afraid to look up.

"Good morning," the man spoke at last.

"Good morning, Master Vincent," all the other women in the room responded. I said nothing.

Tap, tap, tap. The man strutted toward me, stopping just in front of where I was sitting. I could see his feet right in front of mine. The red dress shoes on his feet were shiny. I wanted to reach out and touch them, but I sat there, frozen, too afraid to move.

"I said good morning, slave. Did you not hear me?" the white man said. His accent was different than the man who walked me to the house, his words spoken with an almost nasally tone but still were perfectly enunciated.

Still, I sat there, staring at both our feet, wishing mine were covered like his. I wondered why I never had anything to cover my feet before.

"When I ask you a question, you'll do well to answer me if you know what's good for you. Now say it back to me."

"Good... Good morning," I whispered without looking up.

"Good morning? Is that all you have to say or did you forget something?"

Did I forget something? Well, did I? I wasn't sure. Should I ask if I forgot something? I felt the man's eyes looking down at me. He made me feel small. He was waiting for me to answer him but I was too frightened to say anything. I didn't want to die. I started to cry, again.

"Apparently, this little *thing* doesn't have any manners. When I say, 'good morning' you're to say, 'good morning, Master

6

Vincent'. You know why you call me 'Master', servant?" the man shouted at me. I just shook my head, unable to speak.

"Well," he continued, voice growing louder with each word. "You call me 'Master' because that's what I am and I deserve the respect that comes with the title! I saved you. I saved all of you. You were nothing before I came here. You had nothing. Do I not feed you? Do I not give you shelter? Do I not provide you more than you ever had before? Have I not given all of you more than any of you could dream of? Well?"

"Yes, Master Vincent," the women in the room answered.

"Stop your crying. If we start the morning like this again, I will lash every one of you in here. You teach this little nigger bitch some manners by tomorrow morning or you all will be punished!"

"Yes, Master Vincent," the women in the room answered.

"Now, let us get started, shall we? Why wasn't the fireplace attended to throughout the night? Embers. I told you I want fire from dusk till dawn! Make sure the chimneys are cleaned out this week. We wouldn't want the place to catch fire. As always, meals for the day need to be prepared and served on time. I have a delivery coming in fresh from the market at noon today. Fresh flowers need to be brought in and changed out for every room of the house. For every wilted flower I see, it will be a lashing for everyone. Floors are beginning to look worse than the ground outside. I want them scrubbed. Every room. Spider webs; how has no one not noticed them? The front porch needs to be cleared of them. This needs to be checked on a daily basis; they keep coming back overnight. Until then I will keep bringing in more slaves to get it up to my standards.

7

That would mean smaller food portions for everyone."

Daily chores had started and I caught on quickly, relieved to be away from the man's gaze upon me to whom they all referred to as 'master'. The ladies of the house prepared a grand meal for everyone after the delivery from the market arrived. Never had my eyes gazed upon so much food. All the men got to eat first but there was still enough food for me when it was my turn. I wasn't quite sure of most of the foods that I was putting into my mouth but it was all delicious nonetheless and my stomach grew full for the first time. Everyone was polite to me while eating but they all kept telling me to work hard and to be on my best behavior. Maybe it wouldn't be so bad here after all, I thought to myself as I shoveled more food into my mouth. All the men and women I met were bald and barefooted, like me. It made me feel like I belonged with them. I was no longer sad and afraid but deep down I still missed Mama and Papa. While eating the food, everyone introduced themselves to me. I quickly forgot all their names except for Omari, the man who walked me to the house. He sat beside me, eating his food and made sure I ate all of mine as well.

"They say you're doing a good job, Sassandra," Omari said to me while he was scraping the last bite off his plate. "Keep up the good work."

Much later, after the sun had left the sky and darkness settled in again, I was taken to a room by one of the ladies of the house.

"Master Vincent told me to bring you to this room," the woman said as she opened the door. "You'll sleep here. I guess you're his new pet now," she sneered as she left me standing in the doorway, alone.

I closed the door behind me as I ventured toward the bed. But this was no ordinary bed. It had wooden legs that raised it off the ground and carvings decorated the wooden frame. It had a plush red blanket and a soft pillow for my head. I eagerly jumped into it and snuggled under the blanket as I blew the lantern out that was lit on the bedside table next to the mason jar with white flowers in it.

I had a dream that night. It may have been the first I ever had or perhaps it was the first I can ever recall. I was floating. I saw my body lying in the bed below me, fast asleep. I glided down and out of the room, down the hall, and up a flight of stairs. At the top, there was another narrow hallway with many doors on both sides, but only one door caught my attention. It was at the very end of the hall and a bright red light shined through the crack at the bottom. It reminded me of the alluring red flowers I saw in the fields earlier in the day. I glided down the hall toward the menacing door at the end. That door must lead to the fields of flowers and I wanted to pick one. As I got closer to the door, I heard a man's voice speaking, whispering.

"Do not wake, my child. As long as you listen and obey me, I will keep you safe. Do not think or speak of your parents ever again. I will look after you. You and your blood belong to me now."

I peeked through the keyhole to see who he was talking to. It was Master Vincent leaning over a bed, whispering in the ear of a small girl. She was sound asleep and looked very peaceful. His hand slowly touched her ear and a single finger brushed down her jaw toward her chin. Master raised the girl's chin up, exposing her neck. A wicked grin formed across his face as he leaned toward the girl. His mouth came down on her neck and his eyes slowly closed in satisfaction. A drop of blood ran down the girl's neck onto the pillow, staining the white linen. I then recognized the girl laying in the bed. It was me.

Suddenly, Master Vincent's eyes shot open and he snapped his head toward the door with me on the other side of it. His eyes locked in on mine peeping through the keyhole. I wanted to race back down the hall and down the stairs and back into my room to hide, but I could not move. I was frozen with fear. The vibrant red flowers from the fields, the shine from his dress shoes, the bright light beneath the door. It was all there, in his eyes, glowing red. I became lost in his hypnotic gaze.

I jolted awake from the nightmare, glad to escape it. I was back in my room, laying under the red blanket in the bed I remembered getting into the night before. The sun shone through the curtains onto the wooden floor. The only difference in the room was that a single white flower petal had fallen to the floor. The flower must have started to die when I was sleeping.

CHAPTER 2
YEAR 1857: IMPERFECT

Time passed, as it always had and always will, and I grew up on the plantation into a young woman. Whether it was time that made me quickly forget my parents and what had happened to them, or perhaps it was the distraction of the strange nightmares I seemed to have almost every night that kept running over and over in my head throughout the day while I was awake. Whatever it was, I no longer thought about them or what happened to them.

In my dreams, throughout the years, Master Vincent was almost always there, never aging from the first day I met him, the glow of red within his eyes always watching me sleep. Some nights in the dream he would touch my face, dragging his boney fingers down my cheekbone and across my lips. He would whisper in my ear but I could never remember his words once I was awake. He would lean down to press his lips on my neck, night after night, after night. Other times in the dreams I would see a strange woman with white feathers hanging from her black hair, sitting with her legs crossed, watching a fire burn in front of her. Sometimes the woman would outreach her hand and a black crow would fly down to her, landing in the palm of her hand. She never acknowledged me in my dreams but yet she would smile, as if she knew I was watching her.

When I wasn't sleeping, I was doing everything I could to ensure the house was always kept in order. Fifteen years had passed since the first night of my arrival and most of the lady servants of the house I met my first morning on the plantation were now gone. There were rumors, from time to time, of a few of them being killed by Master Vincent, which scared some of the others into trying to run away. I do not know if they ever got away or if they were killed. It never bothered me enough to ask. Besides, questions were forbidden. What I do know is on more than one occasion I would hear screams outside the house, always after the sun had set. I would hastily pull the curtains shut in my room and jump in my bed, hiding under the blanket until the screaming would stop. I do not know why they were afraid of Master Vincent. If they would complete their work without complaint then he would not be so angry with them. Why couldn't they see him like I did?

But I was happy here. I was given a purpose and a beautiful home to help maintain. The children that were on the plantation would have nightly lessons after supper. As a child, I never attended the lessons with the others because it was outside, down at one of the huts, and I found comfort within the walls that Master Vincent had provided me. Instead, another slave, named Hyenah, would come back to the house and give me private lessons each night. Master Vincent said it was vital for everyone on the plantation to know their colors since we grew and sold flowers. Colors for Master Vincent went beyond primary, secondary, and tertiary colors. Sometimes he would become annoyed that we could not see fine details within the colors of the flowers like he could. I also learned how to cook, how to quilt blankets, and weave clothes for the others. I grew passionate about learning anything and everything Hyenah and Master Vincent were willing to teach me. What more could the world give me?

I was still the youngest of the ladies who worked in the house, but they all knew I was Master Vincent's favorite and that put me above them, therefore I was in charge. I took it upon myself to make sure everything within the house was properly attended to. I did everything correctly. I minded my manners and went above and beyond with my chores. I helped others to ensure their chores were completed on time as well. Something inside of me wanted to please Master Vincent. After all, he did save me. I no longer had questions filling my head as I once did when I was a little girl. Rather, I was the one with all the answers for the new ones who came to live on the plantation.

I had Master Vincent's daily routine memorized. In the mornings he would meet us in the same sitting room next to the dining room for our meeting. Instead of him yelling and pacing back and forth, he would sit and watch me conduct the meetings. I would already have today's chores, meals, and activities planned for the other servants of the house. After they began their work, Master Vincent would sit one on one with me to speak about how the plantation was coming along outside of the house. We brought floriculture to our community. If the first-class citizens needed any type of floral arrangements, they knew to contact us. We were the best.

After talking business with me, he would then ring for Omari, who was in charge of keeping order of the plantation on the outside during the day. Omari would enter the house and speak with Master Vincent about the fields and harvesting.

One morning I had caught Omari half way up the steps that lead to the bedrooms on the second floor. This was odd because once the meeting was over Omari always left the house. He had no business going upstairs.

"What are you doing? Did Master Vincent tell you to go upstairs for something?" I demanded an answer.

Omari gasped and jumped, turning to face me. I clearly startled him. "Um, no. Actually, I was looking for you, Sassandra," he responded, giving me a small smile.

I looked at him, tilting my head, waiting to hear why he was looking for me. I politely smiled back at him.

"Um, I just wanted to see how things were going. Are you alright?" he inquired.

"Yes. I am well."

Omari made his way back down the stairs, stopping at the bottom and said, "Well, if you need anything just let me know. That dress looks really pretty on you by the way. You look so much like... well, just someone I used to know."

"Thank you, Master Vincent gave it to me earlier this week," I said, twirling in a circle to show it off to him.

Omari just nodded and then awkwardly walked past me, sniffling. I could have sworn I saw a tear run down his cheek. I knew the women were jealous that Master Vincent favored me but I never imagined that the men would feel the same way!

"Omari!" I yelled after him.

He stopped in his tracks and turned back toward me. "Ma'am?"

"After you come by tomorrow, I'll have to shave your head. Your hair is becoming too long. Then you can shave mine when I'm finished with yours."

"Yes, ma'am," was all he said and turned to leave the house again. My first week on the plantation I was taught that slaves were to keep their heads shaven due to outbreaks of lice in the past. Master Vincent would be livid if it happened again.

I was ecstatic the night he gave me my first dress. It was yellow with a white floral print on it with a fat blue ribbon to tie around the waist. I tried it on and Master Vincent asked me to spin and spin in circles until I was dizzy, almost falling over. I had a lot of dresses and I proudly showed them off for him. The other ladies never did receive a dress from Master Vincent, only the clothes that were handmade out of burlap. However, he never gave me any shoes

15

to wear with the dresses. But I loved caring for his shoes. I made sure they never lost their shine.

Master Vincent would walk the house, room by room, checking in on all of us. Making sure we were staying busy before retiring to another room where he held meetings with other white men, none who were quite as pale as he, that would visit from time to time. These men did not sound like Master Vincent sounded. I wondered to myself if he was from somewhere else in the world, like me. I would answer the door and walk them to the office. If he had no visitors, he would spend the afternoon reading a book or the daily paper that was delivered each morning. He took an interest in reading about politics and how our country was developing.

Flowers by the bushels would be brought to the house by one of the outside slaves. Master Vincent would pick through them, looking for any with ripped or wilted petals. Imperfect flowers would be sent to the general public to sell for a cheaper price or tossed out with the trash if they were too far gone. Flowers that were up to par were kept for the wealthy. Politicians, bankers, gunsmiths, jewelers. They were all important clients of our plantation. They were the ones to visit and have private meetings with Master Vincent. Fresh flowers would be delivered to them every week.

Language of Flowers was one of the most important and favorite books of Master Vincent's. It was the only book he would reread. I would catch myself watching him skimming through its pages. The book was a few inches thick with a royal blue, hardback cover. He would catch me watching him and he would call me over to him to teach me something new from time to time. Like sunflowers moving throughout the day to follow the sun from sunrise to sunset. Or certain flowers that, if consumed, even a little bit, would bring death to the person who consumed it. Certain flowers even represented words, so you could send secret messages by the type of flowers that would be used.

One morning, the local jeweler brought a package to Master Vincent and later that evening, after sunset, Master Vincent left the house. He wanted to personally deliver a floral arrangement to the local jeweler as a thank you gift. He had me help him pick through piles and piles of tulips of all colors. Finally, he decided on a bouquet of flaming parrot tulips. They were dazzling yellow and white cup-shaped petals that were fringed, twisted, and ruffled on their tips, reminding me of the white feathers that hung in the woman's black hair from my dreams. Bright red petals would snake their way up between the white ones, like a growing flame.

It was that same night that I wished for death. I do not know what came over me. Master Vincent had left to deliver the flowers and I was in his room, scrubbing the floors, humming along to a song the others were singing outside by the huts. I stood up to look out the window. I saw them by a fire, singing and carrying on, without me. I was one of them, a servant, a slave. But I never felt like I belonged with them. I did not have any desire to leave this house to join them. I closed the heavy curtains and turned my back to them, returning to my chores. That's when I saw it, its beauty caused me to gasp. It was a necklace, inside a clear box, sitting on the top of the bookshelf. Its chain was golden and hanging from it was a circular gold amulet with carvings and an oval ruby in its center. I reached up, bringing the box down and sitting it on the desk. I wanted to feel it. To feel gold for the first time. Gently, I removed it from its box and held it within my trembling hands. It was cold to the touch and I turned it over to observe its back. Inscribed was the phrase, "Esprit de la Mere". I did not know what the phrase meant but I knew it had to be a different language. I unhooked the clasp of the chain and went to put it around my neck. I only wanted to see what I looked like in the mirror, wearing it. As I fumbled with the necklace, trying to lock it in place, my reflection showed no one standing behind me but I felt two hands wrap around my own. They were ice cold, boney, and strong. The hands squeezed my own until I felt my fingers break, causing me to scream out in pain.

"You dare try to steal from me?" Master Vincent hissed in my ear.

CHAPTER 3
PRESENT DAY: FANTASY

I gazed in the mirror at my reflection, remembering once upon a time when reflections of vampires were nonexistent, due to their pure silver backing. Every decade my coven, known as the Ooljéé coven, played host to the Bloodfeast and Arubrey gave an exquisite speech about what he was most thankful for. The mirror speech was one of the rare times he had ever shown humor. Most of our kind were convinced that mirrors reflected souls and once turned into a vampire, our souls left our bodies, turning our corpse into the walking dead, who only thirsted for blood. I was one of many who believed I had lost my soul when I was turned. I will always be grateful for my coven for convincing me otherwise.

I learned a lot from them. Arubrey taught me that being a vampire was a gift rather than a curse. Winona gave me back my soul, even though she said I never lost it. And Leslie was and always would be my first true friend.

I smiled as I bent over, braiding my long black hair. Once finished, I stood back up to look in the mirror again, flipping my hair behind me, and watching the braid sway as it fell past my ass. Leslie once warned me that long hair was an easy target during battle but I refused to let her cut it. I went without hair for nearly fifteen years when I was a human, enslaved by a cruel monster. Instead, we turned my hair into a weapon, using silver wiring to wrap around the braid and sometimes, silver needles or spikes, forged with poison, sticking out from all over. I no longer wore dresses, unless it was the night of the Bloodfeast. However, I did become obsessed with shoes. High heels were my favorite. Dress or no dress, I almost always wore heels. No one should be denied good shoes.

Tonight, I slipped on a pair of black stiletto heels with built in brass knuckles between the heel and the sole. All my heels contained hidden weapons and these complimented my leather pants with thick stitching that ran up the legs. I grabbed a plain fitted t-shirt and some brass jewelry to pull it all together. I was on a mission. Tonight, I had a date.

My coven resided in the southern part of the Garden district of New Orleans but I mailed a letter to my date's office earlier this week, telling him to meet me tonight at Black and Blue's, a steakhouse close to where he worked in the East district of New Orleans. I entered the restaurant, fashionably late, obviously, and spoke with the maître-d, who kindly walked me to the table where my special guest was waiting for me. The maître-d pulled out my seat for me and I gave him a kind smile just before he turned to walk away.

My date had short thick brown hair and he was dressed in a white dress shirt and black slim tie and he watched me as I sat down in front of him, mouth wide open like he was missing a chromosome. Forgetting to blink, he asked me, "So, you're... you're real. Like... you're a *real* vampire? I can tell.

"I said nothing. The less I said the more he would talk. He saw this as an opportunity to speak freely because after all, we were in a public environment.

"You're late," he boldly added.

"Were you waiting long?" I asked.

"Just almost an hour. What took you so long?"

I smiled again. "Were you beginning to worry?" I teased.

"I was about to order another bottle of wine, actually. Would you like a glass?"

"What year is it?" I inquired.

He turned the bottle around, about to answer, but paused. "Why do you always answer a question with a question?" my special guest threw back at me.

I sighed. "I guess you're not into games?"

"You're doing it again!" he barked.

"Let's get to business then, shall we, Mr. Devin Green?"

"How did you know my name? How did you know where I worked?"

I smiled again. "Now who's the one asking a question with a question?"

Our server walked up to our table with an ink pen and pad of paper in hand, ready to take our order.

"I'll have the twelve-ounce porterhouse steak, well done with the scallops and risotto and perhaps the chicken for my date," Devin ordered, overconfidently.

I chuckled out loud in amusement. "Actually, his date will also have the steak, but make mine rare. I want it *dripping* with blood," I said to the server as I stared directly into Devin's eyes. "Also, skip the fixins'."

Our server promised us our order would be out shortly and scurried off. Devin probably made him feel uneasy trying to order for me.

I tilted my head to the side and looked Devin in the eyes again, clearly making him uneasy now. "Don't worry, your family is safe," I declared. "I only took photos of them and mailed them to your office to get you here. I never would have touched them. It was a scare tactic."

"Well, it worked. I'm here. What do you want?"

"You run your mouth a lot. I know you don't work late in the office. I know your drug of choice that keeps you up at night. I've seen you at the bar. I've seen you with... our kind. You crave our venom. Tell me, when a vampire bites you, what does it feel like?" I inquired.

"Well, you're a vampire. Don't you know?" Devin asked.

"It's different for everyone. Some experience different types of pain. Others say that it's pleasurable for them. I assume it's pleasure for you?"

Devin shifted in his chair, clearly uncomfortable talking so freely about all of this. "I've done every drug on the market. Pain pills, coke, heroin, shrooms, meth, but only every once in a while. Nothing makes me feel the way being bit by... one of your kind... feels. Like I'm in a different universe. I've always managed to be a functioning addict but it's getting harder. I crave it almost every night now. Every minute at work I think about it. My wife is threatening me. She wants me to quit my job because I keep telling her I have to work late. She's clueless. It's not like I'm out cheating on her. All I want is…" He stops talking.

I lean in closer to him. I had him right where I wanted him. "Tell me, what is it that you want? Perhaps we can come to an arrangement," I suggested.

He sits back in his chair, afraid of my abrupt movement toward him. He looks around the 5-star restaurant, afraid of being watched. No one was paying attention to us. He did not notice earlier but all eyes were on me when I walked in. Once the restaurant staff and guests saw me sit with ordinary looking Devin, their interest faded away.

Our food was served just then and Devin stared at me in anticipation. I rolled my eyes and cut into my steak, letting the red juices seep from the cut. I brought the bite to my lips and winked at him as I popped the steak into my mouth, slowly chewing, pretending to enjoy the flavor. The blood from the steak would never satisfy my thirst as the blood from a human did. The rare steak was heated back up. Once a body dies, the blood always tastes... flat. Blood of an animal compared to a human's taste stale. So even though the steak was served from a 5-star restaurant, it tasted flat and stale. I only ate to amuse my guest of honor.

"I didn't know," he leaned in a bit closer and whispered the words, "vampires could eat food."

"We can do almost anything a human can do," I explained. "But we don't necessarily *have* to do everything a human has to do. Now that I told you a secret about us, won't you tell me a secret?"

Devin sat back in his chair. "What do you want to... Wait, I don't even know your name!" he declared.

"Devin, my name is not important. What is important is a certain rumor you have been told and that you have carelessly spread to others within the vampiric community. I need to know who your source is, of this said rumor. How about a compromise? What if we both get what we both want tonight. Is that fair?"

"Yes. Anything for you. I would do anything for any of you," he declared.

Devin surprised me when he told me what he truly wanted. We chatted a bit about life and death and I shared an anecdote with him about what I really wanted when I first became a vampire. I finished my steak that was served to me before he even touched his, insisting on watching me eat first.

I excused myself from the table and made my way to the lady's room. I had to text the others to let them know my plan and using a phone at the dinner table was just classless. I also needed to puke the steak up but I couldn't let Devin know I only ate it to put on a show for his own amusement. When the bill came, Devin surprised me again. He said that since I declared to the waiter that I was his date that it was his obligation as a decent guy to pay. I probably had ten times the amount of money he could even dream of but he said it was his honor to pay for my lousy meal.

When he was finished eating, I asked, "Your wife thinks you're working again tonight?"

He bowed his head in embarrassment. "Yes."

"We'll take my car," I suggested. "There is a leather hood in my glovebox. I will put it on you and you will not touch it. If you even try to scratch your nose then the deal is off and I will kill you. I will leave your corpse for your daughter to find. She will be scarred for life. If you want to avoid that happening then you will do as I tell you, no questions asked."

"I understand completely," he complied.

The valet pulled my vehicle up as we exited the restaurant. I drove an all-electric Volkswagen SUV. It was a good-sized SUV with a lot of safety features and was excellent for the environment, compared to the vehicles created in the late 1800s. I waited for the valet to open the driver's door for me, leaving Devin to open his own. Once inside I looked at him and then looked at the glove box. He nodded, and opened the glove box, sliding the handgun to the side and took the leather hood out. I took it from his hands and placed it over his head and clipped it to his dress shirt. There were no holes where the eyes would be, only a zipper for the mouth.

"Is this necessary?" he asked. "I won't tell anyone where you take me."

"I believe you," I responded. "But I also believe that if you knew where I took you that you would return, on your own accord and my coven would kill you. But don't worry, they already know I'm bringing you with me and promised to be on their best behavior. Now, stop asking questions."

To ensure that he didn't memorize the route, I purposely randomize my driving in the beginning, in the middle, and at the end, turning endlessly. The drive normally would have taken less than a half hour and I turned it into a two-hour drive. Devin's wife would have to sleep alone again.

We pulled up to the white brick, Italianate, mansion and I pulled my cell phone out of my pocket, quickly dialing the most recent number on my call list. "We're here," I said, then quickly hung up and put the phone back into my pocket.

My coven and I acquired the mansion shortly after President Lincoln's assassination. It was made from white brick, three stories tall, with a grand entrance. It was just over fifteen thousand square feet and one of the first homes within New Orleans to have indoor plumbing. We walked up the stone steps and through the front doors, where black and white marble floors greeted us. Ignoring the large staircase to the left that wrapped around the entire room with a balcony in the middle and at the top, which was above the front doors, we turned right through a single door that led us down a narrow hall. Halfway down the hall, I led Devin, with his leather hood still in place, through the door that took us down a flight of stairs that turned into a 90-degree angle down another flight of stairs into a sub-basement. We walked on the ancient rug that led us to a singular chair, where I sat Devin down and cuffed him to the chair, and removed his hood.

He looked around at his surroundings that were lit by candle light that hung from the walls and pillars that supported the roof over our heads. "Where am I?" he asked.

"Do not speak!" roared Arubrey, who sat across Devin on a throne, fit for a king. On the left side of Arubrey sat Leslie, wearing a sheer short-sleeved white top and blue leather pants with diamond-shaped cuts in them from the knees up to her pelvis. Her short, wavy, brown hair was slicked back tonight and held firmly in place. On Arubrey's right sat Winona, wearing a white gown and purple moccasins. Her black hair was wild tonight, fierce like fire, and was decorated with red and white feathers sticking out from all around her head. Arubrey was dressed in a very fitting suit that complimented his many assets. His black, silk, shirt clung to his muscular chest. He was the most attractive vampire I have ever met. His dark hair was styled messy but his small built frame and the way he presented himself could make the legs of women and men turn to Jell-O. I personally did not look at Arubrey in a sexual manner but one could not deny, even with his burn scars that ran from his neck down to his fingertips on his left arm, that he was in fact pure eye candy.

I stood behind poor Devin, who was shaken by Arubrey yelling at him. I rested my hands upon his shoulders and gave them a gentle squeeze. Intimidation came easily to my coven. This wasn't personal, it was interrogation.

"Your name is Devin Green, human?" Winona asked.

"Um... yes," Devin stammered, afraid of the change of environment.

"And you've been frequenting the nightclub, Seven Nights on a weekly basis?" Leslie asked.

"Um, yes, for about a month now."

"Who introduced you to the nightclub?" Arubrey demanded.

"I... I don't know, she attacked me after work one..."

Winona quickly shook her head and I smacked Devin on the side of his face. "Do not lie to them!" I ordered. "Who introduced you to the nightclub?"

"Alright! I don't know her name. I was leaving a therapy session one night and she grabbed me when I was unlocking my car door. She told me she had the best drug I would ever experience. I was already a mess from speaking with my therapist and I just wanted a quick fix. I didn't ask any questions. I just followed her to her car. We drove to a cemetery and when we got out, she slammed me against the brick wall, trying to make out with me. I... I didn't want that. I only wanted the drugs she promised. She said... she said I was boring and then she jumped over the brick wall. She made it look so easy! I pulled myself over the wall. She knew I was following her. She kept looking back at me and laughing. She opened a secret passage inside a mausoleum and I followed her down the hidden staircase. She paid for us both to get in. But when we got inside, she said she had to leave. I never saw her again." Devin was shaking at this point, either from the cold or from nerves, or withdrawals, probably a combination of all three.

"You have information that we want," Leslie said. "We will give you the choice of doing this the easy way or the hard way, human."

"Arubrey, Winona, Leslie," I spoke. "I have already made a deal with the human. He will give us all the information that we require in exchange for something that he desires."

"Why should we give him anything that he wants?" Arubrey asked.

I stepped around Devin, toward the other three, sitting on their thrones. "We are not monsters. We do not need to resort to torture to get the answers we seek from humans. I believe the word is, 'compromise'."

Arubrey stood, and within a split second, he was nose to nose with Devin. "A compromise is not a few answers in return for eternal life, mortal," he spat.

"Um, I don't want to be a vampire," exclaimed Devin.

Leslie laughed out loud. Winona repeated his words to herself in Navajo, and in confusion. Arubrey was back on his throne, sitting motionless.

I stepped back toward Devin. "He has no wish of being turned. He actually has... a fantasy he would like to have fulfilled."

"I would like details of this fantasy," Leslie said, sitting on the edge on her throne. She always did like to hear the mundane desires of mortals.

"He wants…" I started before being cut off by Leslie.

"No, no, I want the human to tell us what his fantasy is. Tell us, boy, how can we fulfill your fantasy?"

Devin swallowed and tried looking behind himself, looking for me. I placed my hands on the sides of his face, turning it back to face the three vampires who sat across from us. "I… I… well, it's silly now that I think about it," he began. There was silence. No one spoke, waiting for him to continue. "Well, I do love, like *really* love, having my blood sucked. And so, um… I thought it would feel, like, amazing, if I could have a vampire on both of my wrist and on both sides of my neck, you know, sucking my blood. At the same time. Like an orgy but instead of sex, you all, or any vampires for that matter, not necessarily you, could drain my blood, all at once. I mean, unless you would want it to be you. I'm okay with whatever you choose. I've just always wanted a group of vampires to drink from me at the same time. No one at Seven Nights ever wanted to share me at the same time."

Winona and Leslie looked at one another and then they looked at me. I smirked at them then we all three looked at Arubrey, who continued to sit motionlessly.

CHAPTER 4
YEAR 1857: UNWORTHY

I was unconscious, dreaming. I saw a fire, burning bright, illuminating the darkness around me. She was there, watching me laying on the floor in Master Vincent's bedroom. Her eyes were closed and she was crying. It was not tears that fell from her eyes, but small white feathers.

"Help me," I whispered to the strange lady who occupied my dream.

She slowly opened her eyes to reveal nothing but dead white. Her voice did not come from her mouth, it remained closed. I heard her voice speak from within my own soul. "Soon," the voice rang throughout my entire existence.

Soon. I wanted to believe her. I wanted to stay in this dream, with the strange woman next to the warm fire but I could not. I watched as the last white feathers continued to fall from her eyes, turning black once they hit the ground. Soon the flames of the fire slowly died down to embers, leaving me in darkness. I was completely alone.

"The others will rejoice in your fall from grace," Master Vincent said to me.

His voice woke me from my dream, and I was now laying on the ground, back in his room. Master Vincent stood across the room from me and was now putting the amulet around his own neck to wear.

"This amulet is the most valuable piece of property I own. More valuable than this house I took, more valuable than all the money this plantation has earned or ever will earn. This necklace is more valuable than any of you slaves I own, including yourself."

Tap, tap, tap. He walked toward me, coming face to face with me, making me feel small, like I was that little girl all over again fifteen years ago. I could only look at his white dress shoes, afraid of looking into his eyes.

"I'm sorry, Master," I pleaded to him. "No, not yet you're not. But you will be, soon enough." There was that word again; soon. I didn't dare look at him. I knew his eyes would be red, filled with rage. He grabbed me by my throat, lifting me up into the air, my bare feet now dangling above the hardwood floor. Master Vincent carried me in a chokehold, backwards through the door, out into the hallway. I wanted to scream but his grasp around my throat made it impossible; only a gargle escaped my lips. I tried grabbing at his wrist to pull his hands off me, but it was useless; he was much stronger than me. His frigid fingers tightened, strangling me as he continued to saunter down the hall, all the while the *tap, tap, tap,* of his dress shoes echoing off the walls.

Soon. Soon this pain would be over. It couldn't last forever. Could it? Fear coursed through my mind as I imagined just how long forever could be.

My vision was blurred from hitting my head on the wood steps as my body tumbled down them. Was this what he meant by falling from grace? Why did it have to hurt so much? Master Vincent had pushed me down the staircase but when I made it to the bottom he was already there, waiting for me. I was lying at his feet. I saw another glimpse of my reflection within the shine from his shoes before vomiting on them and passing out, again.

Was I dreaming? Master Vincent was sitting across from me in the grass, outside. I never went outside the house in all my years here. A large, fully grown, oak tree was behind me supporting my body as I leaned against it. Many vines of greenery had wrapped themselves around the trunk of the tree and grew up into the tree's branches. The moon was shining down on us and Master Vincent's face was alluring in its glow. I wanted to reach out to touch his pale skin. It reminded me of a white rose. Was his skin as soft as its petals? He smiled, exposing two sharp fangs, amused with the curiosity he saw within my own eyes.

"You humans are so foolish," he said to me. The tips of his teeth reminded me of the thorns on a flower's stem. Would they prick my finger, causing it to bleed if I touched them?

"Please, Master. Please, forgive me. I was only trying it on. I wasn't going to steal it. I promise."

"You are unworthy of forgiveness. You must be punished for your betrayal."

Master Vincent stood up and swiftly came to stand behind me at a speed I had never seen a person move with before. How did he move so fast? He grabbed me from under my arms, pulling me to my bare feet, turning me around and pushed my body into the tree.

"Place your arms around the tree," he ordered.

My body moved without my mind thinking about it. I did as I was told, being careful to not let my hands touch its bark but Master Vincent grabbed them, causing me to scream out in pain, and tied them together with my arms tightly hugging the tree. An instant later he was whispering in my ear, "I just want one last taste before your death," and I felt his cool lips brush against my neck before he sank his fangs into my skin. My legs buckled from the sensation that was coursing throughout my body.

The nights Master Vincent would visit me in my dreams flooded my mind. His piercing eyes, his cool and gentle touch, and seductive words. It made it all so easy for me to let him drink my blood when I was dreaming. So easy, that I did not even realize it was happening. This time was different. This time I was awake. The pain from my broken hands, the pain from his fingers crushing my voice box as he shoved me down the hall, the pain from being thrown down a flight of stairs, it all traveled into my neck. It felt like my flesh was being ripped open and my life was being sucked from my body, drop by drop.

I was weak. I was unworthy. I was a slave to a blood sucking monster.

Master Vincent finished drinking from me and I could hear him smacking his lips together, moaning with pleasure. He walked around the oak tree, fully circling it twice, before coming nose to nose with me. I could see remains of my own blood around his mouth as it slowly trickled down his chin.

"Your blood tastes sweeter when you're awake," he said as he ran his fingers down my cheek, wiping the tears away. I'm going to miss it when it runs cold."

He swiftly disappeared for a few seconds and when he returned, he was behind me again. I tried to plead with him but when I opened my mouth, no words came out. He ripped the back of the dress he gave me, exposing my bare skin for the moon to see. I clung to the tree, afraid. I knew what was coming. I heard it all before. The screams of the others when they were no doubt tied to this very tree.

Master Vincent lashed his hand out, holding a bullwhip. I felt my flesh burn as its leather left its first mark across my skin. Then came the sound of the crackling of the whip. How did I feel the strike before I heard the crack? My head was spinning again. The agony that was in my neck now was seeping from the first gash across my back. The burning became more intense, like a growing fire. The pain was too much. Knowing I did this to myself was too much. I was to blame. It was my fault. I betrayed my master. I failed him. I was unworthy of his love. I deserved to be punished. It all became unbearable and I passed out, returning to my dreams.

I was sitting on a branch in the oak tree that my body was tied to. I saw my unconscious self and I felt sorry for her. Why did I touch that necklace? If Master Vincent wanted me to wear the necklace, then he would have put it around my neck himself.

I floated down from the branch and stood beside my master. I looked at him and bowed my head in shame. "I'm sorry, Master Vincent. I will not ever disobey you again. I don't deserve your love. I am unworthy. Please, punish me. Make me suffer, as I have surely caused you to suffer by betraying you."

Master Vincent's lips curled into a smile as he brought his hand holding the whip back again to strike my limp body. It was all in slow motion for me to witness. His boney fingers were tightly wrapped around its handle as he brought his hand over his head and around in a circular motion in order to get more power behind his second strike. The whip whirled through the air, ripping the air apart as it flew wildly behind him. Leading with his elbow, pointed at the center of my back, he thrust his hand forward. The loop of the whip followed his hand, getting smaller as it reached its target and collided with my flesh. A sonic boom could be heard as the loop disappeared. Master Vincent's motions with the whip were faster than the speed of sound. That's why I felt the pain before I heard the crackling of the whip.

Again and again, he punished me. Crack after crack. Blood flowed from my back. Over and over, I watched him scar my body, his words repeating in my mind as he did it.

"You are unworthy," he told me.

"I am unworthy," I repeated his words to sear them into my mind as the whip itself was searing into my back. Over and over again. Crack after crack. Blood now soaked my dress and it dripped onto the back of my legs and ran down to my feet. "I am unworthy," I told myself.

I'm not sure how long I had passed out. When I woke up again, I felt numb. My body was tingling as if it were asleep, my mind was blank, and my soul felt lost. Who was I? Why was I tied to this tree? It hurt to breathe. Someone told me this would soon be over with. My suffering would end. Who was the woman interfering with my dreams? The sun was beating down on my exposed flesh. It felt warm at first but once I realized the sun was up, it rapidly intensified and started to burn, making me remember the strikes my body had endured the night before. The noise from the whip rang throughout my mind, causing me to flinch and scream again in fear. I sobbed and sobbed. Tears dripped to my feet, leaving wet spots where my blood had dried around my feet.

I finally pulled myself together. I had to compose myself, for Master Vincent. I had to show him that I was sorry. I had to show him that I *was* worthy. I needed to get back in his good graces. I always told the others that if they only listened to Master Vincent, worked hard, and followed the rules, that they would not be punished. Now I needed to listen to my own advice. I would work harder than I ever had before. After all, he said my blood was sweet. He liked my blood. I would let him drink it anytime he wanted, not that I could stop him if I wanted to. I wanted him to drink from me. I would do anything to please him. He was my master after all.

I pleaded my case to the oak tree, to which I was bound to. I confessed all my worries to it. I begged the tree to continue to support my body because my body could not support itself any longer. I had wronged Master Vincent and I could never betray him again. He showered me with clothes and food and I was the only one who got to sleep in the house, in a comfortable bed. I was his chosen one. He picked me out of all the other slaves. I would get back in his good graces. I knew he would taste my blood again, and when he did, that would prove that all was forgiven.

Hours passed and the sun finally began to descend behind the fields. The flowers swayed with the gentle breeze that was in the air. It felt cool on my skin. I heard a man yelling in the distance. I knew it had to be Master Vincent. Why was he yelling? Was he still angry with me? The voice became louder as it came closer but I was wrong. It wasn't Master Vincent's voice, it was Omari's.

"Please, Master, don't," he begged.

"Wrap your arms around the tree, you knew this would come," Master Vincent ordered.

Omari now stood across from me, shaking. I saw fear in his eyes just before he placed his arms around the tree, his fingers brushed up against the sides of my exposed ribs. I shivered from his touch. Master Vincent went behind me to grab his hands and bound them together, making me gasp in agony from the wounds I brought upon myself last night.

CRACK!

Omari began to scream and I had to do everything in my power to stifle my own screams as he was beaten on the other side of the tree that we were both tied to. I closed my eyes after the first whip. I could not watch. Master Vincent whipped him thirty-nine times in a row. Each time my body spasmed, like I was the one being whipped.

"Now tell me, do you still want an extra plate of food, nigger?" Master Vincent spat the words in disgust at Omari.

No one ever asked for extra food. No one ever asked for anything. It wasn't allowed. Why would Omari do that? Master Vincent slowly walked around the tree again, standing behind me.

"No, not yet, but you will be," he whispered in my ear before vanishing into the darkness.

The night was silent for a long time. I didn't know what to say and I wasn't sure Omari could talk. I heard his breath, wheezing. I kept counting in my head. I would count to thirty-nine and then start over again at one. I did this for hours it seemed; my mind unable to think of anything else. I felt like I was going crazy. Why did Master Vincent leave me here, tied up with Omari? He didn't drink Omari's blood like he did mine before whipping me. Did he drink it before and not like it? Was I the only slave he drank from? I couldn't take the silence anymore.

"Why did you ask for more food?" I asked Omari.

He moaned but did not answer.

"Omari. Omari, why did you ask Master Vincent for more food?" I needed to know.

He opened his eyes, looking into mine. The fear I saw before had vanished and an emptiness filled them now.

"You," he mumbled.

"Me what?"

"I asked... for an extra plate. To bring to you," he whispered.

My heart sank. Omari had looked me in the eyes before being brutally whipped repeatedly, all because he asked Master Vincent for an extra plate of food to bring to me. I hadn't even thought about food. It made me sick to my stomach.

"Why would you do that? You know you shouldn't ask him questions," I told him.

That's all that was spoken between Omari and myself. He closed his eyes and drifted off to sleep and I shortly followed him into the dream world.

I was sitting on a branch up in the Oak tree again. Both our bodies tied up below me. I stared down at Omari's body. Was I to blame for his lashings? I didn't ask him to bring me food. He should have known better. I should have known better. Why did I try putting that necklace on? I shook my head in disbelief at both our stupid decisions and jumped down from the branch to the ground.

"Are you coming?" Omari's voice asked.

I looked at his body but it had not moved, still asleep. I looked around and saw dream Omari standing next to a field of red poppy flowers.

"Where are you going?" I asked.

He looked over his shoulder then back at me. "Wherever the fields take me. Any place is better than here."

"No. I don't think it's my time to go. I'm staying."

Omari smiled at me. He looked so peaceful. He turned to walk into the fields of flowers and then turned around again, looking at me and mouthed the word 'soon' before disappearing into the night. I walked back to his body that was tied to the tree and kissed his cheek.

The light from the sun woke me. It was torture to open my eyes. I wanted to stay in the darkness of the night. I wanted to stay in my dreams of red poppy fields. The sun was ruthless and refused to go away. I pried my eyes open and immediately closed them again. Omari was still tied across the tree from me. However, he never woke up again. He got to stay in the dream world and roam fields of flowers, leaving me alone in the harsh reality of life.

The sun was warm on my skin but where Omari's hands touched me remained cool. I wanted this to be over. I knew I messed up. I knew I deserved to be punished. I was sorry! I was sorry! Please forgive me!

No one was there to forgive me. I was alone. I was unworthy of forgiveness. And 'soon' would never come. I pushed the strange woman of my dreams and dream Omari out of my mind. I shifted my body as much as I could to try to get more comfortable. I knew better than to try to escape. I sat there, baking in the sun, without food or water. I kept my eyes closed, not wanting to see Omari's face. I thought of chores I could do and which ones I could do better. I thought of lifting my chin just a little bit higher from now on when Master Vincent would enter the same room as me to expose my neck to him.

I drifted off to sleep again but I did not dream of anything or anyone. I was still alone. When I awoke, the moon was in the sky. I glimpsed at it briefly, but felt betrayed by it so I looked away.

"My, my, what a surprise." Master Vincent's breath was chilling to my skin. "You actually survived. Your companion here was the only other slave who ever survived a beating from me before. I guess this time, he wasn't so fortunate."

Omari. I sighed and spoke with my eyes shut. "He shouldn't have asked you for more food. He sealed his fate. And I shouldn't have touched your necklace. If you want me to die too then I will."

Master Vincent untied Omari's hands, his body landing in a heap, and then my own.

"Get one of the other slaves to wash you off and wrap your wounds. Do not even think of returning to the house."

I nodded yes and watched him walk back toward the house, leaving me alone with Omari's corpse lying beside the oak tree.

CHAPTER 5
YEAR 1857: BURN

I stood there, alone once again. So much had changed in the last few days. I had fallen out of Master Vincent's grace and Omari was dead because of me. I shook my head in disgust at myself. I couldn't allow myself to think like that. Omari died because Omari did not follow the rules. And I was lucky to still be alive. Maybe Master Vincent was showing me mercy. Maybe I could get back in his good graces after all. I smiled, thinking of him holding his arms wide open, forgiving me, welcoming me back into the house. I wanted nothing more than for him to wrap his arms around me and tell me that all was forgiven.

I walked toward the path that would lead me down to the huts where the other slaves lived. I passed fields upon fields of flowers, like I did my first night here when Omari walked me to the house, but I did not pay them any attention. I did not look at their beautiful colors. I did not stop to smell their lovely scents. I did not touch their silklike petals. I kept my eyes to the ground as my bare feet slowly moved one step in front of the other, back to where I originally came from when I first arrived on the plantation.

My body ached in pain with each step I took. I could feel every bone that was broken in my fingers. Breathing was difficult as well. My breath wheezed with each step I took, and every time I inhaled, it caused the gashes on my back to sting. If I could hardly breathe and hardly walk then how would I ever make it to the huts? It seemed to be impossible. One foot in front of the other, I focused on that. It was all I could do to make my body move forward. One... step... at... a... time...

It felt like I was walking for days upon days. However, the moon was the only light in the sky that guided me to my destination. Finally, I looked up and saw the small cluster of huts in the distance. I tried pushing myself harder, walking faster, but I collapsed in agony. I tried yelling for help but my raspy cry was weak and no one heard me. Tears began to fall from my eyes onto the ground. I rolled over onto my side and saw the moon above me. It stayed motionless in the sky, staring back at me, like it was mocking my weakness.

Angry at myself, I pushed my body up off the ground and brought myself to my feet and pushed myself toward the small huts again. Once I arrived at the closest tiny home, I leaned my head against its door for support and banged my foot on the bottom of the door, unable to knock with my hands. A man hesitantly opened the door, catching me as my body fell into his arms, too weak to stand any longer.

"Hyenah, come quick," the man yelled behind him.

A woman who I recognized from the house helped the man move me to a side room where they laid me on my stomach.

"Look at her back, Yahko. She's been beaten. Did she escape? How is she still alive?"

"Shh," he hushed Hyenah. "Help clean her wounds and make her comfortable. I'll go find Omari. He'll want to see her."

They didn't know. They didn't know Omari was dead. I gathered all the strength I had left in my mind, body, and soul. I had to let them know.

"Tree," was the only word I could get out of my mouth before passing out.

When I awoke there was no one in the room with me. My body was shaking but I was able to pull myself to my feet off the ground. I walked toward the window and saw a few of the others working in a field of daisies. Their movements seemed rushed and angry. No one was talking. No one was singing this morning.

I heard the front door of the hut open and close again. I walked from the side room toward the noise to see the woman named Hyenah, the same woman who taught me how to read, write, and many other teachings when I was younger.

"How do you feel?" she asked me.

"I'll live," I replied, with my voice sounding more like a frog than my own.

Hyenah came to me and took my hands in her own to examine them. "I'm no doctor but I try my best. These sticks will act as a makeshift brace for your fingers and will have to stay on for a couple weeks in order for your bones to mend. Your fingers shouldn't be too crooked once they heal."

I looked at my hands where she had wrapped them. I could feel something hard, supporting each finger, under the bandages that made me unable to bend my fingers. The pain was still there but it wasn't as bad as it was before.

"Now, I've made some green tea. I want you to drink a cup every few hours," she said, then frowned before adding, "it's unsweetened, but you can add honey. It will help soothe your throat. And for your back I used some aloe from one of the plants and wrapped it with bandages. Your wounds will heal, but you will have scars for the rest of your life."

Hyenah handed me a cup of tea and watched me until I took a few sips from it. It was warm and the honey was soothing to swallow. I felt safe with her. My body began to calm itself and soon the shaking stopped. I noticed my clothes were different. I no longer wore the blood-soaked dress that was ripped. Instead, I had a loose-fitting gown which I recognized to be made from the osnaburg and jute material I used to make clothing for the other slaves.

The inside of the hut was lit by the sunlight that pushed its way in through the windows, which had no glass or curtains to keep the heat nor cold out. There was a fireplace in the center of the side wall and a pile of tinder beside it. A few candles were spread throughout the hut, some on wooden tables, others on the floor against the walls. The walls were mostly bare and coated with mud. Shovels and hats hung from one of the walls closest to the front door. There was no door that separated the main room from the only other room in the hut, which I awoke from. I felt very privileged growing up in the main house compared to the living conditions in which the other slaves had to endure throughout all these years.

"We're having a funeral," Hyenah said, "if you can even call it that, for Omari later tonight. Yahko found him next to the oak tree, like you said. We knew someone was being whipped but we weren't sure who it was. We thought it was someone new he purchased until you showed up. Omari told us he was going to speak with V after dinner yesterday. We thought nothing of it because he always has meetings with him. If we had known it was him…" she trailed off. "I have work to do, outside the house today. You will come with me. Just because you're in pain doesn't mean you can take the day off; you know the rules. I'm not getting in trouble because of you."

I followed Hyenah out of the hut and we made our way down the trail and through a small clearing in the woods, which led us to a small stream.

Hyenah took off the hat she was wearing, exposing her bald head, as we both walked into the water and handed it to me. "You're gonna need one of these today. Your skin ain't used to the sun, is it? You'll surely burn without it," she said as I struggled putting it on, but finally managing.

47

She waded through the water, over to a large stone that was on the opposite side of the stream, where a pile of clothing laid, and began to dip it in and out of the water, soaking it.

"See what I'm doing? You can do this, just hold them between your arms instead of with your hands and then toss them back onto the rock. I'll do the rest."

I took the various clothing, one at a time, and dipped them in and out of the water a few times each, then passed them to her. Hyenah would then scrub them together and then dip them again and beat them against the large rock before tossing them back to me to dip them into the water for another rinse.

"Washing clothes for V is a lot easier than washing our own. He doesn't let us use anything from the house, so the stream serves a few purposes for us. We're lucky we don't have to walk far to get to it."

I didn't respond at first. I did my new chore without complaint and listened to Hyenah sing, as her humming slowly turned into actual lyrics.

Wade in the water
Wade in the water
Wade in the water, children
God is gonna trouble these waters

See that band all dressed in white
God is gonna trouble these waters
It look like a band of the Israelites

God is gonna trouble these waters

See that band all dressed in red
God is gonna trouble these waters
Look like a band that Moses led
God is gonna trouble these waters

My Lord delivered Daniel well
Daniel well, Daniel well
Didn't my Lord deliver Daniel well
Then why not every man?

Man went down to the river
Man went down to the river, Lord
Man went down to the river
Went down there for to pray

We were half way done with the pile of clothes before I asked, "Why do you call him 'V'? You know we're supposed to call him 'Master Vincent'."

"I call him 'V' because the man is vile. It's my nickname for him. I worked on this plantation before he arrived. He stole it, you know, the property. He killed the previous owners and claimed it as his own. He said he witnessed a group of slaves kill them. Oh yes, they all believed him too."

"You really think Master Vincent did that?" I asked.

"'Course, I do," said Hyenah. "I heard their screams that night and I've heard the screams of many others since then. Ever since you showed up and replaced the last girl, we've felt a bit safer. There has been less screaming. We've feared for you, Sassandra. Being all alone in that house, with that horrible, horrible, monster."

"What last girl? Who?" I asked.

"It was a few years before you came along. Omari had a wife and a daughter, you know. Your precious Master took Omari's family into the house. He told Omari that his wife and daughter belonged to him now. They lived in the house for a while, just as you used to. Omari worked very hard in hopes he would let him see them again. That never happened. One morning, they were just gone and V never spoke of it and that was that. Omari was devastated, but what could any of us do? They could have been sold to another plantation for all we knew. But deep down we all know that monster killed them."

I couldn't believe it. Master Vincent wouldn't have killed a child. Would he? He never harmed me. Well, not until recently but I wasn't a child anymore. I was nineteen now and I deserved my punishment. In all the years of seeing Omari come in and out of the house, not once did he mention a wife or daughter. I wouldn't believe it.

I grabbed the last article of clothing and dunked it in the water, holding it there longer than necessary, wanting to drown my thoughts and questions with it. I brought it back up and pushed it back under the water again before tossing it to Hyenah and walked back out of the water toward the hut. The bottom half of my bandages were soaking wet now but the cool water was soothing to my back. I would ask Hyenah to change them for me once she returned.

Later that night everyone, including myself, had gathered around a large fire outside. Beside the fire, there was a table with Omari's body lying on top of it.

"Tonight, will be the last night we burn one of our own," Yahko spoke to the crowd. "Tonight, we send Omari to the afterlife where he will be reunited with his wife and daughter once again."

I looked at the others standing around the fire. Their eyes filled with sadness but something felt off. Each person had sharpened spears made from branches or pitch forks from the fields. I was the only one standing there without anything in my hands, not that I would be able to hold anything with my bandaged fingers. I looked around for Hyenah to ask her what was going on but I did not see her.

Yahko started again, "Your death will not be in vain, Omari. We will avenge you and your family tonight. We should have done this long ago. No longer will we live in fear."

Yahko nodded toward another man and they both set their weapons down and lifted Omari's body off the table and placed it into the fire. Ashes and embers flew to the sky, lighting the darkness it held.

Everyone started to yell and scream. It was not the sound of fear that came from their mouths, it was years' worth of pent-up rage. They ran in the direction of Master Vincent's house, weapons in hand, where a small cloud of smoke could already be seen forming in the sky.

I tried following them as fast as my body would let me. It was painful but I had to stop them. I couldn't let them harm Master Vincent. I fell behind and their yells faded in the distance ahead of me. I followed the trail leading to the house, almost tripping a couple times along the way. I kept looking to the sky where the smoke grew more and more thick. They were burning the house down; I was sure of it.

The path finally began to widen with small stones instead of dirt and the house came into view. It was almost fully engulfed in flames. The others were cheering and circling the house trying to look through the broken windows.

"Where is he?" someone yelled in the distance.

I recognized the voice that responded. "He isn't here," Hyenah yelled, over the roaring flames. "I just checked and the horses and carriage are gone."

Hyenah was holding a torch. She must have started the fire when Omari's body was being cremated. If Master Vincent wasn't here then where was he? That didn't matter. At least he was safe. He would be furious with the others for burning his house and all his belongings. The amulet! It was still in the house! I bolted up the porch steps and charged through the front door, causing more pain to my body as it slammed through the wooden door. I heard the others behind me screaming my name but I didn't listen. All that mattered was his amulet, his most prized piece of property. I had to save it. I had to show him I was worthy.

I pushed aside the fresh memory of tumbling down the stairs I was now climbing up. The heat from the fire was smoldering. I could hardly see where I was going, the smoke was so thick. By the time I reached the top step, I was on my forearms and knees, crawling and coughing. I stayed low to the floor, making my way down to the end of the hallway. I closed my eyes, hoping the burning would stop, and with my right arm against the wall, I followed the hall to the end. I reached up and searched for the knob to the door. My fingers brushed against it, but with them being bandaged up, I couldn't turn it. I laid down on my back, screaming in pain as I did, and kicked the bottom of the door as hard as I could. I didn't care about the searing pain. Over and over again, I kicked before the door finally burst open and a fresh wave of heat and smoke rushed out of the room into the hall.

I crawled through the doorway. The room was burning like the others below me. The window had been shattered out and the flames were growing closer to it, searching for more oxygen, the same thing my lungs were screaming for.

I used the shelf to pull myself up. The amulet was just out of reach at the top. I felt the scabs on my back begin to break open as I reached for the necklace. I pushed the display off the top shelf with my fingertips and it fell to the floor, shattering even more glass all over. It wasn't easy to do, but I managed to scoop the necklace up in my hands and turned to leave the room again. Just as I made it back to the doorway, the floor beneath me crumbled and the flames below swallowed both my body and the amulet. The crackling of the burning wood and the bright light of the flames that engulfed me did not scare me. If I failed to save Master Vincent's amulet then I was ready for death to take me.

CHAPTER 6
PRESENT DAY: REALISM

The mansion was quiet and the air was still. I don't even think the mortal, Devin, was breathing at this point. He sat, still cuffed to the chair, with his head down, looking at his feet, afraid of what would happen since he just admitted to four vampires that he wanted all of us to suck his blood at the same time. To a human, it would be an erotic fantasy. For four vampires who have lived for a long time, it was...

"Ridiculous! Absolutely ridiculous," Leslie yelled. "Four vampires drinking from one human is not a good idea."

Devin raised his head and looked toward her. "Why is that ridiculous? What's the big deal?" Devin asked.

"If one of us were to drink too much you could, and probably, would die," Winona answered his question. She stood from her throne and gracefully, like a serpent moving in water, moved toward Devin. She smiled at me and I stepped aside, giving her room to unlock the cuffs to free Devin's hands to place them in her own.

Winona kneeled down to his level. "Tell me, why do you crave our venom? Our venom is not addictive. It is your mind playing tricks on you. I can... help you... with your true addictions that you use our venom as a substitute for."

"It's not the venom that I crave. It's the feeling it gives me. It makes me forget." Devin trailed off and looked back down to his feet. "I don't want to remember certain things in my past."

"We all have things that haunt us from our past," Arubrey said as he stood. "We will grant you your fantasy, but first, you will tell us who it was who told you about this so-called army of vampires that you have started to spread throughout the vampiric community. Who was your source?"

"The vampires at Seven Nights never would tell me their names. I always asked but they all refused to answer most of my questions. They would just laugh or yank me in a private booth. It's like... like I was their puppet. I didn't like it at first. But I kept going back... back for them to give me that feeling of being... free."

I put my finger under Devin's chin and raised it up, making him look me in the eyes, and asked, "How did you hear of this rumor then?"

"I'm always taken to a private booth. He pulls the curtain closed and drinks from me. Almost every time I visit there, he drinks from me. He never speaks to me until after my blood has satisfied his thirst. By then my mind is… gone… and I can't focus. But I know he whispers to me after he drinks my blood."

I leaned in closer. "What does he whisper to you?" I inquired.

"That the end for many is coming. For both humans and vampires. That the wives of his master are going to enslave the humans again and kill all the vampires who try to stop him. But he said all the humans are going to be enslaved this time, not just…" Devin trailed off again.

"Vincent," I say out the name out loud.

"You don't know that," Arubrey countered. "What does this vampire look like?" he asked.

"Well, he's black, but pale. And short." Devin hesitated, not wanting to say more. We stared back at him, waiting. "This vampire is a child. A little boy, younger than a teenager."

This wasn't good. Leslie finally stood up and joined us, gathered around Devin. "Here's how this is gonna play out, sugars," she instructed us all. "I'm thirstin' ta' death so we're gonna drink from this cute little human, like he wants us to do. Then we're gonna come up with a plan to get our hands on this vampire child who been whisperin' in Dev's ear." Leslie winked at Devin as she cutinized his name.

"Leslie, you and Sassandra make Devin comfortable upstairs. Winona and I will be up shortly," Arubrey ordered.

Leslie snatched up the leather hood and placed it back over Devin's head and grabbed his hands out of Winona's and practically dragged him up the stairs. I followed behind, lost in my thoughts. Vincent had to be behind this. I knew he would resurface. But why now? What has changed in the past six decades? Whispering in the ear. Enslaving humans. This had Vincent's name written all over it. Wives? Vincent never had a wife when I knew him. And a child vampire? Vincent had waited until I was nineteen to turn me. Could Arubrey be right? Maybe it wasn't him after all.

Leslie interrupted my train of thought, bringing me back to reality. "So, what are you in therapy for?"

"Leslie, we're not diagnosing Mr. Green. You don't have to answer that. She's just being nosy."

"Fine. Which room should we use then?" she asked me. "Do you want to be tied up?" she said, turning her attention back to Devin. "Do you want us to be naked? Do *you* want to be naked? Do you want us to chain you to the bed? You've already got the hood on."

Devin turned his head around, trying to find me, and I knew under the leather hood he had a mortified look on his face.

"Leslie." I chuckled at her enthusiasm. "Third floor, turn left, second door. Check that room. We'll let Devin decide."

The coven of Ooljéé, my coven, lived, if you can call it that, in this mansion. This is why I required Devin to be blindfolded and for the confusing route to get here. He could never see the outside of the mansion or know how to find it. What I was afraid of was if the others were thinking the same as me. Other humans and even

58

vampires had been interrogated here before. Some lived, others not so lucky. I hoped, for Devin's sake, that all would go well. Would Arubrey, Winona, and Leslie insist on killing him? All it would take would be two out of three votes to determine his fate. My vote didn't count. It never had. There were only three thrones and the thrones were built before I joined their coven.

We climbed the stairs, one step at a time, walking at Devin's pace. We finally made it to the third floor and rounded the corner. Leslie opened the door and flipped the switch, illuminating the room. I shut the door behind us and pulled the hood off from Devin's head. He squinted his eyes, blinded by the light, but eagerly looked around the room.

"Oh, wow," he said. "This most definitely looks like I could be comfortable here."

The bedroom was large. It had a cathedral ceiling and a substantial sized window that looked out over the driveway, but Devin couldn't tell from the thick maroon curtains that covered it. There was a modern king-sized bed on the opposite wall from the door, that no one ever slept in. Two gray nightstands sat on each side of the bed with candles on top of them. The dresser was on the left of the room, supporting a large, uncovered mirror, and on the right, next to the bathroom with a walk-in closet, was a chest of drawers, all drawers being empty of clothes. This was a room that no one entered except for the house cleaner every once in a while, to keep the dust at bay. Leslie moved like lightning and had the candles lit and was standing back beside us before Devin even noticed that she moved. I flipped the light off, startling Devin and watching his face change as he looked at us both in the candle light.

"I was only half joking earlier," Leslie said to Devin. "You're in charge of your fantasy. You tell us exactly what you want and we will oblige."

Devin's blood rushed to his face and his cheeks blushed. He was a strange human. He would have these moments of confidence and then a moment later he would get shy again. It was cute, for a human. He took a few steps toward the bed and kicked off his shoes before loosening and pulling off his tie from around his neck. Leslie and I looked at one another, smiling as we both listened as his pulse slowly sped up. We stood there, waiting and watching. Devin tossed his tie on the floor and turned to face us.

The door opened and Winona entered the room followed by Arubrey, closing the door again behind him.

"Before we begin, Devin," Winona said, "I want to ask you a question."

Devin nodded and waited.

"After we are finished, you're more than welcome to sleep here. We will come up with a very believable excuse of why you never returned home tonight to your wife. She will believe whatever we tell her. But if you want, I can help ease your pain from your past. I can help heal your soul, if you'd like. You can have a good life with your wife and daughter. Would you like that? Would you like to erase the pain of your past, Devin?"

Devin closed his eyes and thought to himself for a few moments. "I do drugs to help keep my demons quiet. I know that's a piss poor excuse, but I don't know what else to do to shut them up. My past is a part of me and always will be, even if you can make me forget the pain, you can't change it. What happened, happened. For now, I just want to escape it. Having a single vampire drink from me… that high lasts longer and longer each time and is more powerful than any high a drug has ever given me. It stays fresh in my mind and it distracts me from other things."

Devin started to unbutton his shirt and looked at Leslie. "I'm a lot of things, I know that. But a cheater isn't one of them. All I want tonight is for my blood to be sucked. Just please respect my marriage."

Leslie and I looked at one another again, hearing Devin's pulse begin to beat even faster and faster by the moment now that his fantasy was face to face with him.

Devin dropped his dress shirt, next to his tie on the floor, then laid on top of the pillows and comforter with his wrist facing up and his eyes shut.

Winona was the first to move. She went to the right side of the bed and slipped off her moccasins before climbing onto the bed with Devin. She sat with her legs crossed one over the other and grabbed his wrist, pulling it up to her mouth. "To keep Devin alive, we each can only drink one pint of his blood. Any more can cause severe tissue and organ damage to his body."

Winona did not wait for us to respond. She opened her mouth wide and sank her fangs into his wrist, causing him to arch his back from the sensation of the bite. Winona didn't drink blood often. I could tell she wanted to hurry to get this over with. We instantly could smell the aroma of his blood in the room as she bit into him. I jumped from where I was standing and landed on the bed right next to his other side and bit into his neck, savoring the first few drops of blood that flowed over my tongue.

I sensed Arubrey close to me, on the other side of Devin's body. I opened my eyes to see him closing his and biting into his neck. Like Devin, he had also removed his shirt. Arubrey would never spill a drop of blood, but always preferred to drink without a shirt on, just to be safe. Arubrey lifted Devin's head up a bit and Devin grunted in pleasure, scrunching his toes together.

I felt Leslie lift Devin's other arm up, bringing his other wrist up to her lips. I opened my eyes again, pausing from drinking his blood, and watched as she almost kissed his wrist, but stopped herself. She looked at me and gave me a soft smile before biting into him. I could sense that Leslie also wanted this to be over with, even if she was excited about it earlier. Something was holding her back. She barely moved as she drank from him.

I turned my attention back to Devin as I plunged my teeth back into his neck lapping my tongue over every drop of blood that seeped out from where my fangs pierced it.

One pint of blood was not much to a vampire. Most vampires wanted at least two. So, four vampires drinking one pint would be very pleasurable for Devin. Losing double the amount of blood from four different areas on his body, Devin was probably feeling very elated by now. I pulled off of Devin's neck, having finished my one pint. He looked so peaceful, lying there, asleep.

"You've probably killed him, Sassandra!" Winona said, glaring at me.

"He's fine," Leslie said. "Sass was watching everyone else drink from him. That's why she finished so late after us."

Arubrey picked his shirt up off the ground and stretched with a big smile across his face, something that doesn't happen often. "I don't usually drink from men but that wasn't half bad."

Leslie took the side of the blanket Devin was laying on, fast asleep by now, and flung it over his body, covering him up. She saw us looking at her and rolled her eyes at us. "What? He's human. They use blankets at night."

We all left the room, shutting Devin in. "Meeting in the kitchen," Arubrey said before jumping over the banister to the second floor below us. Winona, Leslie, and myself quickly followed with a bit more class, using the stairs.

"Vincent is not behind this, Sassandra," Arubrey said as we entered the kitchen, another room we only used for its true purpose when we had humans over for a charity event, or like now, a coven meeting.

"Why do you think that he's not?" I asked in disbelief.

"Because a lot of vampires use other vampires to do their biddings. Do you really think he was the only vampire to own slaves or drudges, whatever you want to call it?"

I clenched my teeth together. I hated being reminded of my past. "Vincent never owned me and I will destroy him for what he did to me. I will not allow him to do it to others!"

Winona stepped in front of Arubrey, blocking him from my view. "Even if Vincent created this immortal child, we cannot get ahead of ourselves. First, we need to visit Seven Nights and find the vampire child that Devin spoke of earlier."

"Fine. Once I get my hands on him," I started to say before being interrupted by Arubrey.

"You're sitting this one out, Sassandra. Your emotions are too intense for this mission and we cannot have you compromising it, especially if the rumors of war are true."

"I'm the one who knows Vincent! I killed in his name for him! I know how his mind thinks!" I yelled.

"And I don't think it is Vincent!" Arubrey yelled back at me, slamming his fist into the marbled countertop, cracking it.

"Leslie, what do you think?" I asked, ignoring his outburst.

Leslie stood at the kitchen door, daydreaming.

"Leslie?" Winona touched her arm, snapping her out of her daydream. "What is it?"

"Nothing. I was just thinking. Um, what did you say?"

"What is going on here?" Arubrey said. "I've got Sassandra's head ready to explode and Leslie's head floating in the clouds."

"I apologize. Yes, under different circumstances I would suggest that Sass and I could go to the club and find the immortal child and then bring him back here to interrogate, then destroy. But I also agree with Arubrey, Sass. You're too hot about this vampire's creator being Vincent. We can't jump the gun on things."

"Unbelievable," I say in disbelief.

"Leslie, Winona and I will go to Seven Nights next week to find this vampire child," Arubrey said. "Devin will accompany us to help lure the child out. Then we will interrogate him, without you, Sassandra. Once we get the answers, we will inform you of them. And if you are correct that Vincent is his creator then we will include you in again. But if you're wrong, you need to get your head back on right and forget about Vincent. It's been almost six decades since we've last seen him. He probably doesn't even exist anymore."

I said nothing. I had no words. I stormed out of the kitchen and ran back up the stairs to the room where Devin was sleeping. I needed to escape reality. I needed to feel free from my own mind. I laid on top of the blanket next to Devin. He was still in a deep sleep. I placed my head next to his and focused. This wasn't the first time I'd visited Devin's dreams. I knew they would give me what I was looking for. There were vampires, like Arubrey and Winona, who brought an ability to their immortality that others did not possess. I inherited the ability of dream walking from Vincent. I could enter the minds of mortals when they were asleep and see their dreams and their nightmares. I could even talk to them. At first, they never knew I was there but now I could have conversations with them and even influence and change their dreams if I wanted, amongst other things my mind could do.

All I wanted now was to escape with Devin. If having his blood drunk by vampires put him in a world of bliss then I wanted a part of that world for myself. I concentrated on the darkness, looking for a light, the entrance to his dream world. A white light shone in the distance and I rushed toward it, letting it consume me.

The light entered my mind and as it did, I heard a piano softly playing somewhere in the distance. Its sound was calming to my soul. It moved my feet off the ground and I was floating up. I looked beneath me as I floated away in the sky. Colors swam through the white light toward me, circling me, moving through me, and as each one touched my skin, I felt a different sensation. I felt the feeling I would get as if I was drinking blood again. It was warm and it coursed through my body. The music continued to play as new colors rushed over me. I felt a gentle pressure over my entire body but as it released, it took all my worries with it. A cool breeze came with the notes of the piano's song that caused me to shiver and laugh. The sound that came out of my mouth was a shock. It was like I was a child again, laughing and laughing with my parents. I looked up and I saw Devin floating above me, smiling at me.

"Isn't this amazing?" he asked me.

"Yes. It's nothing I've ever experienced before. Can I stay here forever?" I asked.

I did not hear his answer. Instead, the music from the piano and all the colors and new sensations that came from them was causing me to get lost in my laughter all over again and again, over and over.

CHAPTER 7
YEAR 1857: BLOOM

The floor collapsed beneath me and as I fell through it, I saw the burning light of the fire below, my skin warming as the flames danced around my body. I fell into the fire but I did not hit the floor below. Instead, I felt something cold as ice as it shielded me from the flames that threatened to consume my flesh. My head began to spin as the smoke disappeared in a flash, replaced by the moon and stars in the sky now above me.

"It's a full moon tonight," Vincent, my master, my savior, my everything, said to me as he cradled my body within his arms. I watched as the clouds above shifted very little, revealing a new patch of stars.

I smiled, enthralled by his eyes, burning bright as the fire, as he looked into my own. "You saved me?" I asked.

"I returned just as you were running into the house."

I opened my clenched fist, revealing the amulet that was Master Vincent's most prized possession. "I had to save this for you. You said it was important."

Master Vincent's eyes left my own as he sat me down on my bare feet and gazed at the bright red jewel, encased in gold, as it rested within the palm of my hand. We were standing next to the oak tree as the house continued to burn behind us. Vines of greenery had grown up into the tree and I could see white flower buds, almost ready to bloom. These were not roses, nor lilies. They were a flower I was not familiar with. Slowly and gently, Master Vincent brought his cool fingers to my hand and picked up the amulet. I felt its chain slowly drag away from my fingertips, leaving my hand trembling.

"I know I shouldn't touch such things that do not belong to me. I only did it because I knew it was important to you. I had to save it." I pleaded my case.

"And so, you have." Master Vincent spoke the words more to himself than to me.

He stuffed the necklace into his pocket, focusing his attention back to me. "I understand now," he said, again speaking to himself rather than me. "I knew you were worth saving. There was something about you that spoke to me when I first saw you. You were like a caged animal, trying your damnedest to break free."

"I'm sorry, Master, I don't think I quite understand," I admitted. It's like he had been speaking in riddles for fifteen years now.

"No, I guess you wouldn't. But maybe I can change that. Maybe I can change..." Master Vincent began to say, leaving his last word in the silence for no one to hear.

He was looking at me again, forcing me to get lost in his red eyes as they grew brighter. Instantaneously, he had ripped through the bandages that were still wrapped around my hands and his teeth were sinking deep into my wrist before I even realized what he was doing to me. My head was so groggy. Was it from all the smoke from the house fire that made my head spin? Could this be real? Could Master Vincent really be drinking my blood? I knew he would thirst for my blood again. I knew once he tasted me... all was forgiven. I did not resist. I closed my eyes, letting him savor the taste of it.

I drifted to the sky, joining the stars, watching the scene unfold below. Master Vincent stood, bent over, supporting my limp body in his arms as he continued to drink the blood from my wrist. He drank, drank, and drank some more, until finally lifting himself away from my wrist, searching for something in the sky above him.

He closed his eyes, blood running from the side of his mouth, and licked his lips.

"Drain the body," he whispered to himself, before lurching down onto my neck, drinking more of me. My body lay limp, still supported by his arms. I floated down from the sky to stand next to my master.

I wanted to ask him what he was doing to me. I desperately wanted to know why he drank my blood. I knew better than to ask questions. It did not hurt this time, to be drunk from. Numbness, nothingness, is what I felt. I did not care that my blood was being drained, only that I was happy that it was my master who was the one doing it. I was happy to please him. I knew, if possible, that he would continue to drink from me forever and ever; and I wanted him to.

A gentle breeze came in from the west of the plantation, shifting more clouds in the sky as it did. Master Vincent pulled himself away from my throat, blood running down the both of us as he did. I watched, in the dream, as he brought his own wrist to his mouth this time, biting into it with the sharp fangs that resided on the inside of his bloodied lips. He pierced his own skin, letting his blood run free and brought it to my own lips, pressing his wrist into my mouth.

"Drink, child of mine, drink," he cooed to me. But my body lay still, and I did not drink the red liquid that he offered me.

"You must consume my blood or you surely will die," He ushered me, almost urgently.

I could not let my master down, not again. I moved in closer, but saw no sign of life in the corpse that lay in my master's arms. Was I dead? No, I couldn't be. I closed my eyes and forced myself to rejoin my body. I had to wake up. I had to drink! As my dream merged back to reality, I felt the cold arms of my master that supported my body. I felt the wetness of his blood as it oozed over my lips, dripping onto my tongue. I brought my hands up, gripping my fingers around his arm, trying to pull his wrist further into my mouth. His blood tasted like death, and I was desperate for more of it.

My body was quickly healing. My hands no longer trembled or hurt anymore and I could feel the wounds on my back closing shut. The pain I felt before disappeared and was replaced by a strength I never experienced, more powerful than everlasting adrenaline. I felt the blood of my master enter into my mouth and I gulped it down, swallowing as much as I could. It made its way down through my body, filling it with searing hot power.

My eyes fluttered open to a world I had never seen before. The vines of greenery and flower buds on the oak tree began to move, like a serpent climbing a tree. What I thought were white flowers at first were now a soft blue, almost glowing in the moonlight. As the flower petals awoke, coming to a full bloom, their tops opened up like a trumpet and they released a scent of lemon into the air. Their beauty was nothing but sublime, as if the stars and moon came from inside of them and floated to the sky above. The breeze cleared the last of the clouds from the sky and I saw the moon clearly for the first time in my existence. It was at its fullest I had ever seen and much closer than before. This new version of the moon was watching me as I drank the blood from my master's wrist. It loomed in closer to us, as if it were watching a scene from a play take place and it had a front row seat.

As the moon drew in closer, I closed my eyes, screaming in pain. I was burning. It had all been a bad dream. Master Vincent did not catch me. How could he have caught me and saved me from the fire when I was burning? I was burning! It had to have been a dream and my body must still be in the house. I would surely turn to ash with the walls that once made me feel safe within them.

When would I die? I lashed my body all over the place, trying to put the fire out that was ignited inside of me. I felt the flames grow around my back, reaching my wounds from being punished, tied to the oak tree. The fire burned my old wounds and I wailed in pain.

Omari was in the field of poppies, walking away from me. Why didn't I follow him that night? Why did I choose to stay, choose to burn? The fire was burning and I was standing in the center of it. There, sitting with her legs crossed was the strange woman again. This time the tips of the white feathers that were entwined within her wild black hair were red. They were dripping with blood. She sat with her eyes closed, ignoring the blood and my screaming, and spoke to me.

"Soon," was all she said.

Soon the fire would kill me, no doubt, and my suffering would be over I thought to myself. But it wasn't. The fire continued to burn and I continued to scream, powerless to put it out but still feeling powerful at the same time. The woman vanished from my dream and that was when I became very aware of time. After the second day I realized that even though I was burning from the inside out, there was no smoke. What I thought to be fire at first molded itself into lava that was now flowing through my veins. I burned from the inside out for almost three nights before waking from the nightmare.

"How do you feel?" the familiar voice asked me.

But I was already tired of his questions. I took in my new surroundings. We were in a small room, more of an office, lit by a single candle. I sat up off the floor and stood next to the desk at which Master Vincent sat behind. The layers of curtains that hung over the only window were drawn shut. I didn't know how I knew it but it was afternoon. I could sense it.

"I asked you how you were feeling," Master Vincent said to me again.

"I heard you the first time," I snapped.

"Yes, I was told that newborns could be very moody," he said as he stood and walked around the desk toward me. "Open your mouth."

I could feel my eyes roll in annoyance but I listened to his command. He leaned in close to my mouth, inspecting my teeth. He grabbed my hands, turning them over, then over again in his, before pushing my head to the side to look at the side of my neck. "Turn around, remove your bandages."

I removed my clothing and unraveled the stained bandages in a few quick motions and let them drop to the floor, exposing the skin on my back to his eyes to see. I felt him trace his fingers along my back, his touch no longer feeling cold to me. His fingers ran down the flesh where I was once wounded by his whip. There was no more pain. Whatever he had done to me had healed me completely. I would forever be grateful for his mercy.

I ran my tongue along the inside of my mouth and felt two very sharp teeth, one on each side. They were fangs, like his were.

Next, I flexed my hands, opening and closing them again, as hard as I could, without feeling any pain, only strength. I knew if I wanted to, I could break his desk in half with just my hand.

"What did you do to me?" I asked. I had to ask. I didn't care.

At first, he was silent but then he finally spoke and said, "You have questions. I understand. I also have many questions to which I do not know the answers to. To answer yours, I turned you into a vampire, the same as I."

"What does that mean?"

"It means that you are now an immortal. You will no longer age. You will have new strength, speed, and agility. And thirst. You will crave blood for the rest of your new life."

I was about to ask another question but before I could open my mouth, I realized I had not eaten any food or drank in over six days. I grabbed my throat, beginning to panic yet again because I hadn't been breathing since I woke up on the floor from the nightmare of burning.

Master Vincent smacked me, hard, across the face. It sounded like a glass plate was dropped onto the kitchen floor, shattering into pieces. "Just stop, Sassandra!" he yelled. It was the first time in fifteen years he ever used my name.

"What's happening to me?" I roared in panic.

"I told you, you're a vampire. You don't need to breathe. Stop trying to gasp for air, you don't need it!"

I closed my mouth, still not calm, trying to get used to not breathing, ever again. I licked my lips in anticipation. They were dry.

I closed my eyes and images of Master Vincent's blood dripping from his wrist onto my lips flashed in my mind. I wanted blood. I had to have it!

"We will hunt later tonight. I, too, am thirsty. But first, we must wait for the sun to set."

Wanting to distract myself, I asked, "Why?"

"You'll burn for real this time if it touches your flesh," was all he said.

"I've already burned!" I yelled back, annoyed.

"What you felt was nothing compared to the sun. What you felt was my blood, burning inside of you. It had to run its course through your body to kill the remains of your own blood. Human blood is weak. It cannot support the power of the body of a vampire. Vampire blood destroys the human blood by morphing it into a more unique type of blood. A new type of blood, if you will. I drained your veins as much as I could without completely killing you before letting you drink from my own. The less human blood that is left in your body, the easier the transformation is. But if I were to have drained too much and you died before drinking my blood…" he trailed off.

"Why are you answering my questions now? You never allowed anyone to ask questions before."

"Not anyone. I never allowed a *slave*," he spat the word out. "But now you're a drudge. And I will allow my drudge to ask a few questions."

"What's a drudge? I asked my master.

75

"A drudge is a vampire who serves a more powerful vampire." He saw the concern on my face and answered my next question before I could ask it. "Do not worry, you can still serve me. Actually, you'll be much more useful now. I have big plans for you, Sassandra. Now, that's enough questions for now."

I looked around the room again. A large clock with a small pendulum was on the wall across from the desk. The arms on the clock's face confirmed that it was almost a few hours past noon. I was annoyed. I couldn't just stand here in silence. My mind was racing!

"Whose office is this?" I asked.

"It belongs to me. We are in my floral shop, downtown. I closed it to the public until further notice for us to use since my plantation was burned down. It will keep us safe from the sun during the day."

"What makes a vampire burn in the sunlight," I asked.

"That is a question to which I do not have the answer to," Master Vincent answered me.

"What type of flowers were those," I asked, "that grew around the oak tree where you... changed me."

"They're called 'Ipomoea Alba', or 'Moon Flowers'. They only bloom at night, under the moonlight, and then recede when the sun begins to rise. They're quite intriguing, aren't they?"

"Oh no! Your book!"

"It's okay, books can be replaced. I'll even get you your own copy," he promised.

I looked at him, beaming. I never owned my own book before. Would I really have my own copy of *Language of Flowers* one day?

"Now that you're an immortal I guess you can have some extra privileges. But never forget the color of your skin. Even if I consider you to be almost an equal, now that you're a vampire, the rest of the world, humans, will not. Not only that, but you're also a woman in a man's world."

I glared at him, annoyed by his remark. "If we're immortals then why don't we take over the humans and rule over them or turn them all into vampires?" I asked.

"Humans outnumber us by quite a bit actually. Plus, being immortal is a privilege. Turning all the humans would no longer make us special."

Was I special? Master Vincent called me special. I became lost in my thoughts after that. I listened to the pendulum swing side to side as each second passed. Master Vincent sat back down at the desk, reading random books he would pull from the shelf.

Finally, after eleven thousand, four hundred, and sixty-eight seconds, the sun began to set. Master Vincent stood at the same time as I did.

"It's time," he said with a wicked grin on his face.

"Where are we going?" I asked.

He walked from around the desk and opened the door that would lead us out of the office. "Hunting."

CHAPTER 8
YEAR 1857: BAREFOOT

Master Vincent and I exited the floral shop and stepped onto the street outside. This was the first time I have ever been off the plantation. The world around me was new and thrilling. I was eager to see it all. The sun had disappeared, and with it came an urge of freedom. I desperately wanted to take off running but Master Vincent walked at a leisurely pace, with me following closely behind, barefooted.

"Where did you come from, Master?" I asked as we walked.

"Stop asking questions. It is of no importance of where I come from."

"Your accent is different from all the other men that visited the plantation. So, I was just wondering…"

"I said to stop asking questions."

I wondered why he was so secretive about his past. Maybe one day he would tell me. I waited a moment before changing the subject. "Can we run?" I asked. The new strength I felt inside my body had me on the verge of bolting down the road to see how fast my new strength would carry my body, but instead, I knew to follow my master and do as he did.

"No, not yet. There are others in the area. Try to breathe in again, to smell the air around us. Do you smell that? The scent of mortals? They may see us," he advised me. "A vampire must be patient and we are not to be seen doing things in which other humans would not, or could not, for that matter, do themselves."

I tried to breathe in the air again but choked on nothing as I did. I gasped as I inhaled the oxygen my body now rebuked, but I think I did smell something within the air. Was that what humans smelled like?

I composed myself again, and as we continued to walk down the street, we passed many shops along the strip. There was a plethora of them that sold guns and ammunition, jewelry, clothing for women and men, and sheet music, just to name a few.

"Can I get new clothes?" the question was out of my mouth before I could stop myself.

Master Vincent came to an abrupt stop and turned to look at me, from head to toe, then back up again. He sneered to himself in disgust at my appearance. "Yes, I suppose your appearance is quite off putting. When we return, we shall retrieve you some new clothes. I have a feeling it would be pointless to do so before your first hunt."

"What do you mean?" I asked.

"You'll see."

As the minutes passed, the sky became darker and we were passing fewer and fewer people and the noise of the horse drawn carriages slowly faded in the distance behind us. Master Vincent looked around, and I copied him, looking in each direction that he did. The coast was now clear of all life and Master Vincent took off running ahead of me. I smiled and darted ahead after him. I felt the wind rush past my face as I sprinted. It felt as if I was a cheetah, finally free from the cage of mortality that was holding me back. And I was smiling. I cannot remember the last time I smiled before this moment.

We ran through the woods, in the darkness, startling birds from their nest. We flew past a herd of deer that were walking with the wind. I could hear each of their heartbeats as we flew past them. I could have easily snatched one up to feast on as my first meal but Master Vincent did not slow his speed, completely ignoring the deer, so I rushed to keep up with him.

Moments later, Master Vincent came to an abrupt stop and I copied, now standing beside him, the both of us still hidden within the darkness of the woods.

"What do you smell?" he asked me.

I lifted my nose a millimeter into the air and tried to breathe in, this time without panicking. "I smell burnt wood and a hint of floral. We're back at the plantation?" I guessed.

"Yes, what's left of it."

"What are we doing here?" I pressed.

Master Vincent started to walk down toward the sound of the flowing stream, the same one that I accompanied Hyenah with, to wash clothes on the day of the fire; three nights ago, when I was turned into a creature of the night.

"This is where your hunt begins. Find the slaves who burned my house down. Find them, drink from them, and then kill them," he instructed me.

I gave him a single nod. I understood my mission. I would not fail my master. The others had to pay, as I did, for their betrayal. Their blood would spill and they would pay with their lives. Master Vincent and I reached the edge of the stream. This was where the scent of the others stopped.

"I'll be here when you return," Master Vincent said as he turned his back to the water to gaze upon the moon and stars.

"You're not going with me?" I asked my master.

"I do not go into the water unless absolutely necessary." And with that he started to walk away. I leaped into the air, diving into the water below me. I did not need to inhale to hold my breath as I swam underwater, downstream. I never even learned how to swim as a human; as a vampire it just came naturally. I knew the others swam downstream as well the night I was turned, after catching fire to the house. They used the fire as a diversion in order to get away, to escape to freedom. I thought to myself that their freedom was a disguise. Instead, it was death they would find. As I swam, I thought of how I would kill them. Would I simply crush their skulls with my bare hands? Or, perhaps, I would feed off of each of them, one at a time, draining them dry. I was very thirsty after all.

After fantasizing of my first kill, my first taste of blood, I jumped out of the water. I inhaled the scent of the forest to see if I could smell them, the humans. I leaped across the stream to the other side, inhaling the air once again. I could smell the damp moss that grew along the north side of the tree trunks and pine needles that showered the forest floor. I did not recognize any other scents, besides the one's nature offered me, so I swam further downstream. I recited the song in my head again, as I swam. I knew the hidden message within the lyrics. I knew the hidden message even as a human when I first heard it. The humans would find it easier to travel downstream, rather than against it.

Wade in the water
Wade in the water
Wade in the water, children
God is gonna trouble these waters

See that band all dressed in white
God is gonna trouble these waters
It look like a band of the Israelites
God is gonna trouble these waters

See that band all dressed in red
God is gonna trouble these waters

82

Look like a band that Moses led
God is gonna trouble these waters

My Lord delivered Daniel well
Daniel well, Daniel well
Didn't my Lord deliver Daniel well
Then why not every man?

Man went down to the river
Man went down to the river, Lord
Man went down to the river
Went down there for to pray

I should have told Master Vincent about the song when I first heard them singing it. I heard it a dozen times within the house when the windows were open. I knew its secret meaning. But Master Vincent had to have heard it as well. He had to have known they were planning to escape. Did he let them escape on purpose? Did he plan on turning me and using me to hunt them down? Is that why he left earlier that night before the house was caught on fire? Did he plan all of this?

I pushed the many questions that were swimming throughout my mind away as I left the stream to search for signs of the humans, over and over. In the water, out of the water, over and over, until finally, I caught their scent. I hoped Master Vincent would be pleased that I came this far, finding them. But I knew better. I knew he would only be happy with their deaths.

I followed the scent that lingered in the air. The ground, at first, did not give me any clues to the direction in which they walked but knew they were close. The water that dripped off their bodies washed away their scent on the ground, only leaving the smell of pine cones and the pine needles that covered the floor of the forest. I probably traveled close to twenty miles downstream within less than an hour. I was disgusted by mortality. The humans only made it this far with a three-day head start?

I picked my pace up, wanting to get this over with. I wanted Master Vincent to praise me. I passed a rather large pine tree, and caught their scent all over it. They must have stopped to rest here. I picked up the scents of over a dozen mortals. I knew there were almost double that amount on the plantation but the rest of their scents were mixed up with one another, overlapping.

I left the tree behind me, getting closer and closer to my prey. I felt the power within me begin to boil over. I knew I would succeed. I knew I would taste blood tonight, and that I would relish in what it offered me. I wanted it! My senses became sharper, like my body shifted into a predator that needed to feed. I closed my eyes and envisioned my prey walking through the woods, touching trees as they passed. I pictured myself, drinking from them as the others screamed in horror.

I was probably five miles deep into the woods from the stream when the trees started to open up to the backside of a piece of property where a small house sat. I knew they were inside. I could smell them. I could hear them as they chattered.

"...then tomorrow at sunrise we will head North. My horses and carriage are in the stable. It may have to be two trips. The carriage will not hold everyone at once," an unfamiliar man's voice was saying.

I left the woods and walked to the front door. My instinct wanted nothing more than to break through the door and kill every last person inside the house. I had to contain my excitement before I let it get the best of me. I knocked three times, before swiftly disappearing into the darkness of the woods again. The door opened and a white man who I did not recognize stood there, looking around, searching for the one who knocked. He turned around, disturbed by not finding the source of the mysterious visitor, and closed the door behind him.

In a flash, I was on the doorstep again, and once again, I knocked three times. However, this time I did not retreat to the darkness. Instead, I stood my ground, waiting for him to answer again.

"Hello, dear," he said as he peeked through the cracked door, opening it wider for me. "Please, come inside. Are you ok?" he asked me, welcoming me in.

I crossed the threshold of his home and entered the foyer. The chatter I heard earlier had become quiet. The house was silent, as if this man was the only one inside.

"What's your name?" he asked me.

I gave the man a kind smile and answered, "I am Sassandra. Hyenah told me to come here. Is she here?" I asked.

The man smiled back and lead me through the foyer and opened a door where the group of escaped slaves from Master Vincent's plantation were stuffed into. The room was cramped, almost two dozen slaves were crammed in the room with a bed pushed in the corner of the room at the back.

"Hyenah, it's Sassandra, she made it here," the white man said to the room, announcing my presence to them all.

The group of people parted and made a path for Hyenah and her husband, Yahko, to come forward. They both smiled and seemed delighted to see me.

"You escaped the fire?" Hyenah asked me.

"Yes, and no," I answered.

"Did you get burned? Where are your bandages? Are your hands alright?" she asked, worried.

"You know the rules, Hyenah," I said. "Slaves are not to ask questions."

Yahko stepped forward and spoke, "We're not slaves anymore, Sassandra. We're free."

I tilted my head and looked at the human who stood beside his wife. They helped me when I had nowhere else to go. They bandaged me up and fed me when I could not use my own hands to feed myself. They also betrayed our Master and burned down everything that I ever knew.

Once my mind was set on killing them, time moved very slowly. They stood there, like statues, as I snapped Yahko's neck in one swift movement. I heard seven bones break when I twisted his neck with my bare hands. They watched as his limp body collapsed

86

to the floor, in slow motion, and landed beside his wife's bare feet. Hyena's eyes showed a moment of confusion before I slung my head backwards, headbutting the white man who stood behind me, spilling blood from his nose and knocking him unconscious. I smelled his blood instantly and I turned around, catching him in my arms as he began to fall from the blow. My teeth pierced the flesh of his neck and the taste of warm, savory, blood flowed over my tongue and down my throat for the first time. I grasped his body tighter, pulling it closer within my own, drinking from him.

I heard the screaming from the room behind me as I was drinking. Did they just notice Yahko's lifeless body or were they screaming in fear because I was drinking the blood of the man who promised them freedom in the North? I did not know, nor did I care. All I cared about was blood. And I wanted more of it.

I let the man's body drop to the floor and I entered the room where the others were still crowded in, closing the door and locking it behind me. Their screams bounced off the four walls around us, but one by one they were silenced. One by one, they paid for their betrayal. I made it impossible for them to escape, breaking their bones, as I drank from each of them. They tried fighting me, pulling me off my victims as I drank from each of them, but they failed. They were all my victims and I was their worst nightmare that would bring their existence to an end. I could not just drink from them and leave. I had to end them. That was the mission, their blood was just a perk of the mission in which I bathed in.

I stood in the center of the room, looking around. I was covered in blood from head to toe, but it was not my own. It was the blood of the slaves who I worked with side by side. Almost all of them were now dead. Hyenah wept, covering her husband's lifeless corpse, trying to foolishly protect it.

"What, what are you?" she whimpered with her eyes closed, too afraid to look at me.

I kneeled down beside her and whispered into her ear, "Vampire."

"Please, Sassandra, stop. Why are you doing this to us? We're free. You're free. Be free with us." Hyenah pleaded.

I stood back up and looked down at her, still trying to protect her dead husband's body. "You're wrong, Hyenah. There is no such thing as freedom; only death. Tell Omari I say hello," I said to her just as I brought my foot down onto her spine, breaking it, reuniting her with her husband.

I heard the child's cry. He tried to stifle it by placing his hand over his mouth but I knew he was there, hiding under the bed.

"Come out," I ordered the child.

The boy scooted his body out from under the bed and rose to his feet. I sat down on the bed and patted a spot beside me, telling him to sit with me. I recognized the boy from the plantation. He was probably no older than eleven years of age. I do not know who his parents were but I'm sure their bodies were laying somewhere within this room, no longer breathing. He was silent, looking down at his bare feet, trembling in fear, as I did so many years ago when I first met Master Vincent. The memory shook me on the inside. I could not bring myself to kill this boy.

"What is your name, child?"

The boy was hesitant to look at me but finally did, and stared directly into my eyes. "Jayden."

"Do not be afraid, Jayden. I will not hurt you, but you must leave this place tonight. Come with me."

I stood up from the bed and stepped over the bodies that were broken and twisted, laying on the floor, motionless. I unlocked the door and opened it, revealing the unconscious white man lying on the floor just outside the doorway. I bent over, picking him up and threw him over my shoulder like a sack of potatoes.

"Follow me," I told the boy. We left the house and walked to the stable where I could hear the horses. When I opened the door, the horses went crazy, startled by my presence. I walked in and tossed the man into the carriage. "Get some water to splash on his face. When he wakes up, tell him to take you North like he promised. Do not talk to anyone about what happened here tonight. If you do, I'll know and I will find you," I threatened.

I left the boy to tend to the unconscious man. He was too young to have anything to do with betraying Master Vincent. He was innocent, unlike the rest. I hoped that he would find his way to freedom. Maybe one day, soon.

I left the stable and once I hit the woods, I started to run again. I ran beside the stream, back the way I came. Back to Master Vincent. I hope being covered with blood would be proof enough that I killed the others. What if he wanted to see their bodies? What if the little boy was still there?

I pushed the questions away. I had to be convincing. I couldn't let Master Vincent find the boy. I ran back to the plantation, without stopping, and found Master Vincent standing in the same spot, looking to the sky, when I returned to his side.

"I found them, Master," I informed him.

Master Vincent turned to look at me, my body covered in blood. "I take it that they're dead?" he assumed.

"Yes, I killed the betrayers, just as you ordered me to do so," I answered, justifying that Jayden was not one of them in my mind.

"Good. Did you enjoy your first drink?"

"Yes, it was very satisfying. I drank from all of them. I can take you there if you want to see their bodies," I said to him, smiling again.

"I believe you. Come, let's go back into town to get you cleaned up and some new clothes."

I followed my master as we ran through the woods again, leading us back toward town. The moon and stars were still gazing down upon us as we ventured through the night. We ended back up in front of the dress shop that we passed earlier in the night.

"They're closed," I said to my master.

"We're vampires. We take whatever we want from humans. Sometimes we even take whatever we want from other vampires. Just don't get caught. Go ahead, turn the knob, it will break open for you. Take whatever your heart desires. I'll be back at the floral shop. Do not take too long," he said to me before leaving me standing in front of the dress shop's door.

I placed my hand on the door knob and turned. The lock broke quite easily and I pushed the door open, entering the shop.

Inside, there were dresses upon dresses everywhere. Their colors were much more vivid than the ones Master Vincent gave to me when I was human. I knew it was because my vision improved since he changed me. My vision was sharper, stronger. I could see things now that I have never noticed before. I walked around the shop, picking up a few dresses that fancied me. I could feel the ridges of the threads with my fingers. Material never felt so realistic as it did now. It was like all my senses woke up once I was turned. I rounded a table and then came to a stop, dropping the dresses onto the floor. There, across from where I stood was a small circular table that held a single pair of high heeled shoes displayed on it. They were egg shell white and had stitching in the center that ran from the toe to the top, covered in lace. The simplicity of their beauty held elegance and grace within them.

I returned to the flower shop, walked to the back where the flowers were watered and stripped my slave clothes off. I knew I would never wear anything like that again. I washed the blood from my naked body with the water from the hose and slipped one of the dresses over my head. It was pretty but the dress did not make me feel special anymore like they used to. I slipped my feet into the shoes that I took from the shop from down the street. It was the first time I ever wore shoes and these fit perfectly. I wiggled my toes inside them, letting this new sensation sink in. I walked to the room, listening to the clink of my heels echo behind me, where Master Vincent was sitting behind his desk again, reading.

"Did you find what you were looking for?" he asked me, without looking up, flipping the next page of his book, continuing to read.

"Yes, I did," I answered, as I grabbed a book off his shelf and started to read it, walking across the room from him, in my new shoes.

CHAPTER 9
PRESENT DAY: MESSAGE

Devin smiled, laying in the king-sized bed, before his eyes half opened, waking up from his blissful slumber. He moaned as his eyes blinked a few times, fighting to keep them open.

"What time is it?" he mumbled.

I was sitting on the edge of the bed, beside Leslie, and Winona was standing at the window, looking out. Winona closed the curtains, shutting the night's sky out, and answered, "It's a new night. You've slept longer than we anticipated. But I suppose your body needed the rest."

Devin sat up, still under the blanket that Leslie gave him the night before. "I've never felt better," he exclaimed. "I can still feel the venom from all four of you coursing through my body. I feel like I'm still floating."

Winona glared at the human. "We will never drink from you again, Devin," she said. "We got what we needed from you. Arubrey left a very convincing voicemail on your wife's phone about where you've been and why you never returned her calls yesterday. I took the liberty of breaking your cell phone to make his story believable. We were going to have you come with us next week to lure the vampire child out who frequently visited you at Seven Nights, but I've reconsidered. We will find another way, without you."

Leslie stood, surely to protest against what Winona had just said, but Winona held up the palm of her hand facing Leslie's face to cut her off.

"This is not to debate, Leslie, so do not bother to try," Winona scorned her.

Leslie's body tensed up, almost ready to strike Winona, emotions running rampant, even more so than mine the night before. "You think you know everything, Winona! Just because you have an ability you think you're better than me! You strut around this mansion as if you're the leader of this coven!" Leslie screamed at her. "You're no more in charge than I am and you know it! If I choose to debate it then I will. And guess what bitch, I'm debating it!"

"Silence! Both of you," I interrupted. They both snapped their eyes toward me. "We have to work together, as a coven. And if Leslie wants to debate anything about the plan, then it is her right to do so. And, I agree with her. Any changes should be debated and voted upon."

Winona said nothing and exited the room, surely to head back to the kitchen where Arubrey probably was already waiting to hear the argument and vote. Leslie smiled at Devin, who was still sitting upright in the bed, stunned by the argument between the two powerful female vampires.

"I apologize for that. I forgot you were still in the room, Devin. I hope I didn't scare you," Leslie said to him.

Devin just looked at her, without movement. Was it from fear, or from the venom of four vampires that still lingered in his blood that was causing his high to escalate to a new level? Devin did not say a word, only stared at her blankly, like he had never seen her until this moment. Confused by the human's lack of action, Leslie turned her attention, and attitude, toward me.

"For future reference, I don't need your help, Sass. I can handle Winona myself."

Leslie stormed out of the room, slamming the door behind her.

I rolled my eyes at my friend. "Pay them no attention. Vampires can be overwhelmingly dramatic at times. Now get up. I'll be taking you home soon," I said.

"Will we be going to Seven Nights next week?" he asked.

"That remains to be a mystery as of now. But first, you're going back home to your wife and daughter, so you had better get ready. You can freshen up in the bathroom through that door there." I stood from the bed and headed out the bedroom door to join the others in the kitchen, before turning back toward Devin and added, "Don't forget to make the bed. We like to keep our home in order, as much as we can," before shutting him in.

I heard the debate in the kitchen going on before I even left the room Devin was in. Although my coven was calmly speaking to one another, vampires can pick up sound waves quite easily, even through walls within a gigantic mansion. But eavesdropping was never my cup of blood, so I quickly joined them in the kitchen.

As I entered through the door, Leslie was speaking to Arubrey. "Devin is a crucial part of this plan, Rue. What if we can't find the child? Devin might know where he hides out. He might remember something new when we get to Seven Nights that might be important!"

Winona was sitting calmly on the top of the marbled counter in the right side of the kitchen, listening to Leslie plead her case for the mortal to still join them at the vampire bar.

Arubrey was pacing across the kitchen as he spoke. I chuckled in my head looking at his burn scars as he walked over to stand next to the oven.

"Yes, Devin is a key witness. But we also have to keep in mind that this vampire could just be spreading rumors," he said. "Maybe this vampire is just trying to frighten Devin. Or perhaps, using Devin to spread the rumor to other vampires to spread panic within our community. We have to keep an open mind for all possibilities. After all, Devin said it was an immortal child. You know they're sporadic and love causing mayhem."

"And that's another reason we don't need Devin. All of this could be for nothing at all. This child could have been lying to him, just for fun! So why expose a human, even more to our world, when it may not even be necessary? Plus, his mind is fixed on nothing but the high he wants to feel from our kinds' venom. What if he's high again and somehow ruins everything?" Winona suggested.

"For someone who knows when others are lying, you might want to take a look in the mirror, Winona," Leslie sneered.

"How dare you accuse me of lying!" Winona snapped back.

"How dare me? How dare you!" Leslie interjected. "You may always say you speak the truth, but your motives are nothing but! You act like the human is of no importance but yet you're only mad because he doesn't want to be fixed by you! Face it, you're just pissed because you haven't fixed anyone since you met Sassandra!"

My mouth dropped listening to this argument, which somehow got my name dragged into the middle of it. I wanted to speak up but it wasn't my debate. I did not have a throne to sit upon. Yes, I was a part of this coven but I was brought in as an outsider after it was already established. I loved my coven as if they were family. And they were family to me, the only one I've had for the last sixteen decades. But sometimes, I felt like with Vincent, that I am just a servant for them. I established myself as a powerful asset, but was that all they would ever see me as? I bit my tongue, tasting my own blood, and swallowing it, before Arubrey finally spoke up, ending the argument.

"I've heard all I needed to hear, from the both of you," he said, looking at Winona and Leslie. This debate between Leslie and

Winona would be decided by Arubrey. Three thrones. There would always be debates, votes, and the majority always won, no questions asked. And the one who lost would do as the other two said. We were a coven of four but with only three thrones in the sub-basement. Leslie wanted Devin to accompany them to the vampire bar and Winona wanted to keep the human out of it. What did Arubrey want?

Arubrey strolled across the kitchen again to now stand next to me. "The plan will not change. I'm sorry, Winona. Yes, this all may be just a rumor and hopefully nothing comes of it. But Leslie is right. We can't risk it. As much as I want to keep all humans out of vampire affairs, we need Devin. We have no scent of the immortal child so we cannot hunt him down. And the child may not show himself at Seven Nights unless he smells Devin's scent. We need to use him as bait. That's our best option."

"Bait?" Leslie objected.

"I did not stutter, Leslie," Arubrey said, glaring at her. "Do you think the vampire child will show himself to Devin if we are seen with him? He will sit alone in the club while we watch from a distance. Once the immortal child approaches him and takes him to a private booth, we will make our move. That is the plan. You wanted Devin to be a part of this and so now he is, as bait."

The atmosphere within the mansion, within my coven, was thick like fog, laced with razor blades. Winona and Leslie were at each other's throats, yet again, and I was irate with Arubrey for making me sit this one out. Instead of actually helping, I would now be stuck sitting at home, alone.

"Are you ready?" I asked as I swung the door open, startling Devin. He was just buttoning his pants. He was shirtless, and still wet from taking a shower, water dripping from the tips of his hair onto his shoulders. His skin was pale, for a human. His body did have an undertone of muscle, probably from the training he received in the army. You can tell he only worked out during his deployment. I did well with my research on the human before writing to him, threatening his family, in order for him to meet me. Everything about Devin, including his looks, was nothing but ordinary, all except his past.

"You could knock," he suggested as he grabbed his shirt off the floor and pulled it over his head.

I grabbed the leather hood with the zipper and smiled as I walked toward him. He didn't object. He knew better.

We sped away from the mansion in my SUV. We weren't even a mile down the road when Devin started with his questions, again.

"So, what's the deal with those two?" he asked.

"What two? You'll have to be more specific. I can't read minds you know."

"Leslie and Winona. Why do they hate each other?"

"They don't hate each other," I said. "Leslie is jealous. She'll never admit it, but she's jealous that we have abilities and she doesn't."

"Abilities?" Devin asked, confused.

"Yes. Like there are humans who can run much faster than other humans, or they're artistic whereas others can't even draw a

99

stick figure. Like that, it's the same with vampires. Some of us have other abilities that other vampires do not, but ours are much more intense than human abilities."

"Like what? You said *we* have abilities. As in you? You have an ability? What is it?" he asked, and asked, and asked.

I moaned in frustration. I hated answering questions. But I knew after spending a day with a coven of vampires that he would have tons of questions. I rolled my eyes, this time at myself, thinking of the times I bombarded Vincent with my own questions and how I hated it when he would hardly give me a straight answer. I didn't want to be anything like him.

"Yes, I have an ability. Don't you remember? I was in your dream."

"In my dream? What dream?" he asked as I rounded a corner too fast, squealing the tires.

"I can enter other people's dreams. I see what they see and hear. The music was lovely by the way."

"Oh. That's a unique ability," he said softly. I could tell he was disappointed in my ability. He probably wanted something cooler, but I wasn't ready to tell him what else I could do with the power of my mind.

"What can the others do?" he pressed, eagerly wanting to know the answer.

"You're an outsider, Devin. I can't divulge that kind of information with you. It would be a betrayal to my coven."

"You told me what yours was," he protested.

"Yes, that's because it's *my* information to tell. If you had a one-on-one conversation with Leslie, for example, and asked her what my ability was, she would never tell you."

"Why did Winona change her mind? Why didn't she want me to go with y'all to Seven Nights?" Devin asked, changing the subject.

"Winona sees your suffering, Devin. She sees you struggle with your personal demons. When you refused her help, she decided she wanted nothing else to do with you. She wants to help you. But no one can help you, not if you don't help yourself first by admitting that you need and want help."

"I try my best," he said through the leather hood. "I want to do good for my wife and daughter."

"That's not your best. Doing good for your loved ones will never be enough. You have to do good for yourself. You have to see yourself as others see you. You're an addict, Devin. We both know this. But the only reason you're a functioning addict is because of your wife and daughter. Now, imagine what you could accomplish if you started to live for yourself, not just them."

The last few minutes of the car ride was in silence. Devin did not ask me any other questions as I drove him back home. We pulled up to a blue, two story, undistinguished, house. The houses within his neighborhood were all very similar to one another. It was easy for me to find, having been here before when I first spied on Devin for a few nights before having dinner with him.

My body tensed up and I almost broke my steering wheel as my grip tightened around it. I threw my SUV in park, the engine cutting itself off automatically as I did, on the street in front of his house. I looked into the darkness through the tinted windows of my vehicle, searching. At first glance a human would just think the front door was left ajar, only a crack. A light from the inside of the home could be seen from the opened door but I could see the wood was also cracked at the frame of the door where it latched. Someone had broken into Devin's home.

"I would tell you to stay in the vehicle but I don't think that would be safe for you either," I said out loud to Devin.

"What's wrong?" he asked, panic entering his voice.

I was banking on Devin's military training to kick in. My tone of voice changed instantly with him. "You must do exactly as I say, no questions asked. Do you understand, Devin?"

He swallowed, afraid, not knowing what was happening on the outside of the vehicle because of the leather hood that still blinded his sight. "Yes, I understand," he replied.

"Whatever happens, whatever we may find, do not freak out. I need you to remain calm no matter what. You must stay close to me, within arm's reach at all times. Now, I'm going to remove your hood. Once I do, I will give you thirty seconds to analyze the situation and to compose yourself. Then, you will need to retrieve the gun from the glove box. It's already loaded. After that we will both get out of the vehicle on my side. You will always walk and stand on my right side once we are both out of the vehicle.

He swallowed again then nodded. "Ok, I'm ready."

I had the leather hood removed in an instant and Devin quickly looked around, taking a second to realize we were in front of his house. If a human were to drive, who followed the speed limit, our homes were just under a half hour apart, the city of New Orleans placed between us. With me being the driver and altering the route, we arrived here an hour and a half later.

Devin was pulling the gun from the glove box five seconds after looking at his front door. "Let's go, I'm ready," he said.

"Devin, it could be a vampire."

"I said I'm ready," he declared a little louder, making eye contact with me, and refusing to break it first.

I opened the driver side door and hit the lock button to lock the other doors so Devin, hopefully, wouldn't be snatched out of the vehicle from the other side. I couldn't turn my back to the darkness to help Devin across the seats. I had my back against my SUV, searching the darkness for the one who broke into the blue house. Devin climbed out, gun held up in front of him, pointing to nothing in particular but still at the ready.

We walked to the front door of the home, Devin on my right, facing the house, watching the front and right side of us, as I walked backwards, watching our backs and the left side. Once we were in his home I slammed the door behind me, immediately smelling the distinguished scent of an unfamiliar vampire.

"Vampire. For sure, vampire," I told Devin.

"What do we do?" he asked.

I didn't answer his question. Instead, I proceeded through the house, entering the living room, with Devin walking beside me, where the scent of blood was thick in the air. We saw the bodies, his wife and daughter, lying on the floor, blood spilled on the floor beside them that poured out from both their throats. Devin's heartbeat intensified, beating rapidly. It was the only noise I could hear. He was most definitely holding his breath. His heart continued to slam against his chest as the seconds passed. Devin did not scream in horror at the sight of his family's bloodied corpses that laid in front of us. He did not pass out, nor did he begin to sob. He stood there, looking at them, gun still raised in front of him. I was impressed at his ability to keep his composure. It had to be from shock, or the high he was surely still feeling. Maybe it was his training.

As I waited for Devin's breakdown to come, I surveyed the room around us, again. There were no signs of a break in, besides the front door. No shattered glass or broken furniture, only blood and two cold bodies. The vampire had obviously fed from them both, sloppily. His wife had enough blood to satisfy one vampire so there was no need to feed from the little girl. But the monster did anyway. The living room housed a gray leather sectional and on the side of it, a white circular coffee table with a vase of flowers on top. Across from the sectional, on the wall, was a white brick fireplace with a flat screen TV mounted above it.

I snapped my neck back toward the vase of flowers that sat on top of the white table. The primary flowers within the vase were red rhododendrons, and the secondary flowers that complemented them were yellow tansies. I walked toward the flowers and bent over to smell them. Their familiar scents of sweet and spicy clove and of prickly wood and rosemary were covered with a strong scent of the vampire's flesh. This particular vampire smelled similar to molten glass. It was a vampire who I had never encountered, yet there was something familiar about the scent I could not recognize.

"Message received," I mumbled to myself, looking at the flowers.

"What?" Devin asked, not hearing what I said.

"Nothing. It's time to go."

"Go? We have to call the police," he argued.

"And what would you tell them, Devin?" I asked.

He did not answer, but instead, asked, "Where are we going?"

"Back to the mansion."

Devin told me where the cameras were placed in his home and I quickly grabbed them all, and his computer they were connected to, before getting back in my SUV to drive us back to my home. This was beginning to turn into a mess.

"Do I need to put this hood back on?" he asked, holding it as we sped down the street.

"Don't bother. I'm not taking the long way. Keeping you in the dark from where my coven resides is now far from important."

"Why did you freak when you saw those flowers?" Devin asked. "I saw you staring at them."

I sped down the highway, going fifty over the posted speed limit. My mind was racing faster than my vehicle. I could also tell that Devin was only asking more questions to distract himself from the memory of his family lying dead at his feet.

"I was a slave, when I was human. I worked on a plantation in Savannah, Georgia. We grew flowers. Flowers are very unique.

They can be used for several purposes, communication being one of them. Today, your modern florist would tell you that certain flowers mean love, lust, friendship, empathy, etcetera, etcetera; anything to get you to buy a bouquet of them. But most florists today don't carry the flowers I'm used to working with. The red flowers, in the vase, were rhododendrons and the yellow ones were tansies."

"Who would send you a message with flowers? And what's the message?" Devin asked.

I pushed a button on my steering wheel, ordering my SUV to call Leslie. Her phone only rang once before her voice came out from my vehicle's speakers. "What's up, Sass?"

"It's him. I was right. He sent a message, via flowers. I'm bringing Devin back with me. We'll arrive within five minutes. Devin's family was killed."

My coven understood my obsession with flowers. They respected it and never questioned my knowledge. Each of us had our own obsession. Flowers were mine.

"Sass, what was the message?" Leslie asked.

I looked at Devin and I was grateful that he had served in the army. I knew his training he received was playing its part in helping him keep his composure. He's going to need it, I thought to myself.

"Danger. War is coming," I said to them both before hanging up.

I heard Devin swallow. Was he ready for war? Maybe he was swallowing to push down his own grief, I did not know. He finally composed himself and asked, "Who was the message from? I have the right to know who killed my family."

"A known enemy. His name is Vincent," I replied.

CHAPTER 10
YEAR 1861: TARGET

"You're pathetic," Vincent's voice bellowed.

I sprinted toward him, my master, as fast and as hard as my body would allow me to go. I felt the power as my feet slammed into the earthy ground beneath me as I was running toward him. He'd been training me for years now, but yet I still wasn't able to leave even a scratch on him.

This time I leaped into the air, directly in front of him, and as my body was descending onto him, he disappeared. His speed was uncanny. Where did he go? I searched my surroundings as my body continued to descend down to the earth. I do not know how he was doing it but, again, his hand was on the back of my neck, both of us in the air, falling. His grip was firm and he most definitely was not holding back. As the ground came closer, Master Vincent quickly pushed my head down with his hand still clasped onto the back of my neck. My head slammed into the hard ground and his feet were on each side of my body.

He leaned down to whisper in my ear. "Why did I beat you, Sassandra?" he said to me.

"You're too fast for me," I replied.

Master Vincent stepped aside and allowed me to get back up to my feet, before saying, "I told you, speed and strength are pointless in a battle with another vampire if you do not know how to utilize them. Your attacks are too obvious. You need an element of surprise. Otherwise, you will fail."

"Fail at what? What am I even training for?" I asked my master.

"I told you before, vampires without proper training will be dead within a few decades. You may run across others like us, and I might not be there to save you. Like humans are to other humans, our kind, also, is not kind to one another. We challenge one another to secure our territory, possessions, power, and even mates. You need to learn how to protect yourself. It's either kill or be killed with us."

"Is that all?" I asked, sarcastically. "You told me before you had plans for me. What did you mean when you said that?"

"Yes, I do have plans for you. But considering your current offense and defense skills, I might have to create another vampire and assign the task to them instead," Master Vincent said, with a serious look on his face.

"Please, no!" I begged. "I'll try harder. I did kill the others who betrayed you, and many others since then," I reminded him.

"Yes, but you returned covered in blood from head to toe. You made a huge mess that night and left a lot of evidence behind. The human authorities started asking questions, even about my plantation that was burned down. We were forced to flee the state because you brought too much attention to us. But I guess Jacksonville hasn't taken notice of our presence here yet. Staying close to water is the best strategy a vampire has for a quick escape. You've managed to learn how to eliminate your human targets with stealth and finesse since then, and you must always continue to do so in the future," Master Vincent warned me.

"Yes, Master. I will, Master," I promised him. And I would do my best to keep that promise. I could not fail him.

"I shall strike a deal with you," Master Vincent proposed.

"What kind of deal?" I asked.

"If you can hit me, better yet even a scratch, just once, then I will tell you the reason for your training. But if you fail to do so before sunrise then I will create a new vampire and train them for the mission at hand instead. Maybe they would make a better drudge than you."

I could not be replaced. I would not allow it. I had to prove myself, yet again. I had to show my master that I was still worthy of being his loyal servant.

"You won't be angry if I hit you?" I asked Master Vincent.

"Will I be angry? Is that what's been holding you back?" Master Vincent said, laughing.

Posthaste, I slithered back into the darkness, hiding myself from the glow of the moon, sheltered by the treetops. I went deep into the woods this time, escaping from Master Vincent's line of sight. I knew Master Vincent would stay in the same spot, waiting for me to strike. I could not hit him coming straight at him, I had tried too many times and each time I failed. If he thought I was being serious this time then he would expect me to attack from behind, most likely. But could I risk that? What if he heard me? If I was going to hit him tonight then I needed to make this attack count. Sunrise was in less than two hours. I sat on the forest ground with my legs crossed, brainstorming.

Only a moment's time had passed when I heard something in the trees behind me. I turned around and my body tensed up as two glowing, yellow, eyes stared back down at me in the pitch black of the night.

Almost an hour and a half had passed now and I still had not made my move to land a strike against my master. Would I fail? It's all I could think of, laying in a pool of my own blood on the ground of the forest that surrounded me in darkness. Had I lost too much blood? I screamed out loud, hoping for Master Vincent to come save me. I needed his help. I was exhausted from losing so much blood so fast. I would not make it back to him in time. The sun would surely find me and finish me off if Master Vincent didn't find me first.

The wind continued to blow and I continued to scream, in agony, "Help! Help me!" Would my master come to my rescue and save me again? I laid in a pool of my own blood on the hard ground, searching for the sky, but my view was obstructed from the trees above. I knew the moon was just above me as I laid there, almost dying. I wish I could see the moon again, I thought to myself.

"Sassandra?" I heard Master Vincent whisper my name, standing a few feet away from where I laid.

"Master?" I replied, barely audible to even myself.

"What happened? Who did this to you? Where are they?" he spat the questions out one after another.

"I... I don't know. It happened so quickly. I can't move."

I heard the leaves rustle below Master Vincent's feet. I could not see him but I knew he had to be turning in circles, searching our surroundings for my attacker.

"I can't move. Please, help me," I begged.

"Wait, Sassandra. Just wait, your body will heal."

"No time, sun is coming up," I gasped, reminding my master.

"Merde!" he barked, a word I did not understand. He rushed to my side, picking me up, cradling my limp body within his arms again, and began to sprint back to our new town to seek shelter from the threats of the unknown attacker, and the sun that would surely destroy the both of us if we were caught by it.

As he ran, carrying my blood-soaked body, I looked at his face. He seemed determined to save me. I wonder why he risked his own life to save mine. Did he love me? Did I love him? I could feel

112

my body slowly healing itself from all my cuts. I was still weak from losing so much blood but I knew I would survive. I could see the fire flickering from the street lanterns up ahead. We had to be within a few miles from the new floral shop we set up when we firsts arrived in Jacksonville.

I reached my trembling hand up to Master Vincent's cheek and traced my finger along his jawline. He looked down at me, smiling, which was new, as he continued to run us toward safety. He knew I was still fascinated with him. Just below his chin, where my finger now rested, I used my nail to cut his flesh, causing a single drop of blood to run down from the cut.

He came to an abrupt stop, the floral shop now within our sight and dropped me. I quickly shifted my body, landing on my feet, crouched, ready for him to strike me back.

"Got ya," I bragged. I had won. He stared at me, clearly confused by my actions.

"Get in the shop, now. Before it's too late," he said before rushing to the door within seconds. I followed him, nervous about being shut in with him after what I had just done.

The door clicked shut behind me and Master Vincent was already at his safe, unlocking and opening its door and looking inside it. He was fumbling around, looking at what was inside a small box within the safe for a moment before shutting and locking it again. He seemed relieved as he looked back up at me.

"There was no attacker, was there? Was there?!" he demanded to know.

I was nervous to answer at first. I walked out of his office to the back of the shop to remove my blood-soaked clothes and to change into some fresh ones after washing myself off. I took my time, purposely prolonging the inevitable conversation that was sure to come.

I entered back into his office and he was still sitting in the same spot, patiently waiting for my response.

"When I was thinking on how to successfully attack you, I heard a noise behind me," I explained to my master. "When I turned around, I saw an opossum staring back at me."

Master Vincent held his hand up to cut me off. "So, you saw an opossum and you decided to play opossum yourself? In order to get me to come to you?" he guessed correctly.

I said nothing, instead just nodded my head yes.

"And?" he asked, wanting me to continue.

"The wind was blowing close to the direction in which you were waiting for me. I knew if I could get you to smell my blood that you would come. Well, I hoped that you would. You saved me before. So, I crushed a rock to make its end sharp. I cut myself with it, deep, all over my body. I needed enough blood to get my scent into the air for you to smell."

"So, your plan was for me to come to you instead of you coming to me," Master Vincent stated to himself more than to me. I stood there, waiting for him to say more but he did not. He sat in silence at his desk, looking at nothing in particular but still seeing everything.

"What did you think happened to me when you saw me?" I asked, breaking the silence.

"I told you, there are others, like us, out there."

"Yes, that's part of the reason I faked an attack. You stated that other vampires existed. Did you really think I was attacked by another one of us? I know you know of other vampires, but you never speak of them. Can't I meet them one day?" My excitement overflooded my mind and the questions began to pour out of my mouth. I knew there were others, like us! Would they all want to fight me? Or could we just exchange stories? I had so many questions. Could I make friends with other vampires? Questions galloped through my mind and different questions flowed out of my mouth at the same time.

"Sassandra, shut up!" Master Vincent ordered me.

My mouth closed with a snap. I could feel what little blood I had left inside my body begin to boil over. The anger flowed to my fingertips and I could feel my hands start to tremble.

"Oh, calm down. Stop acting like it's the first time I've told you to stop talking. You always ask too many questions," Master Vincent said to me; which was true.

He was livid with me. "Willingly to lose your own blood is reckless! Vampire blood is very valuable. It's the most valuable thing a vampire has. Never spill your own blood like that again! Now, there are more important questions for you to ask rather than about other vampires," he said, smirking again.

"Like what?" I asked. Now I was the one who was confused. His mood changed faster than the phases of the moon.

"You tell me."

I thought back to earlier tonight and it instantly came to me. "What have you really been training me for?" I asked my master.

"It's quite simple, really. I need an assassin, Sassandra. An exceptional one."

"Assassin? Who do you wish for me to kill now?" I asked my master. I would do it, without question. I owed it to him. He was my everything. I already killed for him. What's one more body? And again, and again? I would kill for my master whenever he asked.

"Tell me, what do you know about our new President of the United States?"

At first, I was taken by surprise but quickly recalled the newspaper I'd recently seen. A wrinkled face with dark facial hair and a high forehead, and a tall hat, flashed in my memory. Under the picture was a quote that read, "In doing this there needs to be no bloodshed or violence; and there shall be none, unless it be forced upon the national authority," followed by his name, declared to be the newest President of the United States of America.

"You want me to assassinate Abraham Lincoln?" I asked, in disbelief.

"Exactly. He is planning to destroy everything I have built for myself in this country," Master Vincent explained. "I know I've already lost the floral plantation years ago, but we can rebuild it, together. We can enslave even more this time. Have a fortune. The power that money buys in this country is unbelievable. This country is just shy of being one hundred years old. It's only beginning to bloom, like a flower." Master Vincent stood up with his hands above his head, illustrating how a flower blooms, letting his own excitement get the best of him this time. He continued, "Just think of the future, Sassandra. One hundred years from now, how much power do you think I will have? I can rule this country and you can be at my side. Don't you want to be by my side?" he whispered to me, looking into my eyes.

"Yes, Master. I will always be at your side. I will do whatever you ask of me. How will I get to him?" I asked.

"We will acquire a carriage for your travels. You will need to set up shop close to the White House." Master Vincent paused, walked to the shelf across the room and touched a single purple iris that was growing in a small pot. "Do some surveillance," he continued, "before you make your move. And when you return, I will expect proof this time. Bring me his head."

Decapitation. My master wanted me to chop off the head of the President of the United States of America and bring it to him.

"You're not coming with me?" I asked.

"No. I have other objectives as well," he said without elaborating anymore. He always had other objectives. Things he needed to do, without me. Sometimes he would be gone for days at a time. But he never offered me an explanation of where he went without me or what he was doing.

"As you wish, Master," I said, bowing my head. Lincoln's blood will soon be spilled. The only question now was…

"Will I have a weapon?" I asked.

Master Vincent tapped his fingers along the top of his desk and spoke, "I will equip you with everything you will need. However, there is a grand weapon that could help you on your future missions. You do not use your hands to wield it, rather your mind." He spoke softly as he continued to drum his fingers across his desk, speaking of this grand weapon.

"My mind?" I inquired. How could my mind be a weapon? I wondered.

"You might possess the gift, but I haven't seen any evidence of it as of yet," Master Vincent said, looking into my eyes. "Do you remember your dreams, Sassandra?"

"We don't sleep, Master."

"No, no. Your dreams from when you were human, when you used to have a soul," he said.

Being human is not something I'd thought of since being changed into an immortal. It's part of my past that held no importance to me now. I strode across the room, thinking about his question. I remembered certain events from when I was human. I remembered the sound of Master Vincent's shoes as he walked across the hard wood floors, the cool touch of the amulet as I tried to fasten it around my neck, the lashings I received from Master Vincent, the smell of smoke from the fire, and the moon flowers blooming under the stars, changing into a soft glow of blue, as my eyes adjusted to their new power. That was my last memory I had as a human.

"No, I cannot recall dreaming. I know what a dream is. I just cannot remember any of them."

Master Vincent stepped away from his desk and was now standing very close, behind me. "Close your eyes and try to remember what I remember," he whispered to me, lips practically touching my ear. "What do you see?"

I closed my eyes and tried to think, tried to remember. Nothing but darkness filled my mind. The only thing I could focus on was how close Master Vincent's lips were to me. The darkness that filled my mind disappeared and an image of myself turned around, placing my lips onto Master Vincent's...

"What do you see?" Master asked me, snapping me back to reality.

"Nothing. I'm sorry, Master. I only saw darkness. What does that mean?"

"It means nothing. I want you to practice. Your mind wasn't ready when I first turned you. The minds of new vampires are scattered, distracted by thirst. Now that you've almost learned to control yours, you can start practicing. Try to remember your dreams. Once you can remember your dreams then we will move onto the next step of using your mind," Master Vincent instructed me.

"What's the next step?" I asked.

"Control," he replied.

CHAPTER 11
YEAR 1861: ENOUGH

At first, I thought traveling by horse and carriage was absurd. After all, I was a vampire, the fastest predator on Earth. I was wrong. The carriage provided shade, I still hid under a thick quilt as well, and shelter from the sun and occasional rain when needed and it gave me a space for my belongings. I had many dresses I stole from multiple shops from towns I traveled through and even more shoes. Master Vincent also gave me a ngulu, an execution weapon, to use. Its blade was made of iron and it cured at the top in the shape of a crescent moon where the outer edge was sharp enough to easily cut through bone, even when used by a human. This would be the weapon I used on Lincoln to sever his head from his body.

When I first arrived in Washington, D.C., I continued to follow the route that Master Vincent gave me and I was soon riding past the White House. I did not slow the speed of the carriage but I did take in its many, beautiful, details as I rode past. I counted ten windows on the first level with the door between the center of them and windows above each of those for a total of twenty-one. The humans made it so easy for an attack. The sun would be rising soon so I decided to circle back to find an isolated place to park the carriage and to feed the horse before anyone would see me. I parked the carriage under a grove of trees beside a large river and settled in for the new day, reading multiple newspaper clippings I collected along my trip, to learn more about Abraham Lincoln. I noticed a big difference in what was printed about him once I entered the Northern states, compared to the articles that were printed in the Southern ones. The South only wrote about how he was trying to destroy them with war and bloodshed where the North showed him as a loving family man with a wife and four children that wanted equality for all the citizens of this great nation. I memorized the words of each article and slowly saw more wrinkles and facial hair on my target's face as I laid the articles beside one another from the dates they were printed. He was only shown smiling in the photographs that were from the Northern states.

After a while, I became irritated from the contrast the articles showed. It was like night and day with the North and South. I folded the newspaper articles back up again and placed them back into my bag and tossed it to the back of the carriage. I laid down, covering all my body and head with the quilt, and closed my eyes; not to sleep, but I wanted to try to remember my dreams again. I laid perfectly still, trying to focus, for just over twelve hours, until the sun had set again. I was upset that I wasn't able to recall a single dream of my human life. Master Vincent said that I might possess an ability, a power, that could help me but I didn't know how to get it to work. Frustrated, and wanting to prove myself to Master Vincent, I stripped my dress off and put on a new one that fit a bit tighter and had much less material to it. It was a simple dark gray gown with black buttons that went from my navel to the top of my breast, that didn't actually button, they were just for show.

I fed the horse again before harnessing it back up to the carriage. I made my way back to the White House and upon my return there were many humans outside the grounds, taking photos of another horse and carriage that was leaving its grounds.

I followed the black, horse drawn, carriage from within the shadows of the night, as it cruised down the street. The carriage had an open barouche top and as it rounded a corner, I could see the hands of President Lincoln holding the reins himself. I did not see his face but I knew it was he who was guiding the horses because of his tall, black, stovepipe hat that he wore in many of his photographs.

Sitting beside him in the carriage were two others who I did not recognize. The first, sitting beside Lincoln, was a handsome man who was wearing a black, long sleeved, shirt with a high collar that covered his neck. He also sported a golden vest with black dress slacks. His hair was dark and very messy and it blew wildly as the wind entered the carriage from above them as the horses trotted along the road. Across from the two men was a woman with fair skin, however, this was not the President's wife. Instead, this woman had short wavy brown hair and was dressed rather floozy for a lady. A shawl made of white fur was loosely draped around her bare shoulders and her corset was the only other thing covering her upper body. One of her feet rested between the legs of the man with the wild black hair. Her black boot that covered her foot was unzipped halfway down, exposing her pantyhose. Why would the President of the United States be traveling with such company?

The horses pulled the carriage and its three passengers, with me following behind in mine, for a few miles before reaching its destination. I read in one of the Northern articles that President Lincoln and his family did not reside at the White House. Instead, they spent most of their time just a few miles down the road in a large two-story home that sat on over two hundred acres of land. There were soldiers close to the property so I did not want to get too close, afraid I would be spotted. I decided to go around and enter the property from the opposite side by foot. I parked the carriage and tied the horse to a tree a couple miles away. I grabbed the ngulu weapon Master Vincent gave me before crossing the open fields from the backside of the house with such speed that if a soldier was looking in my direction, they would only see a blur. I counted on the night and my speed to help disguise my movements from the humans.

I rested my hand on the masonry of the home as I peered through a window. I did not see anyone but I could hear them speaking. I creeped around the home to look into a different window, where President Lincoln was chatting about the casualties of the ongoing Civil War. This time his wife, Mary, was in the room with him, along with the other woman wearing the white corset, who occupied the carriage moments before. Lincoln's face was ridden with stress.

"America will never be destroyed from the outside. If we falter and lose our freedoms, it will be because we destroyed ourselves," the President said, as he paced around the large wooden table that Mary and the other woman sat at, listening to him.

I was taken back by his face. This was the first time I had actually seen him up close. Compared to a picture in the newspaper clipping I had of him, he looked much older. The picture was only a couple weeks old but this war was quickly aging him. I almost felt sorry for the man but I knew I had to destroy him. I knew I could not face Master Vincent again unless I was holding his head in my hands. I gripped the ngulu tighter and was about to break through the window to kill the three occupants within the dining room but just before I did, exhaustion coursed through me. The strength I felt as a vampire was rapidly leaving my body.

"What is happening to me?" I asked myself as I dropped my weapon to use both hands to try and steady myself next to the house. Was I becoming human again? A ripple of gray smoke now clouded my vision and my legs began to buckle beneath me. I felt my hands descending down the house, trying to grasp anything to hold onto as my body collapsed and darkness overtook me, leaving me unconscious.

"One of the strongest I have ever fed upon," said a strange, harmonious, voice. I could not see the one who was speaking nor the ones she was speaking to. They must have me blindfolded, I thought to myself.

"When will she awaken?" asked another, more menacing voice, this time. I could tell it belonged to a man and the first was that of a woman. Was this the voices of the two who were traveling with Lincoln in his carriage?

"Probably in a moment or two," the first voice spoke again. "Do not fret, she will still be weak."

"She was definitely after Abraham," a third voice, from another woman, said. "She was looking at him through the window. She acted like he was the only one in the room. Like I didn't even exist."

So, the voice of the second woman was the one who was in the carriage with the President and the other gentleman, I continued to say to myself in my mind. How did they capture me? What happened to me? Why was I so tired? Whose voice belonged to the first woman that spoke of feeding from me? My body convulsed as I realized that it had not been humans that captured me. The images of the man and woman that traveled in the carriage with Lincoln now flashed in my mind again. Their beauty, their pale skin, they were like me, vampires.

I felt my eyes flutter open. They were so heavy, there was no blindfold. Before me stood the man and woman, vampires, that traveled with Lincoln earlier in the night. Where was the other? I was bound to a wooden chair. I tried pulling at my restraints to free myself but I was too weak. I looked at my hands and they were tied with threadlike silver chains.

"Do not bother to try to break free," said a woman's voice from behind me. "You are currently weaker than the average human. We have some questions for you."

"What is your name, vampire?" the woman who looked like a harlot asked me. I said nothing, still trying to pry my hands free. She leaned down and was now nose to nose with me. "Answer me or I will kill you."

The vampire woman who was behind me now walked around the chair I was bound to, and came to stand beside the male vampire. Her hair was jet-black, long, and braided, and was decorated with feathers and her brown eyes seemed to pierce through my soul. This woman was familiar to me. I remembered her...

"Is it really you?" I asked the Indigenous woman. The harlot stepped aside, away from me and followed my gaze as I stared into the eyes of the one who talked to me from my dreams before I was turned.

The Native woman tilted her head, continuing to look upon me. They all stood there, looking at me, and I sat there, staring at the woman that visited my dreams.

"Who do you think I am?" asked the woman, her voice just as I remembered it from my dreams.

"It *is* you. You're the one who promised to save me," I answered.

"My dear, I have never met you before."

The male vampire stepped in front of me, breaking my view of the woman from my dreams. "Enough of this," he said. "She's trying to trick you. You said it yourself that she's the strongest you've ever fed from."

"Step aside, Arubrey," the Indigenous woman ordered. "She truly believes she knows me."

The male vampire, named Arubrey, moved next to the harlot vampire and the Native vampire now came closer to me.

"I have an idea. A compromise, if you're willing. You answer three questions of ours, since there are three of us, and we will answer one question of yours, since there is only one of you."

I nodded in agreement and waited. The Indigenous woman looked at the harlot and the harlot asked me again, "What is your name?"

"Sassandra," I answered truthfully.

"Most vampires would try to lie, Sassandra," the Native American from my dreams said. "Thank you for speaking the truth. I can always tell when one is lying. This is the only reason that you are still alive. You said you knew me and I can tell that you truly think that you do. I am intrigued to know why it is that you believe this. Now, tell me. Who do you think I am?"

"When I was human, I remember dreaming of you. You were sitting beside a fire. You cried feathers and you held a crow in the palm of your hand. I remember pleading with you to save me."

"Enough! This is fucking ridiculous," Arubrey swore. I ignored him, continuing to gaze into the eyes of the one who promised to save me. Arubrey said something else but I wasn't listening to him.

"You must answer him, Sassandra. That was the deal. You answer three questions and we let you ask one," she said to me.

I broke eye contact and looked at Arubrey. He was clearly annoyed that I ignored him. "What was the question again?" I asked him.

"I said, why would a woman of color, such as yourself, want to assassinate Abraham Lincoln?"

"My master ordered me to," I replied. I had to finish the mission. I could not fail him! I began to panic, trying to escape my restraints again. I was still weak, unable to break the silver that bound me.

"Calm down, Sassandra," the Indigenous vampire said. I refocused my attention to her. I was torn. I wanted to know more about her. About why I wanted her to save me. I couldn't remember. But I needed to kill the President. I could not fail him. Not again. I couldn't disappoint my master!

As I continued to struggle with my restraints, the vampire that was dressed like a whore spoke up, "It's your turn. You gonna ask us a question or what? We ain't got all night."

If they were only allowing me one question then I had to strategize. "What are all of your names?" I asked. Master Vincent would want to know as much information about them when I returned to him.

"My name is Winona," said the Native American vampire. "This is Arubrey and Leslie."

Leslie did not miss a beat and instantly asked her question, "What is your master's name?"

I did not want to answer. He would be angry with me if I told them any information about him. "I do not wish to answer that question." I knew they wouldn't like that answer but it was the truth.

Winona stepped forward and spoke softly to me, "If you refuse to answer then I'm afraid our conversation is over and we will be forced to destroy you. Is that what you wish? Are you really willing to die for your master?" Winona asked me.

My skin was crawling in fear. I did not need to breathe but I began to gasp for air. I was suffocating. I pulled on the silver threads with all my might but they would not budge. I began to scream in fear. Fear from failing. Fear of my master's rage. "Yes!" I screamed at them. "Yes, I would. I would die for him! I will kill for him and I will die for him! Please, let me go. I have to go back to him. I need him! Master! Please, Master, do not be angry with me!" I begged, screeching, and panic driven.

Arubrey stepped toward me, now wielding the ngulu weapon I brought with me. He raised the weapon above his head, ready to strike me with it. Ready to behead me. This time it was Arubrey who looked me in the eyes and I looked into his, accepting my fate.

"Soon," I said the word out loud, ready for death to take me, once again.

It played out in slow motion but it happened very quickly as well. I saw Arubrey bring his hand back and snap it forward again, and the whistle of the iron blade was cutting through the air as

Arubrey swung it, bringing it closer and closer to my neck to sever my own head from my body.

"Stop," Winona ordered.

The curved blade came to an abrupt halt and now rested against the flesh of my neck. Arubrey's stood, glaring at me, like he was chiseled from stone, unmoving, and unwilling to break his glare into my eyes.

"Step back, Arubrey," Winona instructed the vampire to move away from me. "I now understand the situation. She's been entranced."

"Entranced? Can you break it?" Leslie asked.

"Yes, but it's never pleasant for the victim."

Victim? I wasn't a victim. What were they speaking about? I loved my master. And after I killed Lincoln then he would surely love me back.

Leslie left the room and quickly returned with many items in tow. She placed them all on a nearby table and stepped back for Winona to begin her work. I was confused as to what was happening and why the atmosphere in the room changed. No one spoke. We all just watched as Winona started to grind down something in a small clay bowl.

"What are you doing?" I asked Winona.

"Your soul has been tainted by lies and wickedness. I have to cleanse it. I'm going to perform a smudging ceremony on you."

"I hate to break it to you but vampires do not have souls," I informed her.

Arubrey chuckled at my comment and I sent daggers to him using my eyes. Why would he think that was funny? Winona stopped grinding the contents of her clay bowl and turned to face me.

"Vampires do have souls, Sassandra. I will prove it to you one day."

"No. Master Vincent told me that I lost my soul when he turned me. Vampires do not have souls. He wouldn't lie to me." I tried to convince them but all three ignored me.

Winona then slowly walked to stand in front of me and lit the contents of the clay bowl on fire with a single match. I watched as the flame burned for thirty seconds before she placed her hand over the bowl to smother the flame, depriving it from oxygen. Once the flame was extinguished, she removed her hand and a wave of smoke rose into the air. Winona plucked a single white feather from her hair and used it to fan the smoke into my face while softly chanting in a language I did not understand. The smoke changed colors and moved like magic from my face. It intertwined around my neck and made its way down my body, twisting and turning, until it reached my feet. Once the smoke settled onto my feet, it changed to pure white and engulfed my entire body.

This was not the same smoke I saw earlier when I passed out, nor did this smoke try to suffocate me like the smoke from the plantation fire did. This smoke was quite the opposite. Instead of suffocating me, it was breathing life into me. I thought I passed out again but what I was witnessing this time was not a dream. They were memories I had forgotten. Memories of my past.

I was a little girl again and I was sitting on my mama's lap as my papa was poking at the fire we were gathered around. Our entire village was there, with us. Everyone was chatting and laughing under the stars. The warmth the flames provided was more than enough to keep me warm. They made me feel safe and happy.

My papa stood up and our tribe fell silent. His face was painted with white and red lines and symbols all over. He began to speak and everyone was silent, listening to his words.

"Is Papa gonna tell us another story?" I asked, turning to look at my mama's face.

She smiled at me and whispered. "Yes, he is the leader of our tribe," she answered. "Now listen to him, Sassy."

Papa continued to speak. I did not pay much attention until he mentioned my name. "Sassandra, you turn four today. Are you happy about it?" he asked me. I was shy and turned to hide my face in my mother's arms. I didn't want everyone looking at me. Papa laughed and our small village laughed with him.

"I bless you, my child. May the moon in our sky watch over you as you grow into a strong woman. I sense that you will journey far from this land and you will become very powerful. More powerful than even me." Papa walked around the circle of fire that we were all gathered around. I watched as he closed his eyes and continued to speak. "This journey will be difficult and you will lose your way. Be strong, Sassandra. Always remember that you are loved. Not only by your mama and papa, but by all of us within our village. Be one with the moon and its power will protect you from evil."

After Papa was finished speaking everyone cheered and we all got up to dance around the fire as the moon watched over me from above.

A new memory took hold of my mind. This one was different in many ways from the last. We were no longer in our village around the fire, laughing. Instead, I was in a darkened cellar with the people of my village, and others I did not recognize also shared the cellar with us. We were all shackled in chains. The sound of cries from men, women, and other children echoed off the walls that enclosed around us. We were forced to relieve ourselves where we slept. Many of us grew sick and were separated, including Mama and Papa. I cried for them, reaching out as they were unchained and taken out of the cellar, leaving me. I never saw them again after that, but I finally remembered what had happened.

I heard footsteps above us and a man's voice was speaking, "Sir, what should we do with the ones who are sick? Smallpox has spread and many are now on the brink of death."

Another voice of a man answered, "Throw them overboard. We don't have enough food to go around anyway."

I counted to myself as I heard the splashes of the others fall into the water, one after another, after another, until finally, the screaming stopped.

"Wake up. Sassandra, wake up," Winona spoke to me, bringing me back to reality.

Everything changed. I looked at the three other vampires in the room. "I was awake but I was still sleeping," I said to them. "What did you do to me?" I asked Winona.

"I told you; I cleansed your soul. How long has Vincent had you hypnotized?"

Memories of Vincent beside my bed at night when I was just a little girl, drinking my blood night after night. Vincent holding the leather whip, cracking through the air as it hit me over and over. Omari was on the other side of the tree that I was on, dying tied to it after being struck thirty-nine times with the same whip that left its scars on me. Vincent catching me the night the house burned down. Only he wasn't catching me, he was catching the amulet I was clutching onto. Vincent whispering into my ears for me to kill for him, again and again. All those people I killed… they were kind to me. They were Omari's friends and family. They were *my* friends and *my* family."

"Long enough," I said, truly awake from his spell for the first time.

CHAPTER 12
PRESENT DAY: FAMILY

The smell of vomit cascaded throughout the mansion, splattered all over the black and white marbled floor. Winona was attending to Devin, back in the same room he just left a couple hours prior. The shock of the death of his wife and daughter had decided to physically overflow out of Devin's mouth once we made it inside the entrance to the mansion. I wondered how long Leslie would scrub the floor this time.

"What happened to him?" Leslie asked me, entering the kitchen, after I heard Winona reassuring her for the third time moments before that Devin would in fact be okay.

I opened the fridge, which we had converted to keep things warm rather than cool, taking out two clear packs of blood, and looked at Leslie, asking her if she wanted one. She ignored the blood, waiting for me to answer her question. I opened one of the blood packs and poured it into a crystal champagne glass and brought the drink to my lips. I could feel the warmth of the blood on my face just before downing the ten ounces of red liquid in one swallow. The blood stored in the warmer was type O, negative. When discussing flavors of humankind, one of the rare topics almost all vampires tended to agree on, we all preferred this type of blood. It was the purest tasting, compared to the others. Hospitals would easily charge over three hundred dollars for a bag this size for a transfusion. Good thing our coven donated a significant amount of money to the Red Cross each year. Drinking from a human was much more satisfying, but the packs served their purpose of nutrition when we did not feel like hunting. They were a vampire's fast food.

"Isn't it obvious, Leslie?" I finally responded. "His life just hit rock bottom. He was here, getting high from our venom when his family were being murdered. You'd probably vomit too, if you were human."

"What did he do when he saw them?"

"Nothing. He just… stood there. He must have been still feeling high from the night before. Who knows how long it will take for his high and the shock to wear off?" I told her, refilling my glass with the second bag of blood.

"Well, Winona said that he would be fine so there is no need to worry," Leslie said to me, but I knew she was just saying it out loud to reassure herself.

"You care for the human, don't you?" I asked her.

Leslie's eyes darted to mine and I could tell she didn't appreciate the question. Maybe she wasn't sure of an answer. She changed the subject. "Arubrey should be back shortly. He went hunting to prepare for tomorrow night. While you were gone, we decided to visit Seven Nights sooner rather than later. The immortal child is an issue that cannot be put off."

"Did you already hunt? You'll need your strength tomorrow as well," I suggested to my friend.

"No. I'm not going. Going to the bar tomorrow night isn't the only thing in the plans that changed."

I rolled my eyes. Plans seemed to always be changing recently and my input seemed to never matter. "What now?" I asked.

"After we hung up, I told Arubrey and Winona that I no longer intended on going to Seven Nights with them. Arubrey is pissed, of course, but Winona actually agreed with me. You have the vampire's scent that killed his family now, so she's staying here with me to look over Devin. She said she was going to help him, whether he wants her help or not."

I could see the hope in Leslie's eyes. She no longer cared about the war that was sure to come. Her focus was now on the human, Devin, who was brought into all of this by being in the wrong place at the wrong time.

I took a second glass from the kitchen cabinet and took two more packs of blood from the warmer. I opened one of the packs and poured it into the glass, pushing it across the island to my friend.

"Drink, Leslie," I ordered. "You'll need your strength as well if you're going to protect Devin. We never know who could walk through our front door one of these nights."

Leslie nodded and drank the warm blood I offered her. I kissed my friend on the cheek and gave her a hug before grabbing a couple towels and a gallon of bleach. I left Leslie alone with her thoughts and made haste in cleaning up Devin's vomit before Arubrey returned. No vampire wants to see and smell vomit right after drinking from a human. I'm sure Leslie would insist on cleaning the floors again once she processed her thoughts.

I tossed the dirty towels in the fireplace and started a fire to cleanse the stench within the air. I made my way upstairs and quietly entered the room without knocking. Devin was lying on his back on the king-sized bed, resting, on top of the blanket. Winona was sitting by his side, mumbling to herself in Navajo, her first language. I recognized a few of the words she was speaking in her chant. They were almost the same I heard the night I first met her, bound to the chair, when she healed my own soul, setting me free from the spell that my creator had placed and kept me under from when I was just four years old. I stood in silence as she continued to chant and fan smoke using a feather from the same clay bowl that she used on me over sixteen decades ago. I watched the smoke as it moved over Devin's body. It had beauty and grace, just like Winona did. The colorful smoke was kind and gentle as it moved up Devin's body, becoming one with his flesh until it covered him entirely like a blanket would. Once Winona stopped chanting, the smoke faded away into nothingness and the healing ceremony was over. I was surprised that Leslie didn't want to stay in the room to watch this.

Winona stood from the bed and gestured toward the door for me to follow her into the hall. Just at the end of the hall was Arubrey and Leslie, waiting for us. They sat together on a backless bench, upholstered in leather, matching both their outfits.

"How's Devin?" Leslie urged, standing up.
Winona put her hand up in the air to calm Leslie before she worked herself up, like usual. "He will be fine," she assured her. "The healing ceremony is over and now he requires rest. When he awakens, he will be back to his normal self before addiction consumed him."

"I still cannot believe you had the audacity to kick me out," Leslie said, glaring at Winona.

"You left me with no choice," Winona interjected. "You were acting hysterical. It was either that or I was going to feed from your lifeforce to calm you down."

Arubrey cleared his throat, for no other reason but to have the focus put on him. "Plans have changed, again," he said, looking at me.

"Yes, Leslie informed me. I guess it's just the two of us going to Seven Nights tomorrow evening, while Winona and Leslie stay here with Devin." I repeated what Leslie had told me to show that I was fully aware of the drastic changes from the original plan, which was, originally, me staying here by myself.

"Are you ready for this?" was all Arubrey said, looking at me, before leaving the hallway. He was totally pissed at the situation. This change of plans altered our advantage and possibly the outcome of the mission. I understood his frustration. I wanted nothing more than to succeed but dealing with immortal children could be disastrous.

Disappointed as well, I went to my room to prepare. One could say my room was different, to say the least. The walls were covered in floral printed wallpaper from the 1940s. I had various terra cotta clay pots scattered around, in corners, on shelves, and desks, all growing exotic flowers. I had a workstation set up, with burners, thermometers, beakers, and other various instruments, in the middle of the room where I practiced chemistry on flowers I grew from the garden and greenhouse. My closet stuck out like a sore thumb compared to everything else in the room, mainly because of its heavy metal door. I pressed my thumb on the digital print pad, attached to the wall beside it and I heard the bolt unlock. I pulled the heavy door open. "What to wear, what to wear," I said to myself, as I entered my weapons vault. One of the best parts about being a vampire was being able to witness how fashion had changed, decade after decade. I had been a vampire for over sixteen decades now. Sometimes like history, fashion also, most definitely, repeated itself.

I stripped all my clothes off and I let my mind wander to a different time of my past while picking out clothes, shoes, and accessories. I remembered the night Vincent told me of a power that I may possess. A power that would come from my mind. I was hopeful at first but my hope quickly turned to frustration when I was unable to produce results of such an ability. Over the years, Leslie and I became close. She knew how I felt, not having an extra ability such as Arubrey and Winona did. Leslie took me under her wing. She taught me hand-to-hand combat and she was a much better teacher than Vincent ever was to me. She was patient and kind, but still tough enough to never take it easy on me during our sessions. Once she thought I was good enough, she started to train me with melee weapons. Like her, I made using weapons my special ability, although I would never achieve the level of greatness as she had. I wanted to stand out from Leslie, from all of my coven. I started researching flowers and they quickly became an obsession of mine. There was something about certain flowers that I knew was unique to our kind. I just did not know what it was for a long time.

Over time, I was finally able to tap into my mind's special ability, but I hid it from my coven as long as I could, afraid Leslie would hate me for having one when she did not. Because of this fear, I still hesitate to speak about it to Leslie. When I finally confessed, I could see the dreams of humans, like Vincent could, my coven was beyond ecstatic. Although Leslie seemed supportive of my ability, I could still see the hurt within her face. As my powers grew so did the hurt in my best friend's eyes. I caught myself standing in a trance, my naked reflection staring back at me in the mirror. I shook the thoughts of the past out of my mind and refocused.

Any fashionista would tell you that the most important part of any outfit are the shoes. Always start at the bottom and work your way up. I removed a clear box from its shelf and opened it, taking my heeled boots out. Humans would never find my heels on a runway. I always ordered from the same company and then altered the heels once they arrived, making them deadly, one way or the other. This pair of platform ankle boots were made of black leather and had various zippers stitched into them. The heels themselves were one giant spike, made from pure silver. I grabbed a pair of black latex pants that unzipped in the rear and a red, sheer, crop top. I picked out a pair of leather gloves and pulled them over my hands before snatching two thin silver spikes off a shelf and twirling my hair around them, securing them in place. I checked myself out in the mirror then exited my closet, locking it back just as a knock came at my bedroom door.

"It's open."

Arubrey came into my room and gave it a quick look around, and had to readjust his facial expression from disgust.

"I know, you think I have a grandmother's taste when it comes to my room," I said to him.

"I understand why you obsess over flowers, but really? Wallpaper?" he teased, raising an eyebrow as he ran his index finger along the wallpaper to feel its texture. This was the first time he had ever stepped foot into my room. If he kept judging it, I would make sure it was his last visit too.

"Any changes with Devin?" I asked.

"No. Leslie is sitting with him now," he said, before lowering his tone to just a whisper and adding, "I think she has a crush on the human."

I smiled. It's rare that Arubrey ever spoke of anything that wasn't serious. "Yes, I agree. I noticed that as well."

142

"Anyway, we still have plenty of time before sunset. I'll be in my room seeking penance until then." Arubrey turned to leave but I stopped him just before he shut the door.

"Arubrey, how long will this go on? You've been punishing yourself since I've known you."

He said nothing for a few moments, just standing there in his own thoughts. "I deserve it," he finally spoke, before snapping my door shut behind him.

I wished I could help Arubrey. We all did, but he was very stubborn. I refocused my thoughts onto my experiments and went to my workstation. I turned the Bunsen burner on and grabbed a moon flower and started to cut into its stem to pass the time.

Nightfall came and I put my equipment away, pleased with the results of the experiment I performed on myself. I made my way down the hall to Arubrey's room, staggering a little as I walked. I knocked, respectfully, just as he did earlier. Arubrey opened the door to greet me, wearing a black t-shirt with its arms ripped off, showing off his perfectly sculpted muscles. The burn scar that was on the left side of his neck ran down his arm and all the way to his fingertips. His denim jeans were also black, and a little too snug in the front if he would have asked me.

"What, no tie tonight?" I teased him.

Arubrey smirked at my comment. "Well, it is a bar after all," he said, while flexing his muscles as he ran his hand through his thick, messy hair. "I'm driving, by the way."

"I promise the effects will wear off before we make it to the garage."

"I trust you, but I'm still driving."

I wrapped one arm around Arubrey's waist as he started his Arch motorcycle and floored it, hitting over one hundred miles per hour within seconds. I didn't care for having my hair messed up from the wind, but Arubrey loved cruising down the highway on his bike. We flew past a police cruiser and the officers didn't even bother to light us up, not that they would be able to catch us. My mind was now clear again and I looked to the sky, searching for the moon but it was covered by clouds tonight.

We pulled up outside of St. Louis Cemetery No. 1, the oldest cemetery within New Orleans. We both jumped over the filthy brick wall with ease and paused, looking at one another, as we landed. As vampires, we could already feel the vibrations of the beat beneath our feet from the music that was surely blasting within the underground vampire bar. We continued to listen for another second, listening to a group of humans from the other side of the cemetery.

"Tourist," he said, barely audible.

"Yes, I feel sorry for them. The ones who come here, obsessing over the darkness but they're too blind to see the truth."

"And what exactly is the truth?" Arubrey asked as we walked, passing multiple mausoleums, toward our destination, avoiding the humans.

We finally reached a tomb, made from red brick and concrete, with a triangular top. "The truth is that you do not find darkness; it finds you," I said, pushing the tomb's secret bricked door open and closing it behind us as we crossed its threshold, just as a group of humans could be heard, excitedly chatting about a voodoo priestess, as they unknowingly passed by the tomb we just secretly entered.

In the middle of the cramped and darkened tomb was a sarcophagus. Inscribed within its stone lid was a quote: *One thing Death shall never touch is our love.* Arubrey took hold of the lid, which was way too heavy for a single mortal to move on their own, and pushed it open with one hand, revealing steps that led down into more darkness. I closed the lid shut behind us as we both started our descent. At the bottom of the steps sat an empty desk. Arubrey tossed two-hundred-dollar bills onto the desk, adding to the pile of unattended money sitting there, and we walked through an old paneled, wooden, door that resided across from the desk.

The booming of the music we felt above ground was now shaking our bones as we entered the bar. The room was square and was dimly lit with neon lights. It was big in size but the center of the first floor was a loft that looked down below to the second level of the bar. Arubrey made his way around the room to the other side and I followed his lead. We both sat down together at a small table that was next to the railing that allowed us to look to the second floor below.

"If our target comes tonight, he'll have to pass us to get to the stairs that lead down to the bar. If the child doesn't smell Devin's scent outside, he may not come inside. But you'll be able to remember their scent from Devin's place?" Arubrey asked, having to actually speak up for once because of the music.

"Of course, I'll remember. We can go back out in a while if he doesn't show and we can track him. Will you grab us some drinks while we wait? I'll have the usual," I spoke. "You'll have to pay. I didn't want to be burdened carrying a purse."

Arubrey glared at me but he still did as I requested. If we're going to be here, we might as well enjoy some blood. I watched Arubrey's back as he took the second set of steps that took him below to an even darker room where the long bar was. There was only one female bartender tonight. I did not recognize this vampire. The older, powerful, vampires, such as my coven, hardly made appearances at places like this. Not because we were stuck up, but for safety reasons. Vampires with power always had a target on their backs and our coven was the leader of the vampire community in this country.

"So, what's in a Bloody Karen?" Arubrey asked me as he handed me my drink.

"It's the human version of a Bloody Mary but the tomato juice is replaced with blood."

"It sounds fucking disgusting," Arubrey said, making a weird face.

I chuckled at him inside my head. It was odd having a normal conversation with him. "What are you drinking?"

"Deadman's Blood," Arubrey said, raising his glass that was filled with a black liquid in the air for a toast.

I raised my glass and we clinked them together. "What's in yours?"

Arubrey slammed the black liquid down in one gulp before answering. "Black licorice, mint, and blood."

"Now that sounds disgusting!" I yelled, laughing.

We sat together for hours, talking about past events, laughing at different humans we had encountered throughout the decades of death we've lived through. Every once in a while, vampires would trickle in and pass our table, eyes widening when they looked at us, recognizing who we were. Some of them even turned around and immediately left after seeing us. We ignored their looks and Arubrey kept ordering us more drinks as the night grew later. Arubrey and I looked at one another as a human passed our table and made her way to the floor below us. We watched her as she sat at a table by herself by the DJ booth in the corner. A vampire had joined her shortly after and wasted no time in drinking from her.

"I'm surprised they let humans in here. Won't they lose money from us drinking from them rather than buying blood from the bar?" I asked Arubrey.

"No. Leslie told me they make the vampire who invites them here pay triple cover charge for a human to get in," Arubrey was saying just as a black, male, vampire came through the door and was headed toward our table. In my peripheral vision I noticed the vampire immediately, Arubrey did not.

Two courses of action ran through my mind simultaneously. The first being, my body wanted to spring into action and kill the vampire. I knew the laws. Death was the only option. And because death was the only option for the vampire, I had empathy for him. The second course of action was me scooping the vampire up in my arms and running away from this place. Running away from New Orleans, my coven, the world; all to protect this vampire. Why? Because this vampire was just a child. The same child I had met many, many, decades ago.

I sat frozen in my chair. Arubrey must have seen how my body tensed up because he stopped talking. I saw his eyes flicker to the child and back to me. His jaw snapped shut and his body was just as rigid as my own, but only for half a second. Arubrey started to laugh and continue on with the conversation as if nothing was out of the ordinary. After the immortal child passed, without looking at us, Arubrey tapped his fingers on the table. I recognized it as morse code. Arubrey taught the others and myself when we first moved to New Orleans. It was what he used in his past as a human. He was telling me to "wait". An immortal child was against the Vampire Covenant. Death was the only option for him. This immortal child was the same vampire that also killed Devin's wife and daughter. This familiar child walked right past us and Arubrey wanted me to wait. I tapped and slid my finger on the table, asking "plan"?

The vampire child, with short, curly and dyed blonde hair, wearing shiny, black, skin tight, pants, with a yellow netted shirt, made his way to the lower level of the bar. He sat at the bar and ordered a drink, and looked around. "Do you think he's looking for Devin?" I asked Arubrey.

"This child is the same vampire that killed Devin's family?" Arubrey asked, eyes wide.

I only nodded.

"And there is the possibility that Vincent created this child. Still, we must wait. I want to be sure he doesn't have allies here before we make our move."

"Excluding us, there are thirteen vampires here, including the bartender and DJ. And one human," I informed Arubrey.

"Yes, I've been counting as well as they've been coming and leaving. We'll finish our drinks and you can casually make your way downstairs. I'll join you soon after. Clear the room and then you can make your move. The human does not get hurt."

I nod my head in agreement and take another sip of my drink. It would do me no good to tell Arubrey I have history with this child. There would be no saving him from destruction. A minute later our drinks were finished and we both stood up and parted ways. I made my way toward the stairs that took me down to the second floor of the bar. At the bottom of the stairs was an archway that led to the private booths that Devin spoke of and a restroom. I presumed it was a courtesy for the humans that visited the bar. I made my way over to the DJ booth where a microphone was. I flipped a switch on the DJ booth, stopping the music. I now had thirteen pairs of vampire eyes fixed on me.

I smiled and tapped on the microphone to ensure it was on. "Pardon me, I am sure all of you know who I am and I just hate to do this, but I'm closing the bar down. It's time for all of you to leave now," I warned them.

The vampire who was drinking from the human quickly scooped her up into his arms and fled up the stairs. Many others followed them, including the DJ who was standing beside me. The

149

female behind the bar was clearly annoyed with me, glaring at me for causing her to lose paying customers. The vampire child that killed Devin's family smirked at me and started to walk toward the stairs.

"Oh, honey, you're not going anywhere," I said to him, blocking his path.

"My, my, I thought I'd never see you again," he said, smiling at me. "You haven't changed in the slightest."

"The same could be said about you, Jayden," I replied, letting Arubrey know we had history. I knew he was listening close by and would be joining us shortly.

"Have you missed me, my sister?" the vampire said with a mischievous smile.

Sister? I said nothing. The less I said, the more he would talk.

"I can see the confusion within your eyes. Let me elaborate," the immortal child began his story. "I know you remember killing my human parents. Right in front of my own eyes. You slaughtered them and their blood was dripping from your hands. And to make things worse, you let me live. You destroyed my family. That is, until he found me, just days later. He woke me during the night, promising me I could have my revenge. He told me you killed them because you were jealous that I had parents and you didn't. He told me I belonged to him now."

I was in disbelief. Vincent tracked down this child I had spared and turned him? Vincent knew I had let the child live but he said nothing to me about it?

The child turned his back to me, returning to the bar. He picked up a random drink and chugged it down, blood running from the side of his mouth. "Our master says I should forgive you," the boy said, tossing the glass behind him, shattering it on the floor. The vampire that was still behind the bar growled a warning in his direction.

I took a few steps closer to Jayden, closing the gap between us. "I never told you my name all those years ago. Allow me to properly introduce myself. My name is Sassandra of the Ooljéé coven and I have no master," I said to him just before slamming my fist into his chest, sending him flying over the bar and slamming into the mirrored wall. The mirrors shattered into thousands of pieces. Jayden sprung back to his feet and pounced over the bar. I jumped, twisting midair, and slashed his cheek with the tip of my spiked heel. He fell back to the ground and he pressed his hand up against his cheek as blood oozed from the fresh gash.

A cloud of smoke erupted from thin air behind Jayden, revealing Arubrey, now holding a dagger against the child's throat. "Pure silver. You do not stand a chance against her, nor me. Now, we have some questions for you and don't give us any bullshit answers. We can do this the easy way, or the fun way. The choice is yours," Arubrey said, threatening him.

Jayden put his hands up in surrender. He knew he was no match for two vampires of our stature.

"Why did you kill Devin's family?" I started the interrogation as Arubrey removed a couple silver chains from within his jean pockets, securing the vampire to a chair just as I was many decades ago.

"I was told to kill them all but he wasn't there."

"Who sent you?" I asked.

"Our master sent me," the vampire said, smiling.

I was about to bitch slap him but Arubrey interrupted me. "Where can we find your master?" he asked Jayden.

The vampire child said nothing. A flicker of fear crossed his face.

"I'll give you something to fear," I told him as I removed one of my heels, bringing the silver spike close to one of his eyes.

"I don't know!" the child screamed. "He sends all his instructions to the church and I collect my assignments from Pastor John. Our master visits the church sometimes to meet with him. The pastor knows how to find him!"

My blood was boiling. I was ready to kill.

"Where is this church?" Arubrey asked. "Give me an exact address."

"Oh, she already knows its location. Master says her scent still lingers within the closet there."

I looked at Arubrey and we both knew the exact church Jayden was referring to. It was the same church where I sought shelter from the sun during the battle of Antietam. "If you don't have any more information for us then it's time for us to uphold the Vampire's Covenant," I said to the bound child. "Did Vincent not tell you that immortal children are forbidden?"

"No! I do have more information. But I will not give it unless you give me your word that you will release me. I promise, I'll... I'll go into hiding. You will never hear from me again. I just want to live. I promise to be a good boy!"

I softened my expression and forced a fake smile across my face. "Ok Jayden, I promise, it's the least I can do after what I have taken from you. This will make us even," I said to him, lying.

"Our master... he created more than just us. He created mothers for us."

Arubrey stepped forward, almost putting himself between Jayden and me.

"How many mothers?" I asked, clenching my hands.

The vampire batted his eyes at me and smiled. "Master Vincent created many, many mommies for us," he happily squealed. "And he says we're all going to be one big happy family!"

That's it. I was over it. The monster that sat before me was no longer the little boy I once saved. I saw nothing but evil within his eyes. I saw no desire to be freed from the same spell Vincent had put him under that I once was under. It was too late for him to be saved. His mind had been tampered with for well over a century. There was no coming back from that. Was there? It's a risk I couldn't take, besides the Vampire's Covenant forbade it. Death was the only answer for Jayden.

I moved as fast as lightning, tossing my heel I was holding up into the air. I grabbed the silver spikes from my hair and I drove them both straight into Jayden's temples. The child screamed in agony. I caught my heel as it fell from above me and I held it firmly by its sole. I believed every word he spoke. I believed that the same vampire who created me created this one that was now defenseless and bound to this chair. I believed our creator didn't stop and kept changing people, good people, into vampires, brainwashing them as he once did to me. I also believed Winona when she told me the longer someone was under a vampire's spell, the more difficult it would be to break the spell.

"I already have a family," I said just before I was about to slam the spike of the heel into the top of his head to end his existence. But Arubrey grabbed my wrist, stopping me.

"I cannot allow you to kill him, Sassandra."

"What are you doing? He's an immortal child. He must die. The Vampire's Covenant says...," I started to explain to Arubrey before he cut me off again.

"I know full well what the Covenant says. And I am proud that you are willing to uphold it without question. But I will be the one who does it. Let his destruction be on my hands, not the hands of the one who tried saving him all those years ago."

I stepped back, letting Arubrey's words sink in. Yes, this child had to die. But he did not have to die by my hands. Arubrey disappeared into the air, leaving a wave of smoke in his place. He reappeared and disappeared over and over, filling the area around us with thick gray smoke, blinding my view of the child. My high heel was yanked from my hand. I could not see but I could still hear the horrible noise of the silver spike cutting through Jayden's skull. His blood splattered on my face, a few drops landing into my mouth. The familiar taste of Vincent's blood flowed over my tongue and I licked my lips, wanting to taste more. Jayden wailed in agony. I couldn't imagine what a silver spike to the brain felt like. I knew the sound of flesh and bone when a head is ripped from a body. And that is what Arubrey had done to Jayden before taking my hand and walking me back upstairs to the upper level.

"How about a round of drinks, on the house?" the vampire bartender said, coming up the stairs carrying a tray.

"We apologize for the scene, and the mess. We will of course pay for the damages," Arubrey said to the bartender as she brought over our drinks.

"Don't worry about it. We're insured."

CHAPTER 13
YEAR 1861: STAND

Everything had changed and I felt lost, like I no longer had a purpose to live for. Before this, being captured by three other vampires and finally meeting the strange woman who I dreamed of since I was a little girl, I used to have a purpose: to serve Vincent and help maintain the floral plantation. Even after he changed me into a vampire, I still had a purpose: to continue to serve my master. I killed for him, no questions asked. And I would have killed Abraham Lincoln, if I hadn't been captured. But I was just still a fledgling, a newborn vampire without much training. I was no threat to the three vampires who still had me bound to this chair with silver chains.

Arubrey and Winona stood in front of me, watching me, while Leslie went to update the President about the current situation; the situation being me. I could hear them talking about me from the other room.

"If you three are certain in your ability to keep me safe from her then why are you asking me to leave?" Lincoln said to Leslie.

"Yes, Winona says the smudging was successful and Sassandra says she no longer has any desire to harm you. But that still doesn't mean it's not safe for you to meet her. She could be lying."

"Winona told me herself that she can always tell when another human or vampire is lying. So, are you saying she is unsure if Sassandra is telling the truth or not?" Lincoln accused.

Silence. Lincoln had won the argument. We all knew it, as did he. *Click, click, click.* I heard him walking toward the room I was being held captive in. His walk was similar to Vincent's but not as rushed and much softer. The door swung open and in walked the President of the United States of America, Abraham Lincoln. He no longer was wearing his stovepipe hat. Instead, his thick, dark, hair had been combed over to the side. The sun had clearly played its part in darkening and wrinkling his skin over his lifetime. He wore a white dress shirt with a black bow tie, made of wool. I recognized the fabric from the years I worked on the plantation.

"Untie her," Lincoln ordered, looking at Arubrey.

"But Sir," Arubrey began to protest.

"You said that she was hypnotized earlier and that's why she wanted to kill me. You also said she was no longer hypnotized. So now, I am saying to untie her."

Arubrey nodded his head and stepped toward me, looking directly into my eyes. It was a warning. A warning that if I tried anything that I would regret it. I held his gaze, without blinking, the entire time he was unbinding the stringlike silver chains that wrapped around both my arms and the chair's. Once they were removed, I felt a glimmer of strength as it slowly made its way back into my body.

"It is very nice to meet you, Sassandra," Lincoln spoke to me. "I presume you already know who I am so there is no need for introductions. But I must inquire, what do you plan on doing with yourself now?"

I was stumped. I had no idea what to do with myself. "I apologize, Mr. President," I started to say before being cut off.

"Please, do not be so formal with me. You may call me Abraham. Actually, it is I who should be more formal with you and your kind. Yes, I know a thing or two about vampires."

"Well, in that case, can you teach me?" I said, looking at the only human in the room. "You see, Vincent, the one who turned me, wasn't so eager to teach me much of anything, except how to kill," I said as Abraham and the other three vampires all watched me.

"I'm afraid that is not up to me. I may be the President of the United States but I admit that vampire affairs are above my paygrade," he said, chuckling to himself.

I was still confused and I could feel the frustration growing inside me. My voice came out much louder than it had before. "Can someone please just tell me what I am supposed to do? How to live? What do I do with myself?" I yelled at them all.

It was Leslie who came to my side, placing her hand on my shoulder. "Everything will be ok, Sassandra. You're finally free from Vincent and his spell he had you under. Now you're feeling emotions that you probably never even felt before. We can help you," Leslie promised me.

"Like hell we will!" roared Arubrey. "Training a fledgling is not our problem. We didn't create her. I say we destroy her."

Abraham turned to look at Arubrey, clearly agitated with him. "Why would you say that? She isn't going to try to kill me again."

"And what if we let her go and she returns to her master and he brainwashes her into trying to assassinate you again?" Arubrey barked back.

I had enough of this. I sprang up from my chair. "Vincent is not my master! I will destroy him for what he has done to me! You don't know what he did to me! What he made me do to the others! I killed all of them! I slaughtered them like they were cattle!" The anger and pain inside of me was unbearable. I grabbed the chair and flung it into the window, shattering it. Abraham, Arubrey, Leslie, and Winona all watched as I had my meltdown. I was overwhelmed with emotions and my knees buckled and I fell to the floor. I wanted to cry. I wanted to shed tears for the ones who I murdered with my bare hands. But the tears never came. "I'm a monster. I do not deserve to live. Please, just kill me," I begged them, looking at Arubrey as I did.

Abraham approached me and came to kneel down beside me. "I have been driven many times upon my knees by the overwhelming conviction that I had nowhere else to go. My own wisdom and that of all about me seemed insufficient for that day," he spoke softly, just to me. "Now, stand up, Sassandra and whatever you are, be a good one. Do not let your past deeds determine your future."

I looked up into Abraham's eyes. I could see the sadness from his own life within them. But they also held determination. I felt a fire within me that wanted to strive for greatness. I would be great. I was no longer a human hypnotized by a vampire. I was no longer a slave to a master who whipped me, tied to a tree, and left me there to be taken by death. I was no longer property to my creator. I was no longer Vincent's drudge.

I stood up and looked at the other three vampires that were watching me. "Thank you. All of you," I said, looking at each of them as I spoke. "Thank you for not killing me. Even as a human I haven't really lived yet. How is a vampire supposed to live in a world full of humans? Do other humans even know about us?" I inquired.

It was Leslie who spoke first. "Some do. Most do not. Just months ago, it was Abraham who actually helped us find our new purpose in the world. We're not so different, you and us."

Abraham was now standing again and walked over to open the door to the room, and told us to follow him. Arubrey walked out first, the other two making me walk in the middle with them following me.

"Truthfully, it's still a mystery," he said, leading us up a flight of stairs. "I found a letter in the pocket of my jacket one night, before I had even run for office, with two locations written on it. Under both locations were the names 'Winona' and 'Arubrey'. On the backside of the paper was a message: 'Find them, win the war.'"

Abraham opened the door for us and we filed into the small room one at a time. The room resembled a workshop with big wooden tables with saws and carving instruments laying on top of them. On the far side of the room sat three beautiful thrones. The carvings in them were all different from one another but each were also similar to the next.

Abraham continued with his story. "I disregarded the paper I found until after I became President. Once war and death found its way into my life, I sought them out. I had no idea vampires even existed, and they too were clueless on who would give me such a paper. They said there was no scent on the paper, besides my own."

"What are these for?" asked Winona, walking toward the three thrones. "They're beautiful."

Abraham smiled at the compliment and answered, "I made them. With my own two hands. One is for you, Winona, the other Arubrey's, and the last is for Leslie," he said looking at them, clearly pleased with himself. "My job, as President, is to implement and enforce laws written by Congress. It's my job to govern over the people of this country. However, there is no law about vampires. So, I thought to myself, why not you three? Vampires need to be governed as well, but by their own kind. Just something to think about," he said, before leaving the room.

I watched the vampires in the room turn their attention from the thrones back to me. It was like they were unsure what to do with me. "Again, I'm sorry," I said to them, not sure what to do with myself. Was I allowed to leave?

Leslie turned her focus back to one of the thrones while Arubrey continued to glare at me from across the room. Winona looked at him then back to me before walking past me, out of the room, back into the hall. "Sassandra," she said after passing me, "would you like to accompany me for a midnight excursion?"

I took another look at Arubrey and quickly exited the room, following Winona back down the stairs and out of the house through the back door. We walked in the grass toward the woods, along the same path that I came onto the property. She was following my scent from the path I took earlier.

"You have a horse drawn carriage with you?" she asked me.

"Yes," I answered, a little hurt. "I'll leave tonight. I will not bother any of you again."

Winona started to laugh, loudly. "Actually, I was hoping you would stay for a while and discuss the dreams of which you spoke of earlier from when you were still human. We can put your horse in the stable and then I will discuss your

163

stay with the others when we return. The choice, of course, is yours."

"Yes, I think I would like to stay," I said, smiling at being given a choice, for once.

We reached the end of the property and continued down the side of the street until we reached a two-story building. Winona leaped into the air, grabbing onto one of the window ledges above us. Her agility was graceful and unrushed. She pulled herself up and jumped again, landing on the edge of the building's roof. It took me a couple tries, still weakened from the silver, but I copied her movements and finally joined her on the edge of the roof. She ran to the other side, leaping across the street, landing on the roof of the building on the other side. My body was slower than normal but I followed her lead, jumping from rooftop to rooftop, without making a noise as we moved, before finally reaching our destination.

Winona gestured toward the two blocks of buildings in front of us, saying, "Welcome to Murder Bay. This area is known as the slums of D.C. It's where Arubrey first met Leslie after Abraham found us." Lanterns that illuminated the streets were scarce in this area, leaving the streets much darker, and more dangerous.

"This is where we hunt. By choice, we try to only feed from criminals. How often do you feed?" Winona asked me.

"When I was first changed, I fed every night for a couple years. But now, the longest I've gone, without losing control, was four nights."

"For now, you will hunt every other night with one of us. We can't risk you losing control. It's our duty to keep Abraham safe, including from ourselves."

We leaped from the building's roof, Winona landing with much more ease and grace than I, on the street below. The laughter of men could be heard a few buildings down from us. We walked toward the commotion, concealing ourselves in the neighboring ally. We listened as our potential prey continued their argument inside the saloon.

"You're a damn cheat!" a man said, slurring the words out of his mouth.

"I ain't never cheated in my life," the other man countered, "except on my wife!" he said, laughing.

"Show me your cards then."

"I ain't showing you shit!" the man yelled.

A flash of light followed by a loud crack echoed off the buildings around us from within the saloon. The saloon fell silent except for the sound of the legs of a chair being moved. A few seconds passed before the man slurred, "Would ya look at that, he wasn't cheatin' after all!"

The grungy looking man stumbled into the street, still holding his revolver in his hand as he walked, a bottle of booze

165

in his other. Winona and I followed the man from a distance until we were a couple streets from the saloon he just left.

"I'm still full from feeding off your energy," Winona said to me. "This man is all yours."

Feeding from my energy? I would have to ask her what that meant later. But now, I was thirsty and I wanted blood. I rushed the man from behind, grabbing his shoulders, pulling him into my body. I wasted no time and chomped down into his neck, fulfilling my needs. Another shot was fired from his gun, hitting the ground. He struggled to break free, yelling in pain. I continued drinking from my prey as his knees gave out, dropping his gun, and passing out in my arms. When I was finished, I dropped his body, lifting my head to the sky. I felt his blood inside of me as it flowed down into me, finally regaining my full strength.

After licking the blood clean from his neck, I propped the drunken man, now passed out, up against a building, to make it seem like he passed out on his own accord. Winona and I left Murder Bay together, staying on the ground this time, heading in the direction to retrieve my horse. She asked me about my dreams again and I retold, in detail, the memories I had of them to her.

"My people were the first of this land," began Winona. "I was raised to love and respect nature. My people, Indigenous people, were peaceful. I was married at fourteen, to a man whom I loved very much. It was he who taught me how to spirit walk when I was human."

"Was it he who changed you into a vampire?" I asked.

"No. My husband was human. I was turned later after his death. He knew our people were in danger from one of his spirit walks. He knew they would all die, except for me. Spirit walking was only taught to the males in my tribe. But, before he died, he secretly taught me, so the tradition would not be lost in death."

Winona and I approached my horse and carriage, where I left it. I untied the rope from the tree as she jumped into the carriage. We headed back toward the Soldier's Home, the large white cottage where Arubrey, Leslie, Abraham, and his family resided.

She continued her story. "After teaching me the ritual I would complain to him, because as much as I focused and believed that I could continue our people's tradition, it never happened for me. 'Soon,' he would tell me. One night, he packed supplies for me and told me I had to leave him and the tribe. He said it wasn't safe for me. I thought I would never see him again. 'Soon,' he told me, kissing me goodbye. That single word he spoke would echo in my heart for many years after my people were killed. I lived the rest of my human life in hiding for twelve years, afraid I would be killed if I was ever found. It was then when a white bird visited my dreams and I had my first spirit walk."

"What did you see?" I asked, fascinated by her tale.

"Darkness. Souls of the lost and forgotten," Winona said, bowing her head. "When my spirit walk was over, I knew where to go. I didn't know how or why, but I went, nonetheless."

"Where did you go?" I pressed.

"It was the year 1692 when I traveled. I did not know the specific destination of my journey until I found myself blindfolded in Salem, Massachusetts," she answered, as we pulled up to our destination. Winona quickly got out of the carriage before I could ask my next question.

"I'll take your horse to the stables. You can join the others. I will be in shortly when I am finished."

I started walking back toward the front door of the house, thinking of what Winona had just told me, until I saw a group of soldiers running to the backside of the property. I was on their trail in an instant, worried something terrible had happened while we were gone. To my surprise, the soldiers were gathered around Leslie, in the yard, watching her. It was a sight to appreciate. Leslie, still wearing the white corset, was twirling one of the soldier's rifles with her hands. She did not move with the speed at which I knew a vampire could move. Instead, she twirled the gun between her hands, and around her neck and back, at the speed of a human's. Her poised movements had the soldiers drooling over her as they cheered her on, yelling with excitement as she flipped the rifle into the air and catching it again behind her back as it fell again.

She looked at me, still putting on a show, and smiled. We all continued to watch in awe, until she finally stopped, and returned the rifle to one of the soldiers. "Take notes, Sugar, that's how it's done," she said to the soldier, winking at him.

"That was fun to watch," I said to Leslie, as we walked back toward the house together. "And the men seemed to enjoy it."

"Yes, they're fun to tease," she said, smiling again.

"Does that include Arubrey?" I joked.

"Oh, Sass, please tell me that you're not being serious. Arubrey is my complete opposite!" Leslie said, laughing at my comment as we walked through the door. "Or, were you just hinting to see if he's available for yourself?"

"No, no. Nothing like that. I think he'd much rather kill me than kiss me anyway."

Arubrey rounded the corner, stopping me in my tracks. "That can be arranged, if you'd like," he said, glaring at me. "Winona is upstairs, waiting. We're having a meeting."

Leslie and I followed Arubrey up the stairs, passing a couple of human guards as we did. We entered the small room with the wooden thrones Abraham had showed us earlier.

Arubrey and Leslie went to their thrones, sitting next to Winona.

"Have a seat, Sassandra," Winona said, pointing to the same chair I threw out the window a couple hours prior. Someone must have retrieved it and moved it upstairs while we were out hunting.

"Thank you, Sassandra," Winona said as I sat down. "As you know, Abraham presented us with these thrones earlier tonight. Accepting these gifts, the President has made with his very hands, means we also accept the terms that come with them."

Arubrey slightly nodded his head, agreeing, before adding, "And the three of us have all agreed to those terms. From this day forward we will oversee the affairs of vampires within this country."

"What does that mean for me?" I asked the trio of vampires.

"We would like you to join our coven, Sassandra. But, if you want, you are free to leave," said Leslie. "To be honest, we have not known one another for very long. We were all lost, just as you are now."

I looked at each of them, Arubrey being the last, before asking, "All three of you want me to stay?"

Leslie and Winona turned their eyes on Arubrey, waiting for him to answer. He shifted in his throne, irritated to be put on the spot by the three of us. Arubrey looked at me, his eyes turning gray, and disappeared in a cloud of dark smoke. His words were calm and quiet but they held nothing but promise in them when he spoke them, now standing behind me. "Yes, I too, would like you to stay. But only because it will be easier to keep an eye on you. I do not trust you in the slightest. And I will not hesitate to kill you if you betray us."

I knew he was only trying to scare me. But I also knew he meant every word of it. "So, that's the smoke I saw just before I was captured. It was you."

Arubrey reappeared on his throne in a cloud of smoke again. "Yes, that was me. But it was Winona who fed from your life force, weakening you. I only collected your body after you... fainted," he said, smirking at his choice of words.

"How do we feed off of energy?" I asked.

"It's a very rare ability," Winona answered me. "I have met only one other who possesses this same power as I have.

"Vincent said I might have an ability. Something about my mind and dreams. He said he had it and that it may have been passed down to me, through his blood."

Frustrated with the conversation, Leslie stood from her seat and brushed past me, leaving the room and slamming the door behind her.

"Don't mind her," Arubrey said. "She does not have a gift like ours. But to answer your question, yes. You may have it. But it takes a while to manifest and you're still young."

"I wish to kill him. Vincent," I admitted to them. "Will you help me?"

"It's something we would have to discuss in the near future. If what you say is true about him, then you will need more training to defeat him. Your assassination attempt on the President was futile," Winona responded. "You can start training tomorrow, with Leslie. Even without having an ability, Leslie is a threat no one should ever take lightly. As for tonight, I would like you to draw a portrait of Vincent and then give us every detail you know about him."

I stood up from the chair. It was decided then. The next time I met my maker, I would surely destroy him.

CHAPTER 14

YEAR 1862: ANTIETAM

I trained almost every night with Leslie for over a year. We would sneak away from the Soldier's Home after almost everyone went to sleep. To train as a vampire, she told me, I had to let my instincts fully take over. Her training technique was much different than Vincent's. In the beginning her method of training was extremely brutal, more so on my mind than my body.

"You're a pathetic excuse for a vampire," Leslie yelled out at me. "I bet Vincent is ashamed of creating you. If you cannot even hit me then how in the hell do you expect to land a blow on your *master?*"

I knew she was just saying this to provoke me. And provoke me she did. A snarl filled with loathing ripped from my throat. She knew I hated the word *master*. I ran at her, with every intention to rip her head off. A mere inch of space came between us before she easily side stepped my attack. I started to turn to face her again but she was much faster than me. Leslie grabbed me by my hair, yanking my head backwards and down. I heard something snap and before I realized what happened, I was lying on the ground. The bones in my neck were healing quickly, straightening my neck back into place.

"Really? Hair pulling?" I said, appalled. I did not like having my hair touched. Winona taught me her tribe believed hair was the extension of one's soul.

"I warned you about growing your hair out so long. Are you sure you won't let me cut it?"

I ignored her question, tucking my hair down into my shirt, out of her reach and readied myself for the next duel.

"You're weak, Sassandra. Not just your physical abilities but your *mind* is weak. You must control and strengthen your mind. When your ears are more focused on the words coming out of your enemy's mouth then your eyes focus less on their movements. If you continue to let words evoke you during a battle then you will succumb to death."

What could I say? She was right. My mind was weak. Unworthy. Vincent said I was unworthy and I believed him. Did Leslie think of me unworthy to be called a vampire? Vampires were supposed to be strong and fast. At least, the four that I'd met so far were. They were all confident in themselves, and yet here I was

174

feeling sorry for myself. I was a vampire with self-esteem issues, great.

We scaled rooftops of buildings, training me in hand-to-hand combat in its various forms that she picked up over the years since she was turned against her own will. Once I learned to ignore her various insults, she gave me a Samurai sword and ninja throwing stars, all made from pure silver. We would duel under thunderstorms to disguise the sound of our metal clashing into one another as we battled.

I learned that after Leslie was changed, in the year 1732, she traveled the world to seek knowledge from human warriors from different lands around the globe.

"I wanted my revenge, against the one who created me. I knew in order to kill him I had to become better myself. To do anything successful then you must always strive to become better," Leslie said one night as we trained.

"Did you get your revenge then?"

"Unfortunately, no, not yet. I was turned during a night of passionate lovemaking. I was okay with him sucking on my neck at first but then… At the time, I worked in Nueva Orleans, now called New Orleans, at one of the saloons in the French Quarters. You could say I tended to the gentlemen to ensure their wallets remained loose for the night."

I smirked at her. "So you were a saloon girl." It wasn't a question.

"Well, if you want to put a title to it. Anyway, this gentleman had visited the saloon before. I remembered his charm and devilish good looks. The sound of the ticking from his golden pocket watch will forever remain in my memory. I counted over two hundred and fifty thousand ticks when I was changed."

Both of us held our swords facing the ground. Our fight had drifted to a close, getting lost in our conversation of her past.

"It was him who taught you the rules of being a vampire?"

"No. After my transformation he abandoned me. It was me and my own trials and many errors. I didn't know a damn thing about the effects of sunlight until my flesh caught fire shortly after I was turned. It took another few days for my skin to fully heal itself. Hurt more than being changed, that's for damn sure. The most important rule I've taught myself is to do whatever it takes to stay alive."

"What happens when a vampire dies?"

The storm had passed and all was calm. Leslie looked at me, putting her sword away. "That's a question for Winona."

I looked to the sky, the moon covered by dark clouds, threatening to unleash another storm upon us. We leaped from the building to the street below us, quickly making our way to Murder Bay for tonight's hunt. I was now allowed to go five nights without hunting. Any more than that and I would become irritable. None of the others went more than seven nights without hunting. We had each found five or six victims to feed off regularly, to quench our thirst. Feeding from the same prey kept accidents from happening.

I visited the same grungy man I first hunted with Winona at least once a month. His blood was always diluted with whiskey, giving it a surprisingly delightful taste. On numerous occasions I'd fed from him as his wife slept silently in the same bed next to him.

Their home, even though it was in the slums of the city, was always kept clean. I assume she ate dinner almost always alone while he gambled what little money they had away. I decided if he ever harmed her then I would drain him dry and toss his body in the bay, giving my leftovers to the fish to feed from.

Leslie stayed outside the home as I fed from the man while he and his wife were asleep. Arubrey still insisted that I never be left unaccompanied, afraid that I would turn on them. After I fed, I followed Leslie to a different saloon she worked at when she first met Arubrey. The place was still owned by the same people but since Leslie's transformation, they found a new girl to entertain the gentlemen who frequented the bar. She said she liked to check in on the girl who took her place to make sure she was keeping her old customers satisfied.

Leslie easily seduced a man outside the saloon and took him down a darkened ally. The men she fed from never screamed. Instead, I would hear them moaning and grunting in pleasure.

"How do you do that? Keep them from screaming," I asked her one night.

"Oh honey, I just know what men like," she said, laughing.

After we finished feeding, we returned to the house. Arubrey and Winona left shortly after for their hunt. We never left Abraham by himself, afraid of another assassination attempt. I learned that I wasn't the first to try to kill the president, nor would I be the last. Two more assassination attempts came, and failed, since mine. These attempts were of human men, but all were killed by Arubrey or Leslie. I was intrigued one day while Abraham was

177

writing, using a new bottle of ink. I could smell the poison as he scribbled his words across the sheet of parchment. I snatched the bottle up, confirming it was the source of poison.

"Thank goodness for you, Sassandra," Abraham said, half smiling at me. I could see the desperation in his eyes. He was on the verge of a breakdown. I removed the poison from the room and advised the president to step outside for some fresh air while I gathered the others.

We followed Abraham's scent, already knowing where it would lead us. Thousands of white headstones could be seen in the distance where soldiers who had lost their lives now rested. There, watching over them, stood Abraham, with his head bowed.

"Thousands of men have given their lives for this war. The Union has lost more battles than won. What if we lose? My son is very sick and I'm afraid he is going to lose his own battle as well."

"Let us help with the next battle. We can't cure your son, but we can at least help with this," Leslie said, placing her hand on Abraham's shoulder to comfort him.

Arubrey walked to stand next to Abraham, looking over the field of white gravestones. "We can split up for a few days. Two of us can stay with you while the other two go into battle."

"These soldiers did not give their lives for war," Winona said. "They gave their lives for others to have freedom."

Abraham turned around, with tears forming in his eyes. "Yes, I think I agree with that statement. Those who deny freedom to others deserve it not for themselves. The South has already used a vampire to try to kill me. I guess it's time for me to return the favor upon them."

"We will strategize and debate tonight. We will inform you of our decision in the morning. Get some rest, Abraham," Arubrey said, walking back toward the house, soon followed by Winona and Leslie. I stayed behind with Abraham.

"I appointed five seats to the Supreme Court. I have no idea how many vampires exist in our country. I assume it is less than the count of humans. Maybe one day I can build a throne for you as well."

I walked the rest of the way back to the house with Abraham in silence. This was the first time I'd been left alone with him since the night I tried to assassinate him. We walked up the steps and he opened the door for me, like the gentleman he was.

"I do not think a throne is in my future. I believe the only reason I was just left alone with you is because Arubrey thought one of the others would stay behind to babysit me. Maybe he made a mistake tonight."

Abraham chuckled, following me into the house. "I know very little about that vampire. But what I do know is in the three years he has been by my side, he has yet to make a mistake. I trust him completely with my life."

The decision was made and I wasn't sure I liked it. I was glad to be picked to fight alongside the soldiers, but I wasn't thrilled to having to tag along with Arubrey, leaving Leslie and Winona to protect Abraham.

Word of a lost order, number 191, was discovered by Union troops. The order was a general movement order that was issued by the General of the Confederate Army. We now knew when and where to strike. We started our travels a few nights later, waiting for confirmation and for Union troops to move in.

Arubrey and I started our travels, heading northwest. The Confederate army had already made its way onto Northern territory for the first time since the Civil War had started. Abraham was sure they were planning to invade the capital. It was up to Arubrey and myself to stop this. What normally would take a human a full day to travel on foot only took us shy of an hour to reach.

"Battles are almost always fought during the hours of the day. Humans trying to control thousands more is already complicated enough for them. Doing so at night would be disastrous," Arubrey said to me as we continued up the Antietam creek.

"And do not forget that they need their sleep as well, unlike us," I added, following him in the water.

We went another half mile upstream until the woods were thick enough for us to take shelter in. Abraham was the only human who knew we were here and the plan was to keep it that way.

"I'm going to get a feel of the land. You stay here," Arubrey ordered before disappearing in a puff of smoke.

Annoyed, as I always was with him, I dug my fingers into a sycamore tree, climbing up to its top. The view was breathtaking. I saw camps of Union and Confederate troops spread out, split by another stream and a few miles apart from one another. Union troops were hidden behind cornfields whereas Confederate troops could be seen camped out around a small church and close to the outskirts of the town.

"Are you ready for this?" said a voice above me in the tree.

"That's not funny, Arubrey!" I yelled at him.

"I killed a dozen of the Confederate men already. Once the bodies are found, they'll think the Union troops are doing a sneak attack."

"Well, aren't we?" I teased, jumping down from the tree.

Moments later we heard the Confederate troops moving forward. I followed Arubrey's lead as we entered the cornfields. We did not have guns and ammunition or cannons like the soldiers had access to. The first gunshot was fired, followed by hundreds more just yards away from our position, hidden in the cornfield.

"Do whatever you have to do to kill the Confederates. If we cannot find one another when the battle is over, I will meet you back at the sycamore tree. And do not forget about sunrise," Arubrey warned me, just before vanishing into thin air.

Killing this time was different than before. I did not kill because I was ordered to kill. I killed because I wanted to. I had no desire to please Arubrey. I did not need praise from him, or even Abraham. All I wanted was to destroy the ones who wanted to keep my people enslaved. Soon, my people would be free. Soon, I would be covered in the blood of the Confederate soldiers. Soon.

I closed my eyes, letting my instincts take over. I listened to the gunfire on the outside of the cornfield I was hidden in. I counted the seconds it took them to reload and fire again. I listened past the screams of the ones already injured and the war cries of the brave men who stood side by side one another in this war. Once they fired their shots, my eyes snapped open and I rushed the field. I leaped into the air, over the heads of the men who were still reloading their guns in the cornfield. I was out of the cornfield within three seconds. I had twenty-five seconds to go. I saw the Confederate soldiers lined up in a clear opening. I ran straight ahead toward them.

It took me another four seconds to reach them. Twenty-one seconds to go. I slammed the palm of my hands into the hearts of two of the soldiers, sending them flying back into their comrades. I twisted, clenching my fist and slammed it into another two, crushing their skulls. I jumped again, now landing behind the men. They were still reloading their rifles. I snapped their necks and their lifeless bodies fell to the ground. Eighteen seconds to go. I grabbed another man and threw him into the air as hard as I could. I jumped, kicking another in his face. As I landed, a hand grabbed my shoulder, trying to turn me around. My body did not budge. I kicked my foot backwards into the mortal's stomach. I heard him keel over just as the other man I threw landed on top of other Confederate soldiers in the distance. Fourteen seconds to go.

I ran behind the men of the front line, snapping their necks one by one as I passed them. They hit the ground one after another. I jumped, landing on another, my legs wrapped around his neck. I squeezed my thighs together, not releasing until I heard his bones crack. Seven seconds to go. A soldier was laying on his back, holding his arm where a bullet had pierced his flesh. I jumped on top of him, biting into the wound. I could taste something different within his blood. Was it metal from the bullet or perhaps adrenaline from the war that I was tasting? I savored the taste as long as I could, forcing myself to pull away when time was almost up. Four seconds left. I jumped up from the dying man and sprinted back to the cornfields for cover, entering them with one second to spare. I killed over thirty-three men within twenty-eight seconds.

The battle by the cornfields raged on throughout the night. The Confederate army was weakened more and more with each reload and slowly became unorganized. The Union played its part well by staying in sync when firing and advancing on them. Soon we were completely out of the cornfields, gaining ground toward the little white brick church, leaving the blood-stained fields and thousands injured or dead behind us.

We took the church from the Confederate, almost destroying it in the process. Its bricks were riddled with bullet holes and even larger holes from the cannons. I entered the building, covered in blood, pleading for help. I pretended to be a hostage of the Confederates who escaped from one of their camps. The Union soldiers ushered me inside, giving me cover from the sunrise that was coming. The firing soon came to a halt, giving both sides time to regroup. I was hoping Arubrey would also be joining me within the church but he never showed. I wondered if he found his own shelter from the sun.

I made my way to a small closet, locking myself inside, out of sight from the others to wait out the day. Three hours later I heard gunshots in the distance from the church. The soldiers that were inside and around the outside of the church charged in the direction of the shooting, leaving me alone inside. The battle that was taking place outside lasted over four hours. I dared not to open the door, afraid I would surely burn within the sunlight that shone through the windows and holes in the walls. I would have to stay put for at least another five hours to be safe.

Over eighteen thousand bullets and twenty-five thousand seconds had never passed more slowly.

The sun disappeared behind the trees and I burst from the closet and out of the church. I ran toward the ongoing battle, picking up a box of ammunition that laid on the red stained grass as I passed. The sound of gunfire followed by the screams of dying men filled the sky. Soldiers of both armies were once again facing one another, a sunken road between them. Bodies of the fallen from both sides filled the lane, blood pooling around them. I leaped over the Union soldiers, soaring over the sunken road and the thousands of corpses that were filling it as more shots were fired from both sides.

There was the flash of the familiar gray smoke I'd been looking for. Arubrey was standing on top of a pile of bodies, yanking a Confederate soldier down into the pit with him, feeding on him as I passed above them. I landed on the other side, behind a group of more Confederates. I grabbed a handful of bullets out of the box and slung them in their direction, hitting several of them in their backs. The bodies fell into the sunken road, adding to the pile of the deceased. I jumped onto the back of another, feeding from his neck. His body was hit with bullets from the other side and he fell back, smashing me under him. I pushed the man off me to find Arubrey now standing in front of me.

"This is a lost cause. Both sides are almost all dead here. There are more Union soldiers to the south that want to take the Burnside Bridge. They said if they can take the bridge then they can take the rest of the Confederates by surprise from the back. I'll create a diversion. It's going to hurt like hell but you'll have to lead them over the bridge. It's our only hope!"

I nodded my head, understanding what would happen to me. Arubrey disappeared and I left the bloodied mess of thousands behind me. I headed south toward more Union soldiers. Upon my arrival, I heard men arguing with one another. They had tried taking the bridge earlier but failed, having to retreat back.

"This time will be different," I yelled, interrupting their argument. They stopped, all turning to face me. Horror struck their faces as they took in my appearance. I was a strong black woman, covered head to toe in blood. No one said anything. They just gawked at me, unsure of what to do or say. A cannon's blast was heard from across the water that separated us from them. I looked over to see Arubrey standing behind the cannon. He had repositioned it, firing it at a squad of Confederate soldiers. This was his diversion.

"I said this time will be different. Stay close to me, I will get you across the bridge."

I walked west, toward the stream that separated the two armies. I did not look behind me to see if the Union was following. If I had to cross the bridge alone, I would. I would kill every last Confederate soldier by myself if I had to. I would not yield. The Confederates raised their guns as I approached closer to the

185

Burnside Bridge. They pulled their triggers as I took my first step in the middle of the twelve-foot-wide stone bridge that crossed the creek. I opened my arms wide, welcoming the bullets that were blasted toward me. Behind me more guns were fired. The Union had followed my advance. I took another step onto the bridge, getting hit over and over by bullets from the opposing side. I could hear the men breathing behind me, struggling to quickly reload their guns. I did not slow my pace. I used my own body to shield the men of the Union behind me from getting hit. My eyes could see the bullets flying toward us but I moved my hands and arms faster, blocking them from hitting my comrades behind me. Arubrey was right. It hurt like hell. But we pushed forward anyway.

Once we were halfway across the bridge, the Union soldiers behind me cried out, hundreds of men charging past me, guns firing toward the enemy. I was left alone on the bridge. We did it. We took the bridge. I looked around, searching for Arubrey. He was feeding again but someone was sneaking up on him, gun in hand. With all the commotion around us, he hadn't noticed the man behind him. I sprinted toward them as the man was standing just a few feet from Arubrey, gun held up to his head. Would I make it in time? Arubrey was going to get shot in the head. Would he be able to heal from a hit like that? I didn't want to find out.

The man was pulling his trigger just as I wrapped my hand around the barrel of the rifle, moving it just in time as it fired right beside Arubrey's left ear. I ripped the rifle from the man's hands, turned it on him, reloaded the gun faster than any human could, and pulled the trigger, shooting him in the chest. I was showered in red, his blood splattering all over me as he crumbled to the ground.

I turned to face Arubrey who was also drenched in blood. The Union soldiers were now celebrating. The Confederate army was retreating. We had won.

Arubrey approached the Union army. "Spread the word. Let it be known that on this night of September 17th, 1862, that the battle of Antietam was won by the North! Today will be remembered as the single bloodiest day in history!"

The Union cheered at his words, raising their guns to the sky and firing them again in celebration. It was liberating to be a part of this.

"What do we do now?" I asked Arubrey.

"Tonight was nothing short of being a blood feast for us. Leslie and even Winona will be jealous. We will head back to D.C. to celebrate with the others before the sun rises again. Tonight, we will celebrate."

CHAPTER 15
PRESENT DAY: NIGHTMARES

I'd killed our kind before. Jayden was not the first, nor would he be the last. Vincent was right when he told me there would be vampires who would challenge me. Not just me, all of my coven. Every once in a while, a vampire, or another coven of vampires, would start something they couldn't finish. They wanted to be known as the one who destroyed one or all of us. They wanted to make the rules, like we had, and still do, for our community. They wanted the title of being the most powerful vampire or the most powerful coven.

Throughout the decades, we'd met many covens. The stronger ones, like us, who ruled over their own country all had one law that remained the same: children should never be turned. There was a time period in our community where children were turned into vampires. They were all the rage. Everyone wanted to create one, or even sometimes more. Their beauty was next to none. They were the most mesmerizing creatures to have walked the Earth. It still saddens me that we had to destroy each and every last one of them.

In the early 1900s turning children into vampires was very common by then. It gave new purpose to the elder vampires who felt like immortality was a curse or to the ones who no longer had a desire to live forever, and ever. But these captivating immortal children were a curse in disguise to our kind. At first, they gave light to the darkest of our kind. Vampires wanted to raise these immortal children as one of their own. To give them love was easy, but to teach them however, was not. Their minds could soak up knowledge like a sponge but the one thing, the most important thing, they could never learn, was self-control.

The immortal children would throw a tantrum when they thirsted for blood, which was nonstop. If they didn't get to feed, they would go into a frenzy, destroying everything in their paths. There were even stories of children running outside, chasing after a human, in the sunlight, and bursting into flames, because they wanted their blood. They knew they were beautiful and they used that to their advantage, even against their creators, tricking them into thinking the more blood they drank, the more beautiful they would become. They would scream for blood, waking the entire town until they could sink their fangs into a warm neck.

That's when the first attacks against our coven came. When the leaders of each country of the vampiric community, including ours, created the Covenant, stating that all immortal children who were turned before they were fifteen years of age must be destroyed. Most of the vampiric community rebuked this at first. Some tried to persuade us of our decision, to no avail. Others ran into hiding but were soon found because the savage children could not be contained. We found them and we killed them, one after the other. Their creators fought back, trying to save their precious children.

Decapitating a vampire would not suffice to destroy it. One must burn the entire body and head to ensure it remained entirely dead. I would never forget the screams of the immortal children as we tossed their heads into the fires. For years, we hunted and destroyed them, sometimes even the vampires who created them, the ones who were willing to die for their child, the ones who truly resisted the Covenant. At first, we were afraid this would cause a civil war between vampires. But, the majority of the creators who tried hiding the merciless children knew they could not control them. To preserve our secret from the humans, and to preserve their own existence, they willingly sacrificed the alluring adolescents to the flames that would burn in our memories for eternity.

"Do you ever think we'll be able to look at a human child and not see the horrors we have witnessed?" Arubrey asked me as the light turned green. We sped off, leaving the minivan with the unsuspecting family, including a little girl watching cartoons on the built-in TV behind us.

I didn't answer. Instead, I watched the pavement under the motorcycle fly by as we made our way back to the Garden District. Back to our home, where no child, human or inhuman, would ever be welcomed.

"Welcome back," Winona greeted us. "I figured you'd be bringing a guest back for interrogations."

"We decided moving the target would be too risky. We conducted interrogations at the bar," Arubrey replied.

"Without me? How did you know the truth was being spoken?"

Arubrey looked at me, wanting me to answer this question. I headed toward the stairs, wanting to escape the fresh memories of Jayden's death, the same Jayden I refused to kill all those years ago when he was just a child. "I tasted him," I said. "Vincent's blood flowed through his veins, just as it still flows through my own."

"I see."

I could tell Winona wanted to say more. But I knew she was too respectful to push my limitations with questions, especially now. Arubrey could be heard filling in the details of our night as I ascended the stairway.

"Sassandra," Winona called after me. I stopped but did not look back. "If Vincent changed him that long ago then his mind was far from gone. I wouldn't have been able to save him like I did you. And even if I could, the chance of insanity would be too great. He would have had to be put down, one way or the other. I'm sorry."

I jumped over the stair's banister, landing back down in front of Winona. It took everything inside me not to send her flying through a wall. My eyes turned red, releasing my full power on Winona. Chaos unfolded around us as the room was transformed. The plush furnishing with rich upholstering melted away, leaving metal ones in its place. The lighting grew dim. The environment around us was no longer the entrance to our mansion. Instead, I transformed it into the insides of the bar of Seven Nights.

Jayden was bound to the chair again, but this time he wasn't a vampire. This time, he was the little boy I remembered from 1857. Winona looked at the scared little boy as I spoke, my words as cold as my skin. "He was a human, Winona. An innocent child at one point. A child I once refused to *put down* as you put it. He didn't deserve this."

Winona looked around the room, around Seven Nights, astonished with my power, before looking back at me. "I apologize, Sassandra. My choice of words was in bad taste. Truly, I am sorry for your loss."

I closed my eyes, releasing us from my illusion. The room transformed again, back into the mansion's entrance with marble flooring and a large chandelier that hung above us, three stories up.

Arubrey was standing in the spot where the child Jayden just was. "Am I caught in one of your illusions?" he asked me.

"No, it was just for Winona. Shows over. I apologize as well. I think I'm going to go check in on Devin."

"He's still asleep," Winona called after me as I made my way up the stairs again.

"Perfect." I let myself in, finding Leslie gazing out the window next to the bed in which Devin was still slumbering in. "How is he?" I asked.

At first Leslie did not speak or move. She continued to look out the window, as if she did not hear my entrance or question, lost in thought. Or perhaps, she was just ignoring me. Vampire mood swings are a bitch sometimes. I would know. I sat on the bed beside Devin. Even though he was asleep he looked stressed, which was understandable from what he'd been through during his lifetime.

"His face seems different than before, does it not?" Leslie finally spoke.

"It does. But all things considered..."

"Yes, all things considered. Why do I feel this way, Sass?" Leslie asked me.

"What do you feel?"

"I'm not sure. All I know is that I do not wish for him to suffer, ever again."

I looked at Devin and lowered my head in shame. I knew I shouldn't say anything. It would be a betrayal to Devin if I did.

"What is it?"

"Leslie, there are a lot of things about Devin no one knows. No one but me that is."

"Stop, Sass. I don't want to hear anything else. Devin's story is not yours to tell. He may be human but we must still respect the fact that they suffer just as well, in their own way. Don't you dare try to tell his story. It's his to tell, not yours." And with that Leslie left the room.

Mood swings.

I closed my eyes, focusing on Devin. I saw the white light up ahead. I ran into the white light, hoping to find the music and fluid colors like last time. The white light was all around me but I did not find what I was looking for. Instead, what I found was a nightmare. One of Devin's many repeating nightmares. The white light that was all around me quickly changed. Sand started to fall from the sky, as if it were raining. Slowly, the ground filled into a desert. I saw the convoy driving toward me, fast, with Devin behind the wheel. He didn't see it. It was too late. The convoy hit the landmine with its front passenger tire. The sound of the explosion echoed again and again within the dream. The convoy turned on its side, sliding along the unpaved road before hitting a bump and flipping. I watched in slow motion as Devin dunked his head down, his grip tightening around the steering wheel. The convoy flipped three times, shattering all its windows out in the process. It finally came to a stop, with Devin hanging upside down. He was the only one wearing his seat belt. One, two, three seconds passed. I heard the click of the seatbelt as Devin unbuckled it, falling head first to the ceiling. I watched in horror as another soldier crawled out of the passenger side window. The sound of machine guns was being fired nearby. A multitude of bullets flew past my head from behind, barely missing me. Several of the bullets hit the soldier who just escaped the wreck, killing him before he could stand. I saw Devin run, trying to escape, searching to find a place to hide.

I was by his side in an instant. "Devin, it's just a nightmare. This isn't real. You already survived this. Everything is going to be alright."

Devin looked me up and down, worried. "Sassandra. They're still trapped in the convoy. Can you save them?"

I took his hand in my own, bullets still flying in our direction. "I'm going to wake you up from this nightmare, ok? One, two, three," I counted. The nightmare was over in a flash, just as the convoy exploded, killing the other soldiers trapped within it.

"Are you alright?" I asked Devin as he frantically looked around the room, awake and dripping with sweat from his nightmare.

He swallowed and focused his attention on me. "Sassandra, you scared me. Wait, were you just in my dream?"

"I can see why you lost yourself."

"Yes, well, the nightmares are forgotten and my dreams are much better when I'm high."

I stood from the bed and crossed the room, making my way to the door. "We can't run anymore, Devin. Nightmares always catch back up with us."

Devin flung the blanket off himself and climbed off the large bed, wearing only camouflage pattern boxers. His posture was upright and assertive, a habit from serving in the army. I watched as he made his bed again, tucking the blanket edges under the mattress, the way they teach you in basic training.

"I can see why she likes you," I said to him.

"Who?"

I opened the bedroom door just as Leslie stepped into view. I looked at Devin and smiled before walking out of the room, answering his question without actually answering his question.

"Devin's awake," I say to Winona and Arubrey as I joined them in the greenhouse, just off of the kitchen. The greenhouse was shared by Winona and myself. Winona used it to grow her various types of herbs and the other half was where I grew flowers for my experiments.

"That's wonderful, I should go and check in on him," Winona said.

"Actually, Leslie is with him right now and I was hoping you, Arubrey, would stay and speak with him while Winona and I head toward Antietam."

Arubrey looked stunned. "And why in the world would I want to stay and chat with the mortal?"

"Because he lost his wife and daughter. And deep down I bet he's blaming himself."

Silence.

"Vincent or the pastor that Jayden normally reported to isn't going to be hearing back from him tonight, so I figured our best bet would be to strike the church tonight while they're still in the dark. Maybe we can find some sort of clue where Vincent is located."

A few more seconds of silence passed before Arubrey finally spoke. "I'd much rather have all four of us do this together. But, with the human having Leslie on an invisible leash, then I guess we'll continue to work in pairs of twos."

"Thank you, Arubrey," I said, giving him an awkward hug.

"I just booked our flight," Winona said, looking at the screen of her cell phone. "The last red eye flight to Antietam takes off in two hours and seventeen minutes."

I retrieved my passport from my room, stuffing it in my carryon bag with an extra pair of high heels. I would have to charm my way through security, so as to not set off any alarms when they run my bag through the metal detectors and x-ray machine.

I drove Winona and myself to the airport. After enchanting our way through security, we had nothing else to do besides sit and wait.

"I can now see why a few others of our kind want us to be known to the world," Winona said, uncrossing her legs and crossing them again to maintain the illusion of being human to the other mortals around us.

"What do you mean?"

"Airports are so boring. If we were known to the rest of the world, maybe we could have our own bar in airports."

"Winona, you don't even like drinking blood. What would you do inside a vampire bar?" I asked, almost laughing.

"I know that. Maybe I could find a nice human willing to let me feed off their energy. You know I don't like feeding from the innocent."

"Yes, I suppose that would be nice, but the Equal Rights Amendment was for women, not vampires. At least you can vote if you want," I said, teasing her. "Besides, I'm sure there will be an annoying passenger on this flight. You can feed from them until they pass out."

Our flight took off and landed without incident. Winona did seem to calm down once she fed off a teenage girl who had a particularly annoying laugh. I think Winona was just afraid of flying but she would never admit to it. It's not like we would die if the plane crashed.

Once we landed in Baltimore and made it outside, we took off running toward our destination at full speed. It took almost a half hour to reach the church I sought refuge in from the sun many decades ago. I could smell a hint of lilac as the wind blew across my face. The church hadn't changed much since my last visit. Other than the purple lilac flowers, representing spirituality, planted in the landscaping, the green shutters, and repairs on the exterior walls from the battle, it all looked the exact same. Preserved. I wondered if the inside had changed.

Winona and I were perched on the same tree Arubrey and I used in 1862. It made me happy to know it was still alive, still growing. The sycamore tree now had a sign at its base, calling it a 'Witness Tree'. One of the still living trees that witnessed the Battle of Antietam, the battle where Arubrey and I killed countless men, for the greater good of war and peace.

Winona leaped down from the ancient tree. I followed her lead, as instructed, and we made our way toward the church. We passed a white car that was parked just at the front of the church. I placed a tracking device underneath it and switched the device on. We made our way to the single doored entrance, smelling a fresh scent of a human. We veered right, walking around the church, following the scent. At the back of the church, a portly man with a

198

full gray beard, holding a flashlight between his neck and shoulder, was locking a chain around the cellar door's handles.

"Pardon me, sir," Winona said, clearly startling the unsuspecting man. "Would you be able to help my friend and me out tonight?"

"Oh, my goodness! You scared me. No, no. I'm sorry. The church is closed to visitors. You'll have to wait until tomorrow to pay for a tour of the battlefield."

"If I wanted a tour, I would ask my friend Sassandra here. She is a huge history buff when it comes to the Civil War. I'm actually seeking spiritual guidance. I'm in need of a pastor. I feel like I have something dark lurking inside me. Inside my soul. Are you a man of God? Can you help save my soul?"

I'd never heard Winona speak like this before. Was she trying to scare the man?

"Yes, I am a pastor. Pastor John. But like I said, the church is closed."

"I understand. I am sorry to bother you. I guess it's like the good book says: It is better to trust in the Lord than to put confidence in man. Psalm 118:8." Winona turned her back on the pastor and started to walk away.

"Oh alright, come in, come in. No need for guilt," Pastor John said, passing us to walk back to the front of the church. He unlocked the door and flipped a switch on the inside. Four overhead lights and a ceiling fan in the center of the room came on. Electricity, another change. We followed him to the far side of the church where he stood behind his podium, ushering us to sit on one of the front wooden pews.

Pastor John opened his bible, King James Version, shuffling through its pages, and began to read. "But if from thence thou shalt seek the Lord thy God, thou shalt find *him* if thou seek him with all thy heart and with all thy soul. Deuteronomy 4:29," he said, looking back up to Winona, like that should solve all her problems.

"Actually, we are seeking someone else tonight. We're looking for a vam… We're looking for a man named Vincent that visits this church every once in a while. Do you know him?" Winona asked.

"Vincent? No, I don't believe I know a Vincent. You're sure he is a member of this church?"

"Thou shalt not bear false witness against thy neighbor, Pastor John," Winona recited.

"We heard he might be in the area," I said, standing up from the pew, advancing toward the podium.

Pastor John started to back away as I came closer to him. "Please. Don't kill me. I'm just a record keeper for him. I'm harmless," Pastor John pleaded.

"Tell us where we can find Vincent and we will leave you unharmed," I promised him.

"I don't know but I can introduce you to his wife. She's here. Down in the cellar."

I looked at Winona to see if he was lying. She shrugged her shoulders. "He's speaking the truth."

"You're the lead, Winona. I follow you."

Pastor John started to preach again, "If any man serve me, let him follow me; and where I am…"

"Oh, shut up!" Winona barked at the old man, pointing him to the door.

Pastor John grabbed his flashlight and we followed him back outside and around to the back of the church. He nervously unlocked the padlock and removed the chain from the cellar door handles. I pushed him aside and pulled the green doors open that led down to darkness. "After you," I insisted, letting the plump man lead the way.

"She fed earlier so she should be asleep again," the pastor said, leading us down the steep stone steps.

"Vampires don't sleep. And if they did, why would a vampire be sleeping during the night?" Winona asked, following behind me.

Pastor John opened the door at the bottom of the steps, "Come unto me, all ye that labour and are heavy laden, and I will give you rest. Matthew 11:28".

Winona passed us both, entering the room first. I rolled my eyes at the pastor as I passed him, still holding the door open for me. Pastor John struck a match and lit a lantern that was hanging from the wall, illuminating the cellar. The floors of the room were made from concrete and the walls were covered with beadboard panels. The moisture in the room was thick with mold and sitting in front of us were caskets. Thirteen closed caskets, to be exact.

"Wherefore he saith, Awake thou that sleepest, and arise from the dead, and Christ shall give thee light. Ephesians 5:14,"

Pastor John whispered behind us, just before slamming the door shut and locking us in.

I turned around at the door, ready to break through it. "I'll go get him. He probably hasn't even made it back up the steps."

"Um, Sassandra," Winona said, "I might actually need your help."

I turned back around and faced the room that was occupied by the coffins. Thirteen coffins that now were slowly opening simultaneously, by thirteen pale hands, pushing each of their lids up. Thirteen pale women, all dressed in white, sat up from the inside of their coffins with their eyes still closed. Their heads snapped up, turning toward us. Blood began to pour from their mouths, soaking and staining their white shirts and dresses, as they all let out an ear-splitting scream directed at Winona and myself. The sound waves that were coming from their bloodied mouths were high pitched and deafening. Their screams lasted for exactly thirteen seconds before they abruptly stopped. The thirteen women snapped their eyes open, revealing nothing but pure hatred and evil as they stared at Winona and myself, piercing us with their eyes.

The thirteen vampires all chanted together, "For whether we live, we live unto our Lord; and whether we die, we die unto the Lord: whether we live therefore, or die, we are the wives of Vincent, our Lord."

CHAPTER 16
YEAR 1862: BLOODFEAST

Arubrey and I returned to D.C., close to midnight, after the battle of Antietam was over to deliver the news to Abraham about the Union's victory, with our help. Abraham immediately called for celebration. The atmosphere within the White House was filled with exhilarated chatter and some folks were already elegantly dancing around the room. The battle of Antietam was the victory that Abraham and the Union were hoping for. The soldiers needed the motivation and Arubrey and myself were able to give that to them, by fighting side by side with them, not that the surviving soldiers remembered seeing us. Everything had happened so fast on the battlefield that when it was finally over, there was little chatter about me leading a group of soldiers across the bridge, using my own body to help shield them from flying bullets. What rumors were going around would be exaggerated and soon forgotten. The press had been silenced by order of President Lincoln. They were no longer allowed to print about the Civil War to keep vital information away from the Confederacy.

Arubrey and I had cleaned ourselves up upon our return and joined the others at the White House, where Abraham and the other government officials and their friends were celebrating in the East Room. We spotted Leslie and Winona standing idle in a corner when we entered the room. It was queer to see Leslie dressed so formally. Her royal blue gown was puffed out at the bottom making it impossible for someone to stand close to her. The East Room was the largest room within the White House and the room itself looked faded and worn, as if it was already hundreds of years old, including the furniture. Even the chandeliers looked dated.

"Welcome back," Winona greeted us as we made our way toward Leslie and her.

"It's good to be back," Arubrey said. "And wearing dress clothing again."

"Yes, Arubrey is quite upset. Bullet holes and gallons of blood ruined his outfit during the battle, mine as well," I explained.

"That, and I had to burrow myself underground to avoid being killed by the sun," Arubrey added to the conversation.

I looked at him, bewildered. "I was wondering where you hid. You should have joined me in the church's closet," I said, wanting to blush after the words left my lips.

"Oh, that is quite alright, Sassandra. I much rather bond with the worms."

I glared at him. Why did he always have to be such a prick? "I was hoping your opinion of me would have changed by now, seeing as how I saved your head from getting blown off," I snapped back, turning on my heel and starting to leave, annoyed.

"Oh, come back. I was only kidding. I promise not to tease you ever again," Arubrey yelled after me. He grabbed my hand, pulling it back toward him, making me turn to face him. "Sassandra, truly, I thank you."

"You don't have to thank me; we both know you would have survived it."

"True, but it would have been very painful and messy, nonetheless. Would you like to dance?" Arubrey asked me.

"I thought you said you were done teasing me."

"I tease you not. May I have this dance?" Arubrey asked again.

"Arubrey, I never danced before," I confessed to him.

"It's quite simple. Just do as the other ladies do. Your mind will be able to predict their movements, your body will be quick to follow, and your soul will get lost within the music if you let it."

"Everyone already stared at me when we first arrived. What will they think? I'm the only black woman here."

He smiled, continuing to look me in the eyes. "Then let's really give them something to stare at."

I gave in, letting him pull me to the floor for the next dance. The humans called it the Romany Polka dance. We all lined up, men standing across from the women, almost all of them kept looking at me. When the music began, all the women, including myself, stepped forward toward their partners, then back again with the men following us, taking our hands and twirling us around and around. Arubrey was right, within minutes my soul soon was lost within the music as the musicians strummed on their instruments. Even Leslie and Winona found a couple of gentlemen to dance with. Abraham chose not to dance, which was nothing new, Arubrey told me. Instead, his wife danced with their eldest son while he sat with other government officials, chatting about the ongoing Civil War. Just because this battle was won did not mean the war was finished.

After our dance was over, we all made our way over to Abraham.

"Why aren't you dancing?" I asked the President.

"I shall dance once this war is over. Until then, there is much work to be completed."

"You're always working, Abraham," Leslie said. "You should take the night off and come celebrate with us."

"Perhaps another night. I will not be needing your assistance tonight. You've all earned a night off. Now, if you will excuse me, I have a speech to write."

206

We were all stunned by Abraham's dismissal. Since I met him, there had always been at least two of us guarding him. Had he thought the assassination attempts would yield now?

"Abraham is right. We do need a night for ourselves," Arubrey said to us.

With that we left the White House and made our way East, arriving within the slums of Murder Bay. Leslie took lead, jumping from building to building, with us following her. We arrived in front of a rundown, brick building. 'Fallen Angels' was painted in red on the wooden sign that hung above the door. One of the windows on the second story was busted out.

Leslie turned around, smiling. "I hate this thing," she said, ripping her dress and crinoline off and tossing it around the building's corner. She looked at Winona and myself, waiting for us to follow her lead. I tossed my dress with Leslie's but Winona refused. Arubrey removed his tie and yanked his dress shirt off with one swift movement, ripping his buttons off.

"Leave the suspenders. It makes you look classy," Leslie said to him, smirking. I took a quick glance at Arubrey and I had to agree with her, he looked very classy tonight. Arubrey caught my eye and I quickly looked away. I thought we were going to go inside but instead, Leslie jumped up, grabbing a hold of the second story's window ledge. I guess Leslie had other plans for us tonight.

"Isn't it beautiful up here?" Leslie asked, looking out at the view of the city.

Winona laughed. "If by beautiful you mean the buildings are decomposing and the air reeks of dead fish, and probably a few corpses, then yes, by all means, it's quite beautiful."

"Oh, Winona, our world is growing. Humans have to build up to accommodate. Although, Lord knows they breed like cockroaches."

"That is precisely what worries me," Winona whispered to herself.

"Did we come up here to bicker about humans, our food source, or are we celebrating tonight?" I interjected. "And just why are we on top of the building instead of inside of it?"

Leslie walked to the ledge of the rooftop and peered her head over, looking down. "Fallen Angels is a brothel. Tonight, I want to feed on some men who refuse to follow the rules. Naughty men always taste better."

"How about we watch you and Winona hunt tonight? Hunt however, whoever you please," Arubrey suggested to Leslie.

As the sky slowly grew darker, we watched as man after man went inside the brothel. A few came back out, accompanied by a woman. We watched Leslie watch them, unsure of what her definition of the word naughty meant. Moments later a group of four men were making their way over to the brothel. Three of them stopped a block away and went down a narrow alleyway between two buildings. The fourth man, with a scruffy mustache and beard, made his way into Fallen Angels. A few minutes later he made his way back outside with a lady wrapped around his arm. The man guided his new friend back toward the way he came, back to the alley where the other three men were waiting.

Leslie said nothing as she followed them with her sharp eyes. She took a single step off the rooftop, falling to the ground below us, landing gracefully. She calmly walked toward the alleyway. Arubrey, Winona, and myself jumped over to the building beside us to peer down on the scene that was about to unfold below us in the alley. The lady from the brothel just began to scream as Leslie rounded the corner of the alleyway.

"Release her," Leslie ordered the men who were already circled around the woman.

"My, my, what do we have here? I pay for one and get us two it looks like," said the man with the scruffy facial hair, taking a few steps closer to Leslie.

Leslie advanced on her prey, coming face to face with him, their lips almost touching. "I do not ask twice," she said loud enough for everyone to hear before slamming the man's head into the brick wall, crushing the man's skull and killing him instantly. His blood began to pool at her feet as she reached down, pressing her hand into it and bringing it back up to her lips. She looked at the men who were still holding the woman and smiled at them and licked the palm of her hand, savoring the flavor of justice. "You boys give her all the money you got. Now."

The men did as they were instructed, in silence and in shock at what they just witnessed. "Come on, sweety, it's ok, I won't hurt you." Leslie took the dead man's money out of his pockets and gave

209

it to the woman as she came closer to Leslie. "You take the rest of the night off. Go home."

As the woman left the alleyway, she started to run, never looking back. Leslie turned her attention back to the three remaining men. "Strip."

"What? No way, lady!" one of the men yelled.

Leslie looked down at the body laying at her feet and then back up at them, tilting her head and licking her lips again. The three men quickly changed their minds and started to strip their clothes off.

"All of your clothes," Leslie instructed the men, looking each of them in the eyes. They were shaking with fear but they obliged, removing their socks and underwear as well. Leslie walked toward the men and ran her fingers down the chest of the tallest of the three. She grabbed him by the throat, lifting him into the air. The man struggled to free himself from her grasp but she ignored him, looking to the other who was closest to her. "You, come here. I would like you to put your wrist up to my lips."

The man was in a trance and did as he was instructed. Leslie bit into his flesh, drinking his blood while still holding the other man up by his throat.

"What are you doing to us?" the third man said, coming back to his senses.

Leslie continued to drink from the wrist that was offered to her. She drank from the man until he grew too weak to stand on his own. His legs gave out and he laid at her feet beside the deceased, landing in his blood. "It's a Bloodfeast, Sugar. You be good now and do as I say and you might die quickly."

Leslie pulled the man she was holding in the air to her mouth, biting into his neck. She kept her eyes open, watching the last remaining man who was still able to stand on his own as she drank. Once she was done with him, she dropped him beside the other two men at her feet. "Come hither," she said, beckoning him forward with her finger to the naked man. She had him back under her control. He walked forward, stepping over the bodies to get closer to Leslie. She bit into his neck but released him quickly. "Your blood is vulgar. How unsatisfying." She tossed him back and came to stand over one of the men laying at her feet with their head between her feet. She closed her feet together and twisted them, snapping the man's neck. She did the same to the other man lying beside him before making her way to the end of the alleyway where the last man, now standing again, watched in fear as his friends were each murdered in front of him.

"Now, what shall I do with you? Life has already been so unfair to you. Bad blood and a small penis? You poor thing. You have nothing to offer me."

"Please, let me live. I will never harm a woman again. I beg of you. Have mercy!"

"Sorry, Sugar. Fallen angels don't show mercy to the undeserving. Besides, we're standing in a dead-end after all," Leslie said laughing, just before thrusting her hand inside the man's chest and out the other side, grasping his heart in her hand. The man gasped for air twice before dying on his feet.

"That was intense," Winona said as Leslie rejoined us.

"Please. I did less to them than they would have done to the girl. Besides, weren't you just complaining about overpopulation?"

Winona took us toward the docks of the bay. The Georgetown Waterfront was flooded with tobacco factories that delivered their products across the Atlantic for trade.

"The men that run the docks here work overnight, so most of them are always refreshed with energy at night because they sleep during the day. They're the perfect prey for an energy vampire, such as myself," Winona explained.

She sat down, crossing her legs with her hands on her knees and closed her eyes, just in front of us. I'd seen her hunt before and watching her never grew old. A white aura began to glow around her body, steadily growing brighter. The white energy she was emitting took the shape of Winona's body. It did not cast shadows or light up the dark. Her energy, or Ka as she called it, was invisible to the human eye but could be seen by vampires. The first time I watched her hunt was how she proved to me that vampires had souls. How else could one explain what she could do?

Winona's spirit glided toward a group of men who were unloading cargo from one of the many containers sitting on the docks. Her spirit touched each of the men on their chest, just for a few seconds before moving on to the next, draining a portion of their energy from each of them. Her spirit did this to twelve different workers before rejoining Winona's body. She opened her eyes, smiling. "I only took a little from each of them. That way they can continue with their work."

"Sassandra, you're up next," Arubrey spoke.

"Actually, I'm still full from earlier tonight on the battlefield."

"Yes, as am I."

I looked at Arubrey in wonderment. "I've never seen you actually hunt. Are you sure you're a vampire?" I teased him.

"Yes, quite," he replied, smirking.

"It's just that in the year I've known you, I don't actually know much of anything about you."

"Sassandra, you are still a very young vampire. Still a newborn. One year to elder vampires is like one month for a human. We do not count years but decades. And you have only been a vampire for half of one decade."

"Well, how old are you?" I asked him.

"In human years I am twenty-nine. I have been a vampire for nearly twenty decades."

I did the math in my head. "Wait, you were turned in the 1600s?"

"Yes. I was turned, without permission, in the year 1666."

"1666? You were turned the same year Winona was born? Do you not find that to be... odd?"

"Yes. And we discussed it shortly after we first met. But we found no connection. We drew portraits of what we remembered of our makers, just as we had you do shortly after we met you, and there was no resemblance. Nor was there any resemblance in how we were changed."

I had to press my luck. "How were you changed?"

213

"He tortured me. A lot of torture. The one who created me was made from pure evil. My wife and I were both held captive, as humans that is. I never knew his name. He is the one who gave me these scars," Arubrey explained, waving his scarred and blackened hand in the air. "My wife was not as lucky. When I escaped, I left London and I have no desire to ever go back there." Arubrey began to pace, putting some distance between himself and us. "After my escape I was alone. I kept my distance from society most of my immortal life, up until Abraham found me at least. I still find myself uncomfortable in the presence of others, whether they be dead or alive." Arubrey turned around to face us again, continuing with his story, "I was and still am afraid. Afraid that one day I will meet my maker again. Afraid that he will finish what he started in 1666. I think he created me just to have something strong enough to torture without killing it."

"That's horrible!" I yelled. "Why would they do this to us? Are they incapable of creating a vampire out of love?"

"Calm yourself, Sassandra," Winona said. "The humans will hear you."

"If it makes you feel any better, Sass, I was making love, so to speak, when I was first bitten," Leslie added, lightening the mood and making us laugh.

"I did not care much for you when I first met you, Sassandra," Arubrey started again. "Truth be told I would have killed you if the others would have let me. I did not trust you. I thought you would run back to Vincent and his cause. We're quite similar when it comes down to it. We were both ill-treated beyond belief before we were changed into what we are today. I've fought with you in battle and danced with you in celebration. Abraham has become very fond of you. I am glad I did not kill you, even though I've had multiple opportunities. I am glad to now call you my friend and my sister. I am glad to call all of you my friends and my sisters. I am nothing without the three of you."

"He's still drunk on all the blood he had, isn't he?" Leslie teased.

"And you are our brother, Arubrey," Winona said, beaming with happiness.

"That is very kind of you to say. I believe that is the most I have heard you speak," I added.

Arubrey looked down for a couple seconds, becoming shy from what he had just admitted. He raised his head back up, smirking. "If any of you try to hug me, I will be forced to kill you."

We all laughed together at his response as the moon shined its light down on the four of us.

The night continued and with it came a new bond between us all. We competed against one another, seeing who could run across the city the fastest, who could jump the highest and furthest. Before the sun rose, we decided to make Bloodfeast a recurring event once every decade. It was this night of the first Bloodfeast when we declared ourselves as the Ooljéé coven, the coven of the moon.

CHAPTER 17
YEAR 1865: HORIZON

Arubrey was right. Years had passed but it seemed as if it were only months. Slavery had been abolished. Abraham was now fresh into his second term of presidency. The Union had finally prevailed against the Confederacy and the Civil War between the North and South was now over. There was an unspoken understanding that peace was on the horizon and with it we knew our relationship with Abraham had to come to an end. The humans were beginning to whisper about how fast the presidency was aging Abraham. How long would it be before the whispers would start about the ones who guarded over him, ceasing to age, as the years passed?

"I sure am gonna miss the soldiers," Leslie said, looking out to the grounds as soldiers marched by, guarding the White House.

"The soldiers? What about Abraham?" Winona replied.

"Oh, you know I will miss him just as much. We can always write to stay in touch."

"Abraham was the one who brought us together. A letter just seems so impersonal."

I listened to Leslie and Winona go back and forth. They acted like tonight was our last night with Abraham. "Arubrey said we need not leave for a few more months, at the earliest," I reminded them.

"Sassandra," Winona said, looking at me. "A few months to me is a few hours to a human. Give it a few decades, your perspective on time will adjust."

Leslie and I looked at each other and we both rolled our eyes and started to laugh just before Arubrey entered the room.

"Ladies, the show will begin momentarily. Sassandra, Winona, I would like the two of you to secure the building before Abraham and his guest arrive. They will be riding with Abraham and the First Lady. Leslie, you are to ride in front of their carriage and I will follow closely behind."

The Ford's Theatre was just five blocks away from the White House. Winona and myself set off on foot shortly after sunset to secure the building for the arrival of the President. The 3-act play of *Our American Cousin* was sold out, mostly due to the fact that the President would be in attendance tonight. The public wanted to see him more than the play itself it seemed.

"Welcome to Ford's Theatre," the dark-skinned gentleman greeted Winona and myself as he held the door open for us. "I was informed two beautiful ladies would be showing up shortly to ensure the safety of the President tonight. If my eyes are not deceiving me, I assume the two of you to be part of the newly formed Secret Service?"

"How very kind of you," Winona replied to the man as we passed by him. "President Lincoln should be arriving within the hour. It is of our understanding the Secret Service has full access to the building entirely?"

"Yes, ma'am. Would you like a tour?"

"No, that will not be necessary. We will manage on our own. Thank you for your hospitality."

We left our greeter behind and ventured into the building. The entrance was a rectangular room with three sets of double doors that led to the main floor seating and stage. At both ends of the entryway was a curved staircase that led to the second floor, the staircase on the right would be the one Abraham and his guest would soon climb to make their way to their seats for the play. The other staircase would be used for the other members of the audience.

"We shall start at the top and make our way back down," Winona commanded. The third-floor balcony was the smallest, mainly holding only a few chairs, ladders, overhead lighting, and a singular spotlight in the center for the performers on the grand stage down below. This area was only for the lighting crew, off limits to guests. The second floor was full of singular wooden chairs, all lined up in rows. At the back two corners were doors which led to the upper state boxes. "Abraham and his guest shall be seated there," Winona said, pointing to the upper right state box. The main floor, excluding the building's entrance, was set up like the second. Wooden chairs set neatly row after row for the audience with a large stage that spanned from both sides of the state boxes. The Ford's Theatre workers had draped flags across the outside of the upper right state box in honor of President Lincoln's visit tonight.

Winona and myself made our way back down to the building's entrance while discussing the plan. "Once they arrive, Leslie will check all exits to ensure they are locked from the inside. That way if anyone comes inside, you will see them. Arubrey will be seated across the stage from Abraham in the other top state box," Winona explained. "You know how he likes to try and see and be everywhere at once. Leslie will be seated below, on the main floor, closest to Abraham's state box. You can stay down here in the entryway and guard the entrance and the left staircase to the second floor. The other stairs will be only accessible to Abraham and his party for tonight. I will be stationed at the top of that staircase, just outside the door which leads to their box."

"What about intermission between acts?" I asked.

"Dinner and refreshments will be brought to me to inspect before serving. Arubrey and Leslie will usher them to the restrooms if need be."

"Tonight will be great for them. A time to get away from politics and to just relax. A time to laugh and be happy. Abraham needs this."

Soon the lobby was filled with eager citizens of Washington, D.C. They happily showed their tickets as they passed by. Once the last of the paying guests took their seats, Abraham and the others finally arrived. Arubrey led the way up the opposite set of stairs across from me while Leslie went through the double doors to find her seat close to the stage. *Our American Cousin* was a humorous play, or so, at least the humans found it amusing. Their laughter could be heard through the closed doors and echoed off the walls of the entrance.

The outside entrance doors opened and in walked a man, making a beeline toward the staircase which led up to the area Winona was guarding. "Excuse me. Sir? You must use this staircase and I will need to see your ticket," I called out to the man. He turned, looking at me, then to the stairs just behind me. He smirked and then turned back around, ignoring my instructions completely.

I moved forward toward the man, calling out, "Sir!" before hastily stopping in my own steps.

Tap, tap, tap, was all I could hear. The human man continued his way up the stairs and I let him, frozen in fear from the sound of a different man walking toward me from behind.

Tap, tap, tap. "Good evening," the man spoke to me. I said nothing, still standing with my back facing him. "I said good evening, drudge. Did you not hear me?"

I gritted my fangs and turned around to face him. Just like the words he first spoke to me when I was a scared little girl, his appearance was unchanged. His dark hair was slicked back and he still wore pointed dress shoes. "I knew you would come for me soon enough," I said to Vincent.

"What makes you think I'm here for you?" Vincent replied, as his eyes began to glow red, just before disappearing up the stairs, the stairs I was supposed to be guarding, leading to the second floor.

"Damn it!" I cursed out loud to myself, quickly rushing up the curved staircase after him. Although my body moved at an accelerated speed compared to humans, the time it took me to climb the steps seemed to take ages. Something had changed. The abundance of steps grew to an unspeakable height. I could hear a man speaking on stage as I climbed.

"Don't know the manners of good society, eh? Well, I guess I know enough to turn you inside out, old gal – you sockdologizing old man-trap!" the stage actor said his line, followed by a roar of laughter from the audience.

I climbed and climbed up step after step as if I were going up a thousand flights rather than just one. The audience's continued laughter began to fade down, followed by the unmistakable sound of a single gunshot. The stairway shifted, returning to normal and I was shocked to see I had only climbed three steps during this entire time. I swayed to the right, my hands pushing into the wall beside me, trying to keep my balance. What the hell was happening to me? Once the world quit spinning around me, I flew up the remaining steps until I finally reached the top.

Chaos. Unadulterated and undiluted chaos had broken loose within the theater. The audience was no longer laughing, no longer having a good time. Instead, they were all on their feet, screaming and panic driven. Some seemed drunk, stumbling around trying to escape while others were pushing forward, trying to see what was happening on the stage down below. I pushed past them, literally pushing the humans out of my way. I had to find Vincent before it was too late. It was useless. The sea of humans that were in my way seemed to never end. I clearly remember being told the theater was only allowed to hold a maximum of 350 guests at once. Why did it seem there was triple this amount and all of them crowded on the second balcony? I closed my eyes, trying to refocus my mind. This was a trick. It had to be a trick. I reopened my eyes; the crowd of people had lessened back to its normal size.

I found an opening to the left of the remaining people. I looked over to Abraham's state box. Abraham was sitting in a rocking chair, slumped over. His wife was holding onto his hand, hysterically crying. Winona was standing behind Abraham, both her hands cradling his head, with a white glow illuminating from her body. I spotted Leslie on the main floor below. She was slowly and quite awkwardly making her way up the few steps to the stage. Why was she moving so slow? It was then I saw a man standing on the stage, holding a gun in one hand and a dagger in the other. This was the same man I saw moments ago. The man who refused to listen to me just before Vincent made his presence known. "Sic semper tyrannis! The South is avenged!" the man yelled to the onlooking crowd of people. Vincent was behind the man, standing at the back of the stage, eyes glowing red.

I leaped over the balcony and started to descend down to the stage. A flash of smoke appeared in front of me as I was falling.

222

Arubrey slammed into me, pushing me back away from the stage. We crashed down just behind the mass of humans, breaking a couple wooden chairs as we landed on top of them.

"Arubrey, what the hell!" I roared in anger. Why would he stop me from going after Vincent?

"Sassandra, stop! You will be trapped in his spell!"

"What are you talking about? Vincent's going to get away!"

"You need to forget about him and save Leslie! Go! Now!" Arubrey yelled. "Pull her away from Vincent!"

Arubrey vanished, leaving a cloud of smoke in his place. I looked at my friend, still leisurely climbing the few steps up to the stage. She was moving slower than a turtle! I gasped as my perspective changed. I was no longer watching Leslie climb the steps. Instead, I was now in her mind. I could see what she was seeing, hundreds of steps laid before her. She was running up them, trying her damnedest to reach the mortal and Vincent. With each step she climbed, a new one formed at the top, making her efforts meaningless. I knew what she was seeing was not real. This was an illusion, cast by no other than Vincent himself.

Leslie continued up the steps, trapped within his spell. I did not know how I did it but I was able to pull my mind back out of hers, back to reality. A golden flagpole was hurling through the air, heading straight for Vincent's chest. The red glow of his eyes receded, changing back to their natural color of dull brown. Vincent caught the pole that was thrown at his chest, its pointed end was inches away from his heart. Leslie swayed on the steps, just as I had moments earlier. Vincent's illusion was temporarily broken. I did as

Arubrey commanded of me and rushed toward Leslie, grabbing her to yank her away from the danger that awaited her on the stage.

We were at the double doors that led back into the entrance of the theater. "What's happening?" Leslie asked, confused as I held onto her arm, steadying her balance.

"You cannot trust what you see, Leslie. Not with Vincent being close by," I explained to her.

"The man. He shot Abraham, Sass. He shot him!"

"Go up to Abraham. Winona is up there with him. Help her."

Leslie left my side and using caution I made my way back toward the stage just in time to see the red glow of Vincent's eyes again as he closed the door that led to the backstage area. Arubrey now stood on the stage alone, his back facing me, but he was not moving. I pushed my mind into his, instantly blinded by thick, dark, smoke. He was trapped in Vincent's lingering illusion. I left his mind and joined him on the stage. "Arubrey?" I said, touching his shoulder.

Arubrey jumped, startled by my touch, the illusion breaking. "Sassandra. Where are they?" he asked, looking around.

"They're gone," I answered, sounding defeated.

"Arubrey!" Leslie yelled from up above, standing in Abraham's state box that overlooked the stage. "Abraham is still alive. Winona says to find a secure place nearby to move him. We cannot stay here!"

Winona carried Abraham cradled in her arms across the street from the theater. Traveling any further was too dangerous for him, she warned us. We laid the President on the bed diagonally. His height was too much for the small bed that took up most of the room that was offered for us to use by a civilian. Beside the bed, Winona was sitting in a small chair, with her eyes closed, focusing her energy into Abraham, helping him stay alive.

"Will he survive?" Arubrey asked, concerned for the President's wellbeing.

"I do not know," answered Winona, without opening her eyes.

"You must save him," Arubrey urged.

"I must *focus*, Arubrey. Now shut up and get out. All of you."

Seconds turned into minutes and the minutes turned into agony for us. Abraham was like a father to all of us. He was the one who brought us all together. What would happen if we lost him? Was there no other way to save him if Winona was unsuccessful?

"What if...?" I started to say before stopping, hesitating.

"What is it, Sass?" Leslie inquired.

I looked at Leslie and then onto Arubrey. "What if we turned him?"

Leslie's head lifted up, eager to hear more of this idea. Arubrey remained calm as he spoke. "You want one of us to turn Abraham? Turn the President of the United States of America into a vampire?"

"Yes," I replied. "That would save him, would it not? If Winona cannot..." I trailed off.

Arubrey left us in the hall, rejoining the room with Abraham and Winona, closing the door behind him.

"Sass, we have to find them," Leslie began. "Vincent and that man that shot him! They have to pay for what they did."

"I know. Don't worry, we'll find them. But first, we must focus on Abraham."

Arubrey rejoined us in the hall. More minutes passed, turning into hours, before Winona finally emerged from the room. "He is awake now," Winona said, closing the door behind her. "His breathing is also normal again, no longer strained. He is still very weak, as am I. I do not know how long the energy I gave him will stay inside of him. Without it I am sure he would be dead by now. I talked to him momentarily. He does not wish to be turned."

"What?" Leslie almost shouted. "He has to! If it's the only way to save him!"

"It's his choice," Arubrey quietly said.

"He wishes to speak with each of you, separately."

Leslie entered the room with Abraham. We could not hear what was being said. Outside, a crowd had filled the streets earlier. They were all chatting loudly amongst one another, eager and waiting to hear updates on their beloved President.

Leslie's visit with Abraham did not take long. Arubrey took her place next. Leslie did not speak to any of us upon her return. Instead, she passed us by and left the hall and building altogether. Hopefully she would not do anything stupid.

I stood in the same spot, motionlessly, waiting as the minutes ticked by. The door creaked open as Arubrey reentered the hallway. "You're up, Sassandra," he said.

I sat beside Abraham, still laying on the bed with his feet hanging over the bottom of the mattress. He looked at me and gave me half a smile. "It is good to see you again, Sassandra," he said with a weak voice.

"Abraham, please. Please stay with us. Will you not reconsider letting one of us turn you? We can make you into a vampire, like us. You can live forever."

"Oh, come now. You were not the first to try to kill me, you know. You were not even the second. My wife has always been afraid for my safety since I took office. And I told her, if they do kill me, I shall never die another death. And I must keep that promise to her. In the end, it's not the years in your life that count. It's the life in your years. And I have had 57 years to live by this. I am already on borrowed time, Winona tells me."

"What will we do without you?" I asked, pleading.

"You will do your best at whatever it is you wish to do with your existence. And you shall succeed, I am sure of it. I was told it was the same vampire who created you who was behind tonight's attack."

"Yes, it was him. I saw him. And I'm afraid I will not be able to ever defeat him. He is too strong."

"You are correct, Sassandra," the President said, coughing in pain.

"What do you mean?"

"Whether you say you can or cannot defeat him, you are correct."

I took his hand in my own and held it there, saying nothing. We sat like this for just a minute before he broke the silence. "After I am gone, I promise to watch over you. Sunrise is coming soon and I believe these curtains to be too thin for your liking."

I squeezed his hand. "Thank you, Mr. President." I released his hand and gave him a quick kiss on his forehead before leaving his bedside. Mary was waiting outside the door and went to her husband's side after I left the door open behind me. Sunrise was coming and we needed better shelter. Arubrey, Winona, and myself left the building, following Leslie's scent. While running, we all three looked at one another. Another scent soon was mixed with Leslie's. A scent we were all now familiar with. It led us a few miles South to the edge of the Washington Channel where Leslie stood.

"He's gone. Vincent and the human split up just outside the back of the theater," Leslie explained. "I decided the human would be easier to find later so I followed Vincent's scent here. He did not linger. He made a beeline straight to the water after he left the theater. He could be anywhere by now."

"You should not have followed Vincent. He's too strong!" I said, scolding my friend.

"I don't care, Sass. He has to pay. We all know he used the mortal to kill Abraham."

"Abraham is not dead, Leslie," Arubrey said to her. "Not yet at least. And Sassandra is right, Vincent is too strong for any of us. We only survived because he let us."

Silence fell between the four of us. We all knew sunrise would be threatening the horizon soon enough. We turned our backs on the water, turning our backs on Vincent, for now at least, and made our way back home to seek shelter for the day. And what a long day it would be.

CHAPTER 18

PRESENT DAY: EMOTIONS

Vampires were unable to sleep, or so I believed until I was bemused by the thirteen pairs of eyes that opened and were now staring at us. No, not at us, but *through* us, like we did not exist to them. The wives of Vincent, which they had just proclaimed to be to Winona and myself, were transfixed in a state of somnambulism. The way they each exited their caskets was indistinguishable from the next, yet they did not move in a manner which suggested they were awake!

A single oil lamp was mounted onto the wall and the small amount of lighting it offered within the room bounced off their cold, pale faces as they arose from their slumber. The vampire closest to us was the first to stand on her feet outside of her coffin. I rushed the undead creature, shoving her as hard as I could back into her casket and slamming its lid shut. I jumped up onto the top of the casket standing tall and looking down on the scene that was unfolding. The vampire was shrieking within her casket and I could feel her trying to claw her way back out through its lid.

"Stay where you are!" Winona ordered the wives of Vincent.

Her command fell on deaf ears. The women hissed at Winona, warning that we were in their territory and that we were now their prey. A vampire flung itself at Winona, crashing into her. The force knocked Winona off her feet and they slammed onto the floor just outside the door that led back to the stairs, becoming entangled in the tattered wedding dress the vampire was wearing. I was flung from the casket's lid, hitting a wall and landing in a heap on the floor, as it blasted open again. The vampire I had trapped inside of it and another six went after Winona as the other six began to close in on me.

I grabbed the oil lamp that was hanging from the wall and threw it at the doorway. The glass shattered as it hit the floor spilling oil and flames that now illuminated the room. The barrier of fire separated Winona and myself but it also split the group of vampire wives in half. The fire spread, growing wide and high, as it burned.

The six vampires all watched as the flames grew out of control. One of the wives started laughing hysterically, turning to face me. "You trapped yourself in here with us," the vampire said.

"Oh, on the contrary," I replied, taking my eight-inch platform heels off and pulling two hidden blades out of the heels. "I locked all of you in here with *me*. For I am Sassandra of the Ooljéé coven, and none of you are going anywhere."

The six enraged vampires lunged toward me. I jumped, diving over them. The wives of Vincent were fledglings, slow with their movements and uncoordinated. I soared through the air with my arms reaching straight out in front of me. As I flew over them, I sliced the throat of one of the vampires. My blade sliced all the way through her neck, including the bone. I landed behind the group of vampires on my feet and the decapitated head fell to the floor beside me, blood splattering as it landed with a thud. I kicked the head into the flames, feeding the fire that was growing more and more out of control. The headless body collapsed and lay motionless. I took advantage of their slow movements and raked my blades down another's back, staining her white gown with fresh blood. The vampire screamed out in pain but the scream did not have time to bounce off the walls before it ended. I snapped her neck, not having enough time to finish the job. The vampire fell to the ground but was not dead. Breaking her neck just pissed her off even more.

My back was to the flames and the smoke was pouring in, filling the cellar. Another vampire lunged for me but I twirled my head, lashing my braid of hair and silver spikes into her face. The spikes sliced open the vampire's face and she hissed in agony as poison now entered her bloodstream. I bounced up on top of a closed casket again just in time. The vampire with the broken neck was now on her feet and she moved with such speed I barely had time to react. I kicked my bare foot straight into her face with all my strength. Her severed head rolled into the fire. I smiled as I heard the shrieking fade away into nothingness, leaving another corpse on the ground.

I looked at the chaos of my surroundings. The fire was spreading around the room and I was trapped in the middle. The four remaining vampires were each in a corner of the cellar. I had just killed two of them. Were the other four afraid? They should be.

I hurled both of my blades in opposite directions, diagonal from one another, with fierce precision. I hit my two targets directly in the forefront of their skulls and as their knees buckled beneath them, their blood poured from the backside of their heads where the tips of my blades were sticking out of. The wound was not fatal to them but it did buy me what I needed, which was more time.

I locked eyes with one of the remaining two vampire wives that were still left standing. Her eyes grew wide with fear. I anticipated her to try and attack me but she did something unexpected instead. She ran toward the flames that towered over us and as she entered the fire, she screamed in agony as it turned her white dress to ash and her flesh began to tear away from her limbs as her body was baked in the fire.

I looked at my last adversary and smiled. Her eyes never left mine as I pulled my blades out of the heads of the two collapsed vampires and used them to sever their heads, putting them out of their misery once and for all. I tossed both heads into the fire, then dragged the screaming vampire wife out of the flames. Her body withered in pain as it continued to burn. I put my blade to her throat, still looking at the other vampire, and pushed down and all the way through to the floor. I broke eye contact with the last vampire and I tossed the head into the fire with all the others.

I turned my attention back to the corner of the cellar where the last vampire should have been. She was gone. Where did she go? There was only one way out and it was blocked by a roaring fire and charred skulls. She was hiding. There were twelve open caskets within the room, some were on fire, and there was one which was closed. I opened the lid and the vampire that laid inside the casket stared back at me. Her eyes did not resemble that of someone who was afraid. In fact, her eyes were void of emotion all together.

"Please, do not kill me. I wish not to die!" said the voice of the remaining wife.

I smiled at her. "Do not worry, you're already dead," I taunted.

The vampire grabbed the side of the casket, ready to pounce up to attack but I was quicker. I slammed the lid down as hard as I could. The force behind the action severed four of the vampire's fingers. I felt blood running down my thigh. Had she gotten me? I looked down to realize that shards of wood from slamming the lid shut so hard had broken off the casket. Damn, I impaled myself.

I readied my blade and opened the casket's lid once again. I slit the vampire's throat. The top of her white garment quickly stained red as it soaked the blood up that was gushing out from her wound. She just laid there, drowning in her own blood. She did not try to fight anymore. She closed her eyes, welcoming an eternal sleep to take her. I grabbed her head and gave it a hard yank.

After I pulled the shards of the casket's wood from my thigh and put my heels back on, I tossed the last head into the flames with all the others. With uncanny speed, I jumped through the fire and made my way back up the cellar steps, into the cool air and night. My burned flesh and leg wound was healing and the cool air of the night was soothing to my skin as it did. The bodies of three wives that followed Winona laid just outside the cellar doors. They were still alive but unconscious, their energy drained by Winona, just as mine was when I first met her. I removed their heads from their bodies to finish them off, one by one, and tossed them back down the cellar's stone steps where the flames were starting to reach, searching for more oxygen. I followed the scent of Winona and four other vampires back around to the front of the church. Laying on the front steps, unconscious as well, was another three of Vincent's wives. I did the same as before and detached three more heads before opening the double doors to the church.

Winona was on her knees, facing the large wooden crucifix. The last wife of Vincent was sitting on the right frontmost pew, speaking to her. "Tell me, why is it not fear that you are feeling? Others I have met were all filled with fear. Only Lord Vincent himself has not shown fear, and now you."

"One feels fear when one is afraid," Winona replied to the vampire. "Quite simply, I am not afraid of you."

I shut the doors behind me as I entered the church and made my way left, watching them in silence. Winona was the kindest vampire I had ever known, but that did not make her weak.

"Your friend has joined us," the last wife said. "Yet, I do not feel fear from her either. Why is this?"

"Only Sassandra speaks for Sassandra. You should ask her, not me," Winona said, still facing the cross with her back facing us.

"Sassandra. Lord Vincent has spoken of you to me before, when he first created me."

I walked forward toward them, new emotions emerging from within me. "You speak of Vincent like I used to, long ago. You think of him as your savior? He is not!"

"Lord Vincent is a lot of things, I know this. As do you. I do not see him as my savior any longer. I have been surrounded by negative emotions since the night he created me. I've only experienced positive emotions moments ago when I awoke. Emotions that the two of you have shown me."

The vampire turned to face me and I too fell to my knees. An overwhelming feeling of helplessness consumed me. I looked at her and I wanted to sob my sorrows away. The vampire stood from the pew and came closer to stand in front of me. She placed her hands on my cheeks and smiled as her red eyes looked into mine.

"You do not fear me, yet you are afraid, unlike your friend," the vampire said to me. "Tell me, what is it that you are afraid of?"

I did not know why I answered her. I should be killing her, like the others. Was she hypnotizing me? Did it matter? All I knew was that I was indeed afraid of something. Something that I did not wish to admit, not even to myself. But, for some incomprehensible reason, I was compelled to answer. "Failure," I replied. "I'm afraid of failure."

"Failure. Lord Vincent struggles with this emotional experience just as much, if not more," the vampire said to me.

"I am nothing like Vincent!" I yelled, struggling to stand on my feet once again. "Release her from your spell!" I say, pointing to my friend.

"I am under no spell, Sassandra," Winona said to me, without looking at me.

I went to her and her face seemed to be at peace, unworried.

"I wish to thank the both of you," Vincent's last wife said.

"Thank us? For what?" I replied.

"You freed me. I never knew feelings of goodness, not until now. Lord Vincent is filled with hatred, anger, and greed, just to name a few. I have not experienced positive emotions since I was human, before he changed me, not until tonight. And the emotions of humans are so much weaker than the emotions of vampires."

"And you think that will save you? You think of yourself as healed?" I asked.

"I think of myself as free. I no longer am drowning in negativity. Instead, I am swimming with hope," the vampire said.

"Hope will not save you. Not from me."

"Your friend is very compassionate. I take it that you are not the same?" the vampire asked me.

"Sorry, I'm not that kind of vampire," I answered.

Winona stood and turned to face us. "Sassandra, this one does not need to die." Winona approached the vampire, unafraid. "She was the only one out of them all that has an ability. It seems she can sense the emotions of others. Am I correct?"

"Yes. You are correct. But your friend Sassandra is also correct. I do need to die. I don't want to be whatever it is he turned me into. I do not want to be a monster."

Her words had enthralled me. She was appalled by immortality. It reminded me of the night when Devin had said he had no desire to become a vampire.

"Why did Vincent create you?" Winona asked.

"I do not know," she answered, sitting on the pew where she was before, looking at the cross. "It was the pastor who kidnapped me and brought me here when I was human. The others, and sometimes a child, drank my blood night after night before Lord Vincent came. I remember the feeling of death when I first met him. Then he turned me, among other terrible things…" the vampire said, trailing off.

"We can help you. You can come with us," Winona offered.

The heat from the fire below the church was growing. I could feel it through the floors. Soon this entire church would be engulfed. The vampire stood back up from the pew and approached the large wooden cross at the front of the church. She placed her hand on it, without looking at us and quoted the Bible. "Jesus said unto her, I am the resurrection, and the life: he that believeth in me, though he were dead, yet shall he live: And whosoever liveth and believeth in me shall never die." The vampire turned to look at Winona and me. "Although we are dead, we are still alive. And I still believe even after this death, my soul will remain. That is my hope that you have given me. So please, I beg of you, kill me."

My body instinctively moved, grabbing a golden antique offering plate from the front pew. It soared through the air as it left my hand, cutting through the vampire's neck and severing her head.

Winona bowed her head and began to pray in Navajo as I took her hand and guided her out of the church. The floor below us began to bend and snap as the flames from the hell below us were rising up. I had no wish to fall through a burning floor again.

Outside the church, Winona was still praying and I reminisced on the memories I would forever be burdened with of the feelings I once had for the monster that raised and created me. The feelings of wanting to be recognized and praised by him grew into lust, a toxic emotion. This lust was a feeling that was planted in my head by him through trickery and power. He did the same to these women.

I got lucky. Lucky enough to be saved by Winona and the others. Would I have been one of Vincent's many wives if I had not been? Images of the innocent people I killed when I was under his control flashed in my mind. I quickly pushed them out again as I watched the historical church go up in flames. I vowed a long time ago to destroy Vincent. I would burn everything he ever touched down to the ground.

The church went up in a blaze, destroying the remains and all evidence of our presence within it from the humans. Winona remained quiet as we began to make our way toward the direction in which Pastor John's vehicle was traveling. Although some vampires may accuse my coven of being traditional, we found that modern technology does have its advantages. Sirens could be heard in the distance behind us as we ran further west.

"Are you upset that I killed her?" I asked Winona as we made a beeline to Pastor John's location.

"I have existed for nearly forty decades, Sassandra. You have existed for almost twenty. To some vampires, the ancients, we are still quite young. Others perceive us as their elders."

"Me? An elder?" I said, laughing at the thought.

"Yes, even you are considered an elder within our country. You have to remember, our country is only seven decades older than you," Winona said, amused.

"Well, when you say it like that, you make me feel ancient!"

"But, to answer your question, no. I am not upset that you killed her, nor the others. Death is part of life. We will all meet Death in the end. I was quiet because I was pondering what happens to us, to vampires, after we perish."

We caught up to Pastor John's vehicle parked in front of his house. All the lights in the house were turned on. We went in through the front door and made our way to the master bedroom where we found the pastor, packing a suitcase.

"Going somewhere?" Winona asked, startling the man.

"Please! Don't kill me! I'll do anything!" Pastor John begged us.

"I do not kill and I believe it's safe to say that Sassandra has had her fill of bloodshed for one night, so you're safe for now. But we're taking you to someone who might not be so merciful. Grab your bag, our flight takes off soon," Winona instructed.

We took the pastor's car, Winona sitting in the back with the pastor as I drove us back to the airport. Pastor John was worse than a child in the backseat, never shutting up. He kept pleading with us and asking what was going to happen to him. Truth was, I wasn't sure. It was not my decision to make. I am sure Winona wanted him to be judged by Arubrey, Leslie, and herself. The three of them would decide his fate, after interrogating him first. We still needed information about Vincent.

After parking the car, I hypnotized the pastor into silence. We couldn't risk him causing a scene in the airport. We made our way to our gate with time to spare and we all sat in silence, waiting for them to start boarding us. The plane took off on time and we made it back to our home in New Orleans before sunrise.

"Take him downstairs while I meet with the others and fill them in on what happened," Winona instructed me, talking about Pastor John.

I took him down to the lower levels of our home, to the same chair where Devin was interrogated. "Sit," I instructed the pastor. He did as he was told and I cuffed his arms and legs to the chair, like many others before him, and then we waited for the others to join us.

The others took their seats on the three thrones. Arubrey was seated in the center with Leslie on his left and Winona on his right. It was Leslie who spoke first.

"Tell me, Pastor John, did you receive thirty pieces of silver when you betrayed Jesus, just as Judas did? Or did you do it for free?"

"I beg your pardon?" Pastor John said, confused.

"Let me tell you something about your *Lord* Vincent…"

"That's enough, Leslie," Arubrey said. "He is only here to tell us what we want to know. Not for us to convince him that he has been brainwashed by a demon."

"Lord Vincent is no demon! He will save me! And if you let him, he can save all of you as well!" Pastor John proclaimed.

Leslie stood from her throne but Arubrey grabbed her by the wrist, stopping her. "Calm yourself, Leslie."

A snarl started to build in Leslie's throat. I knew her emotions were running high, which was not uncommon for her in general but was uncommon for her during a judgment. Once she realized Arubrey was not going to release her, she regained her composure and sat back down.

"We need answers, Pastor John. And depending on those answers will determine your fate," Arubrey said.

Pastor John snorted. "I only answer to God."

"What if I told you there was no God?" a voice from the top of the stairs yelled out. "What if I told you I prayed multiple times a day for years upon years for forgiveness and for mercy, yet your God never answered me. He never showed me an ounce of hope," Devin said, making his way down the stone steps.

"Devin?" Leslie said, surprised by his appearance. "You're not to be down here."

"Please forgive my intrusion but I ca sit upstairs and let the four of you determine the fate of this man when he's part of the reason that my family is dead."

"And who are you?" Pastor John asked.

Devin did not wait for Arubrey, Leslie, Winona, or myself to interject. Instead, he walked straight toward Pastor John and punched him in his jaw, as hard as he could. "I may not be God but damn it, you will answer to me!"

The pastor swore out loud after being struck. We watched Devin, letting him take control, for now, to see where this was going. Humans could be amusing at times. This was one of those times.

"Now you listen to me, you son of a bitch, I didn't serve five years in the US Army over in Iraq to come home and have my family be killed by a creature that isn't even human on my own soil. Now, when I ask you a question, you will answer it, because I'm your God now. You got that?"

The pastor looked dumbfounded as Devin bellowed out his rage, almost nose to nose with him. Devin pulled back his fist again and slammed it in the pastor's jaw again. "I said do you fucking hear me?"

"Yes… Yes. I hear you."

"Good. Because I am sure these vampires behind me know how to get answers out of a hostage when they want answers. And trust me, as do I. I'm sure I can even teach them a thing or two about torture they haven't thought of in all of the years they've been alive. Trust me when I say that if you do not answer me, I will cut your tongue out and have my way with you and you'll wish you were able to beg the vampires to kill you."

Pastor John said nothing, staring back at Devin with wide eyes. Leslie shifted in her throne, crossing her legs and smiling at the scene that was unfolding before her.

"We know Vincent is behind all of this. Where is he?"

Pastor John looked at Devin and then to the three vampires who sat across him. He knew there was no escape. He knew we would get the answers out of him one way or the other. "I overheard him on the phone once. He was talking about a place that was under new construction and he wanted an update on their progress."

"Where was this place?" Devin asked.

"Savannah, Georgia. He called it a plantation when he was talking to whoever was on the other end of the line."

I froze. A plantation in Savannah, Georgia could only mean one thing. Vincent rebuilt the house I was raised in as a slave. I moved around the chair to face Pastor John instead of standing behind him to see his face as he spoke.

"How many more vampires has Vincent created?" Winona asked.

"I don't know. Honestly, I was only in charge of feeding the ones at the church."

"What about Jayden?" Arubrey asked.

"Jayden was an informant. A vampire child placed in New Orleans to spy on the Ooljéé coven. He missed his last appointment with me and I have not heard back from the child," Pastor John admitted.

"How long was he spying on us?" I asked, without permission from the others. It was no doubt a question we all wanted to know the answer to.

"Just over three months. His assignment was to find out as much as he could about each of you and then report back to me once a week."

"Why…" Devin's voice broke. He tried asking his question again. "Why did Jayden kill my family?"

"The child was very fond of your blood. He grew attached to you, always returning to you to have another taste. Vincent wanted to break that attachment and ordered him to kill all three of you. Only you weren't home. No, you were safe here with them while your wife and child were being slaughtered. So, he had Jayden return to your home with flowers. But the flowers weren't for you. They were for your new family, the Ooljéé coven," Pastor John's words struck hard and Devin's body started to shake.

"Jayden was turned into a vampire long before you were even born," I said to the pastor, taking over the conversation to give Devin a moment to recompose himself. "Whatever Vincent has planned, he has been planning it for nearly fifteen decades now. You are but a pawn to your Lord."

"What's going to happen to me?" Pastor John asked.

No one said anything at first. The silence grew second after second before Arubrey spoke. "Devin, I would like to hear your input on this. What would you like to happen to the man that took part in the killing of your wife and child?"

245

"The old me would say to turn him over to the police," Devin answered.

"And the new you?" Leslie asked.

"The new me knows better. He knows too much about vampires and it would be a risk to turn him over to government officials. Besides, Vincent would be able to get to him and it could backfire on us. Call me apathetic if you want. Letting him live or killing him will not bring back what I have lost. Do as you please. I don't think I care anymore." With that, Devin left us and made his way back upstairs.

Winona's eyes turned white as snow as her spiritual energy left her body and forced its way into the mouth of Pastor John, possessing him. The pastor's eyes turned white and his shoulders relaxed as Winona's soul took over him completely.

CHAPTER 19

YEAR 1865: ILLUMINATED

News of President Abraham Lincoln's death came early in the morning. The energy Winona had transferred into him that was keeping him alive throughout the night had faded away within the hour after we left his bedside. He had passed with his wife at his side, hand in hand. Winona warned us he would not survive but it still came as a shock, even to her. We all looked at one another, unsure of what to say, knowing there was nothing we could do to change the past night.

"What is done is done," Arubrey softly said.

What does that mean?" Leslie responded.

"It means we move on. We must cut our ties with the humans, especially the ones within the world of politics. I fear they will not be eager to keep paying us after we failed to protect their leader."

"He was our leader just as well," Winona added to the conversation.

"So, you expect us to wash his blood off our hands and move on?" Leslie asked.

Arubrey looked deep into Leslie's eyes. He felt her pain because it was the same as his own. It was the same as Winona's and the same as mine as well. We may not have pulled the trigger of the gun that killed him but we were the ones who failed to stop the bullet.

"And what of Vincent?" I asked.

"I believe last night to be just a test," Winona stated. "His primary goal was to kill Abraham, which he succeeded, with the use of the human. I believe his secondary goal was to test our strength against his own. Some may see his inability to kill any of us as a weakness. But for being so young, we are stronger than most."

"Excluding Sassandra," Arubrey added.

I shot a glare in his direction. Was he blaming Abraham's death on me? "What in the hell does that mean?" I demanded.

"I said what I said, Sassandra. And I mean what I say, but allow me to slow it down for you." Arubrey stepped closer to me and looked directly into my eyes. "You. Are. Weak. Therefore, I blame you for last night."

"Me?" I retorted. "I tried to stop them!! That was Vincent and whoever the hell that man was who killed Abraham, not me!"

Leslie and Winona stepped between us, forcing our bodies back. I felt my blood boiling. How could he accuse me of killing Abraham? Did he still think of me as one of Vincent's pawns?

"I am not accusing you of being in cohorts with Vincent. But I do find it odd that in these last four years you failed to mention that Vincent can control images within our minds! Or perhaps, I am saying that if you had been stronger or perhaps even *smarter,* you would have stopped at least one of them!"

"What Vincent was able to do last night was new to me, Arubrey. I swear it, I have never experienced that type of power from him. When I was human, it was different. He was there, in my dreams, controlling my mind, twisting it. But when he turned me, he never messed with my mind. Not like that."

"Maybe. Or maybe you failed to recognize his hallucinations and have been blinded all these years."

I wanted to run, I needed to escape. I had to get away from him. I hated him! How could I remain in a coven with someone as audacious as him? My thoughts ran wild in my head, with nowhere to go, locked in the room with him because of the damn sun. Leslie nor Winona said a word to defend me. They remained quiet, lost in their own thoughts. Did they too secretly blame me? I was beginning to blame myself.

Leslie started pacing around the room, looked at Arubrey, opened her mouth then snapped it shut again, as if she changed her mind about wanting to say something to him.

"What is it, Leslie?" I asked.

"I begged him," she started saying before taking another lap around the room. We all patiently waited for her to continue. "I begged Abraham to let one of us turn him. I am not religious by any means. Just look at me, a prostitute turned into a vampire. And that's just the tip of the iceberg. Abraham looked past all of my sins and welcomed me with open arms. Not once did he ask me to dress more formally or to stop flirting with the soldiers. He accepted me as I am. Abraham was my Jesus."

"Yes, he was good to all of us," Winona said.

"After failing to convince him to stay with us as a vampire, Abraham squeezed my hand and told me to take care of my family once he was gone," Leslie said, looking at the ground. "We are family. And we must not fight amongst one another."

I went to my friend's side and took her hand into mine. Winona was there too, holding her other hand. But it was Arubrey who spoke to her first. "We are here for you, Leslie. You are not alone in this." Arubrey turned to me, almost ashamed. "I apologize, Sassandra. I was out of line. I supposed my emotions…"

"I forgive you, brother. But what will we do now?" I asked.

Arubrey explained to us that Abraham wanted us to live separately from the humans, as it should be. And so, a plan was erected and it was decided to be executed tonight by the four of us. Abraham had told Arubrey names of certain politicians who took interest in the four of us. To be safe we had to eradicate ourselves from their world, erasing all evidence of our existence.

Sunset came and Arubrey, Winona, and myself left the Soldier's House, leaving Leslie behind. We each were given a specific location to infiltrate and destroy all evidence of ourselves and using the power of persuasion, we had to make the humans forget we were ever close with the President. Arubrey gave himself the Capitol Building, Winona was taking the White House, Leslie remained at the Soldier's House, and I was headed back to the Ford's Theatre.

I took my time crossing the few streets across D.C., making my way toward the theater, giving myself time to reflect. Ripples of emotions were now waging a war within my mind, all against one another, but were kept in check by the realization that whichever emotion would succeed and emerge, it would be greeted by nothing more but loneliness. Abraham meant something dear to each one of us. For me, Vincent was and is the darkness that forever will run through my veins. Without Vincent, I never would have met the honorable President and surprisingly that thought brought peace to my unbeating heart. But it wasn't enough. Vincent was also the one who took Abraham away from me. How cruel life and death can be, especially for a vampire.

I looked to the sky and the moon was there, greeting me. I stood in the middle of the deserted road, staring at all its beauty and watched as an oddly shaped cloud passed over the top of it, as if it were a hat. If Vincent was the darkness within me then Abraham was now the light that emitted from the moon that now watched over me from above. Quite suddenly, the feeling of loneliness no longer held its sway over me.

As I drew closer to the Ford's Theatre, I pushed my thoughts to the side and focused on the mission. I could hear two men chattering with one another just outside the theater's entrance. I scaled the building which was connected to the theater itself, my movements shadowed by the night. I peered over the ledge of the theater, looking down to two men, whose voices I heard moments ago, that had been placed at the theater's entrance to protect it from public civilians. I remembered the door attached to the stage that Vincent and the human assassin used to escape. The two men placed at the front of the building were in luck; there was only one guard at the back door. I dropped from the theater's rooftop, landing gracefully, directly in front of the now startled guard.

The man looked at me, eyes wide from shock, and looked to the sky before looking back at me. "Where did you come from?" the man asked me, ignoring his gun that was holstered to the side of his hip.

"Oh, you poor thing," I responded, touching his cheek and gazing deeply into his big blue eyes. "I do not like questions. Now, won't you be a dear and open a door for a pretty lady?" I kindly asked the man.

He fumbled for a few seconds with the button on his shirt pocket before pulling out the door's key. The man held the door open for me, allowing me to enter into the theater's back hall.

"What a true gentleman you have been tonight. I thank you for your kindness," I said, looking into his eyes once again while running a finger down his jawline, something Leslie taught me. "And now I want you to forget all about me. I was just a figment of your imagination. Perhaps, I was in a dream you had. Do you understand?"

"Yes, ma'am."

"Good. You can close the door now and lock me inside. Once you do so, you can go back to guarding the door. But if anyone else wants to come inside the building, I would like you to fire your gun into the air before you open the door for them."

"Yes, ma'am," the bewildered human said before locking and closing the door with a click and a glazed look over his eyes.

The back hall was pitch black, for humans at least. For my eyes not so much. Vincent's scent was still strong within the hall, slightly diluted with the human's scent that had shot Abraham. I easily maneuvered my way down the hall before reaching three closed doors. The first two doors both opened up to medium sized dressing rooms; one for the women and the other for the men. The last door at the end of the hall was the connecting door that opened to the stage, the same door Vincent escaped through the previous night. I could still smell his aroma as I reached the door and it repulsed me. My own venom started to salivate within my mouth. My body was tense and was ready to strike. The only problem was I had nobody to strike.

I opened the door and stepped onto the stage, which was slightly illuminated by a singular arc lantern, which shone down from the third level balcony. I found the environment of the theater to be quite different from what I witnessed on my first visit. Unlike the night before, there was no show tonight. The wooden seats were now empty and the silence within the theater was deafening. I stood center stage, gazing up at the state box where Abraham was accompanied by his wife and friends to watch the play. The yellow curtains which were draped over the cutout of the state box were no longer opened, instead they now obstructed my view from what horror took place beyond them the previous night.

In one swift movement, I leaped from center stage and landed on the second-floor balcony in the main aisle between the rows of seats. I did not hear nor see any other guards within the theater. I closed my eyes, trying to push the feeling of loneliness away. Yes, I was alone. But that did not mean that I was unloved. My eyes snapped back open and I made my way to the door that would lead me to the state box. Would I find anything that the humans had missed? I entered through the door that Winona had guarded and rounded the corner at the end of that hall, entering the luxurious state box. A hint of gunpowder still lingered in the air. A plush crimson sofa sat at the right side of the box with a cushioned wooden chair beside it, in the middle. Sitting in front of where I stood, closest to the entrance, was a dark wooden rocking chair. Its back was tall and upholstered with crimson fabric and matching buttons. This was the same rocking chair which Abraham sat in to enjoy the play with his wife and friends. It was this rocking chair in which some of his blood now resided within the crimson fabric. I stood in the entryway of the state box, mere steps away from the rocking chair. I outstretched my own hand, as if I were holding a gun. The human had shot him point blank in the back of his skull. He never saw it coming. It sickened me. Why was there such evil in the world?

My body jumped as a loud crack came from outside the theater. Gunfire. I divided the yellow curtains, revealing the view of the stage and I quickly scanned the theater to make sure I was still alone within the building. The human had shot his gun to warn me. Someone was coming. I leaped from the state box, landing on the stage, just as the human who murdered Abraham had done the previous night. I could hear the human men outside the back of the building yelling. If they were the same men who were at the front of the building that I saw earlier then I now had a perfect way to escape. I cracked the far-left front doors open and peeked outside. No sign of them. I slipped out the doors, quietly shutting them behind me, and made my way across the street, slipping into the shadows.

"Sass!" a voice hissed somewhere close by.

"Leslie?"

"I'm up here. Did you find anything?" Leslie asked, perched on a thick branch in a nearby tree.

"No. The state box was cleaned out and empty, besides the furniture. I wonder if Arubrey or Winona found anything about us."

Leslie dropped from the tree, landing with grace. "Well, if they have then they're not the only ones."

"You found something?" I asked, eager to know what it was.

"Yes. But we shall discuss it later. First, we need to find that human who killed Abraham."

"Arubrey told us…" I started before being cut off.

"Arubrey is not here nor is he our superior. Besides, I just want to have a little fun with him. Oh, don't you dare give me that look, Sassandra. I promise. Once I'm finished with the boy, I will turn him over to the proper authorities."

"No. I'm sorry, Leslie. But we mustn't. What if Vincent's with him?"

"All the more reason to go! Don't tell me you're still afraid of your master?"

"I have no master! You'll do well to remember that, Leslie," I snapped back at my friend.

"You know I like to tease. Oh, come on. I'm going with or without you. Better you come with, by my side, is it not?"

The three men who were on the outside of the theater earlier were now gone. I assumed they were on the inside of the theater now, searching for intruders. Leslie and I followed the scent of the human from behind the Ford's Theatre. It was not long before the scent changed from human to animal.

"He must have ridden horseback from this point," I said.

"Splendid. Animals are much easier to track than humans."

We followed the trail of hoof prints as they led us out of D.C. The night was still young and hopefully Arubrey and Winona would take their time with their searching. The hoof prints led us to the countryside northeast of D.C. We slowed our pace as we saw a large fire that illuminated the darkness around a small farm. Flames had engulfed the large red barn and were growing higher by the second. Local authorities had already arrived on scene and the animals were scattered outside the barn, running wild, and a family of four stood outside their two-story home, watching as their livelihood burned before their very eyes. Leslie and I watched the police force that had the burning barn surrounded and a few of the officers were shouting orders to the others.

"Do you think the assassin is inside the barn?" I inquired.

"Yes, I dare say so. The humans did well at finding him. I wonder if they're going to…" Leslie was saying just before a gunshot was fired at a man that had just emerged from the barn, trying to escape.

"They killed him!" Leslie shouted. "They shot him in the back of the head, just like he did to Abraham. Did you see?"

I said nothing, only nodding as the flames grew higher and more out of control, taking me back to the floral plantation, where the house I grew up in went up in flames. Memories of me falling through the floor into the flames below flashed through my head.

"Let's go, Leslie. Shall we? I would like to go home now."

"Yes, he isn't moving. Well, I'll be, they killed him the same way he killed Abraham. How fitting."

"What will we do now?" I asked Leslie, as we turned our backs to the flames and started our way back to D.C.

"I found the letter, Sass."

"Letter?"

"Yes, the letter. Abraham's letter. The letter he said he found in his pocket one day, telling him to seek out Arubrey and Winona to end the war. I found it."

"So now what?" I asked.

"Well, the war has all but come to an end, hasn't it? The only scent on his letter is Abraham's, and now my own. So, I guess it's a dead end. Nothing else to do now but start our existence over, some place new."

CHAPTER 20

1865: HOME

The water of the Atlantic Ocean climbed its way up my flesh as my body submerged in its depth. As we swam in the darkness, a weight was being lifted off my mind. The weight of worry, self-doubt, and loneliness was being washed away from me as I swam underwater, following my coven somewhere new and unfamiliar; somewhere we would call home for the rest of our existence.

Arubrey and Winona also found documents pertaining to us and our relationship with Abraham. It seemed as if the government was building files on each of us, and they seemed to have more questions than answers. I guess they wanted more information than

Abraham would give them about us. The files were burned and the minds of the politicians who created them were wiped clean. Nothing more came from the letter Leslie had found within the pocket of one of Abraham's jackets. It gave no clues on who its author was or how they possessed knowledge about Arubrey and Winona's existence. There was no scent, besides Abraham's, and no signature. "Find them, win the war," was all that was written on the piece of paper with Arubrey and Winona's name and their current location written on the backside. Abraham did as the letter instructed after winning the election. He found them and the war was won. Now what?

Leslie had stuffed the paper inside a mason jar with the little cash we were given from working for Abraham for the past several years and screwed its lid back on, securing it from the threatening waters in which we would be traveling. It was the only item we brought with us, leaving everything else behind in D.C., including the three thrones Abraham had built for the others. As vampires we could move within the water faster than we could on land. Although swimming was a longer route to New Orleans than running, we would arrive faster and still have time to find shelter from the morning's sun.

New Orleans was in shambles. Losing the Civil War had left a bad aftertaste in the mouths of the scorned citizens of the deep South, and the Crescent City was still suffering from the military command from the Federal Government. With the city in dismay, it was the perfect cover for us to blend in, unnoticed.

And so, we swam, guided by the light of the moon, traveling down to Florida, and swimming around the state making our way into the Gulf of Mexico. Even at night, the temperature change of the water could be felt, warming about five degrees higher than the Atlantic as we entered the Gulf.

"Welcome to New Orleans," Leslie said as we emerged from the water.

"Leslie," Arubrey said, "can you acquire us new clothing, with haste please? Something which speaks money, if you will. We will need to look the part of a gentry before we can play the part. Do not use money. I will need the cash to gamble."

Leslie nodded, handing the jar to Arubrey, and took off down the street without a word.

"You're going to gamble with the only money we have?" Winona scolded him.

"Well, yes, naturally. It is the fastest way to grow our finances. When Leslie returns, we will find shelter and rest while the sun is up. Then I will join a few card games during the evening. Do not worry, I do not lose."

"Well while you're playing cards, Leslie, Sassandra, and I will scout the area to see if we find any other vampires, just to be safe," Winona declared.

Leslie returned shortly after with her hands and arms full of clothes. "I got us each a couple things to wear, including shoes," she said, beaming with happiness.

"Your love for shoes almost surpasses my own," I said to Leslie as I helped her with the garments and accessories.

The four of us made our way alongside the Mississippi River until we came across the port of New Orleans, mainly used for the trade of cotton at the time. Dozens upon dozens of steamboats were docked and were being loaded or unloaded as we watched from afar.

"There," Leslie said, pointing to a large warehouse in the distance. "We can stay there. I am sure no one will find us, as long as we stay quiet and hidden in the shadows."

The warehouse was not abandoned, quite the opposite. Men were coming and going through its doors every few minutes. Even the side entrance was being used by its workers.

"This isn't going to work, Leslie," I said. "It's too busy. We will be found out."

"Relax, Sass. We can go through the roof and hideout in the rafters. Buildings like this always have useless space up top."

We scaled the building, climbing the attached ladder made of iron until we reached the roof. There was no door at the top nor a hatch open, no way in. Arubrey walked the perimeter of the roof, looking over the edge, until he stopped at the backside of the warehouse.

"Over here," he said. "There's a window."

I peered over the ledge and watched as Arubrey laid down and pushed the top of the rectangular window, opening it to the inside as the bottom window pane pushed out to the outside. We slithered through the opening like snakes, closing the window behind us once we were all inside.

"Hang the clothing over the window so the sun will be blocked," Winona instructed as she looked around, searching her surroundings. "Over there, Arubrey, go get some cotton. We can stuff it in the cracks. And see if you can find anything else we can use to make it darker."

Leslie and I tied a rope over the window and hung the outfits she picked out for us over the glass. Arubrey returned quickly with a crate full of dirty cotton, probably forgotten or lost over the years. We stuffed the cotton anywhere we could see glass that the clothes could not cover.

"Are there more of these crates, Arubrey?" I asked.

"Yes, but I do not think we will need more. No light should be able to come through."

"I know but we could use these crates to hide in, like coffins. Just to be safe."

Arubrey smiled at my idea and pointed to where more were. We all went together to pick out a crate to slumber in during the day, like it was completely natural. And for us, it was. We each emptied a crate and carried it back toward the now covered window, placing them side by side. Sunrise was coming soon and so we each sat down inside of our crates, pulling the lid up to our necks, like a blanket, and started reminiscing about Abraham and past good times we each shared with him. After a while the conversation died down and we could hear more of the humans coming and going in and out of the warehouse from down below. The morning crew must be showing up to relieve the night crew.

I laid down inside my crate, closing the lid and the rest of the world out. It was peaceful, enclosed inside a wooden box. The ocean had washed all my worries away and now this crate helped by keeping them at bay and out of my mind. I closed my eyes, wishing sleep would take me. I thought about asking Winona to drain my energy, to force myself to sleep. But I figured she would say no to the idea so I did not bother to ask.

The hours of the day dragged by and I became restless within the confines of the rectangular crate; we all did. I heard one of the others slide their lid off, followed by two others, so I slid mine off as well. Leslie was already out of her crate pacing back and forth.

"Sorry, I cannot just lay there," she said.

"I thought laying on your back was customary for a woman of your stature," Arubrey teased her.

"Oh, Sugar. Do you find yourself to be amusing? Because we all know you use your sarcastic, and to be frank, uncivil, humor as a disguise for your own insecurities about yourself. When was the last time you laid down with a woman, Arubrey?" Leslie was the only person I have ever known of who could talk to Arubrey like that and get away with it.

"Would you ladies be interested in learning morse code?" Arubrey asked, changing the subject.

"Morse code? Why would we want to learn that?" I asked.

"I learned morse code before coming here to the United States, when I resided in England. Not many are willing to learn because they think it is of no importance and will soon be obsolete, and I quite agree with them."

"If you agree then why did you learn it?" Winona asked him.

Arubrey clasped his hands behind his back and began to walk, every so often with each few steps he would tap the tip of his shoe or slide his foot a couple inches instead of taking a step, each time it would be a different, and then he would continue to walk as if he had not done anything out of the ordinary.

"You were just using morse code, were you not?" Leslie asked.

"You are correct. But can you tell me what I have said?"

"No. I haven't the slightest idea."

"Well, I will not tell you. If you wish to know the answers you seek then you must be willing to learn," Arubrey said with a smirk.

"I would like to learn," I said.

"The message can be sent via a machine that the humans have created, called a telegraph. Or one can use sound or light to give your allies critical information. I believe morse code will be obsolete within the next century. Human inventions are growing. They love anything new and shiny and morse code has already begun to collect dust. This can be useful in our future if ever a situation of secrecy calls for it."

"How?" Winona asked, taking the question out of my own mouth.

"If ever we were in the presence of an enemy, I could be talking to him or her, just as I am talking to the three of you. While I am talking, a trained eye and ear in morse code would already have deciphered the message I said by using my feet."

"What do we learn first?" Leslie asked.

"The basics. Dits and dahs. Dits are dots and dahs are dashes..." Arubrey explained, in detail, step by step, everything he knew about morse code. We all found it very boring, but I loved learning and it also helped the day pass by.

When night finally came, we promised Arubrey that he could continue with his lesson the following morning and reminded him he had a poker game to join and money to win. We changed into our new clothing that Leslie had picked out for us the previous night and removed the rest from the window and stuffed them into our crates for safekeeping, just in case a curious human made their way up here.

The four of us each leaped from the horizontal window and fell to the wet ground below us. The sky was dark with clouds and our new clothes quickly became immersed with rain. I looked at Leslie in disbelief and she just shrugged, as if the weather was completely out of her control, which it was. Winona had her head held up to the sky, letting the rain fall upon her flawless skin. I watched the raindrops run from her high cheekbone down the side of her face. We all stood in silence as the rain fell down on us, just for a few seconds, before Arubrey raised his head.

"Ladies, may the darkness of tonight fill you with light. Now, if you don't mind, I shall be off to find a poker game."

And with that, a cloud of smoke filled the void where Arubrey stood just one second earlier.

"We shall split the city then," Winona declared. "Leslie, you can go west. Sassandra, you can go east and I shall head north, no more than eight or nine blocks, I would say. If you pick up a scent of another of our kind, do not follow it. Come back to the warehouse and wait. We do not want to provoke any other vampires that may already be in the area. Remember, we are in unfamiliar territory."

And so, we went our separate ways within the night. It was liberating being in a new city. D.C. was full of politics and with that came lies and secrets. This was our fresh start. We of course would still keep our existence to the humans a secret, but losing Abraham felt as if we all lost a father. Now we were left alone in the world and hopefully we would succeed in finding our way of life within it.

I headed east as Winona instructed, in search of others, like us. How many more of us could there be? Vincent did not elaborate on much of anything after creating me. In the eight years of living in darkness, never sleeping, I still had questions. Questions even my coven did not have the answers to. Maybe if we met another coven, they would know more of our history. Vincent never spoke of his past and I doubt he would ever tell me, at least not willingly. Arubrey, Leslie, and Winona had each met other vampires in their past but they never became friends with any, besides amongst one another.

I continued searching, block after block, to no anvil. The only sign of vampire life was my own reflection in the puddles of water left in the street from the never-ending downpour of rain. If there was a scent to be found, it was quickly being washed away. Giving up, I decided to search for something else. Something I desperately wanted to find; a book. *The Language of Flowers*. I wanted a copy to pursue my quest of knowledge. Flowers from the plantation were indeed beautiful but why did the color of the moon flower change after I was turned? The moon flowers were white, like the moon. Yet after my transition into becoming a vampire, the pedals of the flower changed to blue, almost glowing. What did it mean? I believe Vincent did not have the answer to this question. I do not think he ever gave it any thought, until I mentioned it to him. Perhaps he had never seen a moon flower until after he was changed.

I knew a city this size must have a library somewhere. Perhaps it was in another part of the city. I decided to go up one more block and around to make my return back to the warehouse to meet up with the others. Maybe one of them had succeeded where I did not. I rounded the corner of the street and before me stood a giant building made of brown brick. It had steps on both sides that led up to the front entrance and above the entrance were two giant flowers, carved into the masonry with a Public Library sign posted in the middle, just above the door. I was up the steps in half a second and stood at the door. Another sign was posted, this one on paper, that read, "No colored people allowed." How kind of them to refer to us as people. Was this the progress of change that Abraham promised us? I grabbed the sign, ripping it down from the door.

Human rules and laws were just that, for humans. I had no obligation to follow any rule or law set by mankind. I was not that kind of vampire. I smashed the window pane out with my fist and reached inside, unlocking the door, letting myself in. I was amazed. I had never seen so many books in my life. It was humankind who wrote these books throughout the ages. I wonder if vampires ever wrote any books. But, did this library have the book I was looking for? I ran the tips of my fingers across the spines of hundreds and hundreds of books as I walked the aisles, searching for it. The library indeed was home to many books but the building was not overly huge so it did not take me long before I found it.

Le Langage des Fleurs by Charlotte de la Tour. Here it was. Written in a different language, one I did not understand. I flipped through its pages, comparing the photographs from memory, confirming it was the exact same book, just written in another language. I snapped the book shut, tucking it under my arm for safe keeping. I knew I was not permitted to come back to check it out so I had no other choice but to steal it, along with multiple other books pertaining to growing and caring for flowers.

The rain had died down when I exited the library and I started to make my way back toward the warehouse, our temporary residence. Hopefully Arubrey would succeed in his quest for riches. Living in the top of a warehouse was not something I was thrilled about. I was not the first to arrive back at the docks. I ran across Winona's fresh scent upon reentering the area.

"I found no others like us," I admitted my failure to Winona, who was sitting by the water gazing off into the distance. "Did you find anyone?"

"No, not a soul. Only humans," Winona said.

"I wonder when the others will return."

"Leslie probably found herself a bar full of drunken men."

"Winona, are you alright? What you just said about Leslie is out of character for you," I said, worried about my friend.

Winona stood up, turning to face me. "I apologize. I have not been myself, not since Abraham…" she trailed off.

I set down the pile of books I acquired, free of charge from the library, and hugged her. It was all I could do to comfort her.

"What are those?" she asked me, looking down at the stack of books.

"Oh, I am so thrilled!" I exclaimed, my voice almost sounding childlike. "I found the book I told you about a long time ago. You know the one Vincent had about flowers? But it is not printed in English. I do not understand it, but I just had to have it!"

I handed the book to Winona and she examined its cover for only a second. "This book has been printed in French."

"French? Why French?" I asked.

"Do you not know about the Louisiana Purchase?"

I shook my head. My education on the floral plantation did not cover much history.

"In the year 1803 the United States bought Louisiana from France. And what a bargain the deal was. Only three cents per acre of land!"

"Three cents an acre? Are the French mindless?" I said laughing at the deal. Winona started to laugh with me, her spirits lifting from recent events.

"Am I interrupting something?" Leslie asked as she was approaching.

"Did you come across any others like us?" I asked Leslie.

"No. But I did find a delicious human who I..."

"We do not need details, Leslie," Winona said, cutting her off.

"What's got her feathers in a tangle?" Leslie asked, looking at me. I just shrugged and Leslie rolled her eyes.

"Arubrey almost tripled our money. I ran across his scent and followed it. I overheard him speaking to a mortal man on the west side. They call it the Garden District. Beautiful homes, each with their own garden! But what would we ever do with a garden?" I looked at Winona, making eye contact with her and we smiled at one another. We both knew exactly what I would do with a garden.

Winona and I followed Leslie to the house in which Arubrey had apparently struck a deal, with our money and without us having any say in it.

"Well, how do you like it?" Arubrey asked the three of us as we approached him standing just in front of the house. It was quite large and made of white brick, although it looked as if it had been abandoned for many years. The property was overgrown with weeds and the large stacked fountain in the front had a broken basin. Many of the windows were busted out as well. I could just imagine what the inside looked like.

"Please tell me you did not pay for this atrocious structure!" Leslie took the words straight from my mouth.

"Paid in full and signed for."

"Signed for? I do not recall signing anything," Winona hissed at him.

"Oh, do not fret, my friends, I will send the deed off to the bank and add all your names to it just as well. I promise."

"How much did you pay for this… house?" I inquired.

"Well, the seller had actually lost the house to me in poker but I felt bad for him. More like embarrassed, I should say. He started to cry when my royal flush beat his four of a kind, saying his wife was going to divorce him for losing another one of their properties. So, I struck a deal with him."

"What kind of deal?" We all three said in unison.

"I gave him five thousand dollars for the property and he is letting me assist him sell the other properties he has in the area for a cut of the profits. He said his family is in real estate and that is how he acquired their fortune."

"Five thousand dollars?" I asked. "You do realize the United States purchased all of Louisiana for the price of three cents per acre. You overpaid."

"This mansion will be worth millions one day, you'll see. We will have riches beyond measure," Arubrey promised, looking smug.

We entered our new home, the door squeaking very loudly as it was pushed open. A large staircase was on the left which wrapped around the entirety of the entrance hall as it went up. A dirty rat scurried across the room, startled by our presence.

"It needs some work," Arubrey declared.

"Clearly. I would like to start in the garden tonight. Would you like to share the garden with me, Winona?" I asked her. "You can grow some herbs and I can grow flowers."

"That sounds lovely," Leslie said, walking further into the dark mansion. "Perhaps we can throw parties here, if we ever find more vampires that is. We can host Bloodfeast parties here, once every decade to bring our kind together and celebrate our way of life. Does that not sound wonderful?"

We all looked around the mansion, imagining the possibilities of our future. But, for now, there was much work to be done in our new home.

CHAPTER 21
PRESENT DAY: PLANS

Throughout the decades of my existence, Winona had planted the roots of her soul within my own mind. She was not just a friend; she was the teacher of life and death I never knew I needed. She gave me strength and hope that things would get better if I held on just a little bit longer. "Soon," she told me during my dreams when I was human.

She had taught me about different components of one's soul. The most intriguing of the five was Ka. It was the very essence of which made the difference between the living and the dead; between the warm touch of your lover's hand when you reach out to hold it, to the cold, rotting flesh of their corpse when they die. Ka was the spiritual life force within our bodies. It was the white form of energy that Winona could manipulate and control as she saw fit. Winona believed when a mortal dies, their Ka leaves their body to find a new home, never dying. She believed when a human was turned into a vampire that their body died but was now strong enough to continue to home their Ka.

"Speak the truth of all you know about Vincent," came Winona's voice from Pastor John's mouth.

Pastor John was still bound to the chair, eyes burning white from Winona's Ka that had now taken home within his body. Arubrey and Leslie sat in their thrones with Winona's body still sitting in hers with her head bowed and eyes closed. I took a step back from beside the chair, unsure of what could happen. Could two souls occupy one body at the same time? I wasn't sure. What I was sure of was the fact that human bodies are much weaker than vampire bodies. Was Winona going to kill this man? She had never killed anything, not even a spider, in all the time I had known her.

"Vincent came to me thirteen years ago," Pastor John started. "I was working late at the church, writing next week's sermon. I did not see him with my own eyes for several weeks. But he would visit me each night, whispering promises in my ear of a better world. Vincent was no prophet of the Lord. No, no, no. Vincent *was* the Lord. Resurrected once again in his image. He showed me his power. He showed me beautiful worlds he had created within the universe. Planets of all shapes, not just round like our Earth!"

Pastor John was looking up at the ceiling and laughing. "Oh, the magnificent things he can do. We are not worthy of his love! I begged him to love me. I would have done anything to serve him! And just like when Mary birthed Jesus in the barn, he asked me to give shelter to his wife. He brought her to me, dressed in an all-white gown. She was an angel. Oh, she was beautiful, just as he was. He told me she needed sacrifices in order to survive. That she, and twelve others he would choose, were necessary to help stop the others."

Stop what others? Was Vincent creating an army to take down our coven? Why would he wait after all these years? He probably could have done it the same night he had Abraham assassinated. I yearned for Vincent to be the one strapped to this chair instead of one of his pawns.

"I only saw Lord Vincent every so often when he would stop by the church, unannounced, to check in on his wives he gifted me to care for. They needed their rest, he told me. He would speak to each of them, whispering his love to them as they slumbered. I was quite annoyed when he brought me the child, Jayden. He was totally out of control and it was one of Lord Vincent's worst creations to ever walk this green Earth. But nonetheless, he told me to care for the child. I had no choice but to obey. I let the child feed off the wives while they slept. It was the only way to calm him down! And once he drank from them, he became very obedient."

I looked at Arubrey and Leslie. They seemed to be thinking the same as me: what did it all mean?

Winona's voice continued flowing out of Pastor John's mouth, "The last time I saw Lord Vincent was last month. He did his normal routine of checking in on his wives and picking up his reports I wrote out from the information I collected from Jayden. His phone rang and that is when I overheard the conversation about the plantation being built. I remember he told the other person on the line that his very first creation would love to see her old home."

I had heard enough.

A puff of smoke blinded me as my hand was a centimeter away from Pastor John's chest. I had intended to rip his heart straight from inside him but I was stopped before my fingers could invade his body. Arubrey's hand grasped my wrist in an ironlike grip. He was much stronger and faster than I would ever be. It was not fair. All I wanted to do was kill this evil man.

I could feel the vibrations of Arubrey's whisper in my ear from standing so close to me. "Calm yourself, Sassandra."

"He deserves death," I replied without emotion.

"It is not your decision to make, Sass," Leslie said from her throne. Of course, it wasn't my decision. It never would be because I did not have a throne. They would never see me as their equal. I relaxed my arm and Arubrey finally released my wrist. He did not move from my side until I stepped back away from Pastor John.

Pastor John's mouth opened and expelled the white light of Winona's Ka that had invaded his body. Winona's spirit took the form of her body just in front of the chair in which his now lifeless body slumped over into. Her spirit looked directly at me as it glided toward me. My body stiffened, afraid of what was to come. Was she going to drain my energy? Were they going to judge me again? Winona's Ka now stood parallel to me. The translucent white hand reached up and touched my cheek. If vampires could cry, I would have cried a river. Winona's soul was trying to comfort my own. I looked at each of my friends and nodded. I knew they cared for me and I knew they understood my rage.

Winona's Ka returned to her body and Winona's eyes opened once again, back to their natural deep brown. The pastor's body twitched and awoke with a jolt as his own consciousness took charge of his mind and body once again.

"Pastor John," Winona began, "I would like to apologize for the intrusion of your mind, body, and soul, but it was a necessary evil in order to collect the information my coven needed. Let it be known that the Pastor's soul has been warped and twisted to do unthinkable sins. His mind was brainwashed, just as Sassandra's once was, and that alone has damaged his soul."

Pastor John glared at Winona as she spoke about himself. His soul was keeping his mind and body alive, like all souls do, but no human soul could heal a mind or body, not without a little help from others that cared, such as family and friends. Although our coven was neither of those things to Pastor John, the one who compelled him to do bad things throughout the years was the same one who brainwashed me into doing horrific acts when I was human. I knew his pain all too well because it used to be my own and it is a pain I have yet to fully recover from, even after all this time.

"Pastor John," Winona continued, "Although you have done terrible things that have led you to be seated before us, you have not done them on your own accord. The evil you carry inside you was placed there by another. If my coven agrees, I would like to heal your soul."

"I don't need your healing!" Pastor John yelled at her.

"Yea, yea, we've heard it all before," Winona said, looking over to Arubrey and Leslie.

Leslie recrossed her legs. "When you heal him, Winona, I would like for him to take the fall for murdering Devin's family. Yes, we know the truth, but the humans that know Devin do not. Since Devin has been here, the media has reported him as the main suspect of the murders of his wife and child. I would like to clear his name. That way if he chooses to, he can go back to his normal life, outside of our world."

I knew Leslie had feelings for Devin. Could she so easily let him walk out of her life if he was cleared of all charges? She cared for him so much she was giving him the option to. If he did leave, it would devastate her. I had never seen her this way with anyone, vampire or human. Was this what being in love looked like?

Arubrey nodded. "Then we are in agreement. Winona shall cleanse the human's soul. Leslie and I will plant new evidence to indict him. At least this Pastor will not be behind bars due to sexual misconduct, like so many others. But before we point the police in his direction, we will have to alter his mind, just a bit. We cannot risk him telling authorities about vampires framing him. It may land him an insanity plea but it still poses a threat to our existence. Do we all agree on this?"

279

"Agreed," Leslie and Winona said simultaneously. Although I agreed with them as well, I said nothing.

I started to leave the sub-basement now that questions were answered and decisions of his fate had been made but I was stopped by Arubrey. "Sassandra," he called for me, "when the time comes, I would like you to be the one to make him forget us."

"Why me? Any of you can persuade his mind."

"True. But your mind is much more powerful than ours. If you are the one to do it, then it is almost guaranteed to last for the rest of his lifetime. Our persuasion will fade overtime."

I nodded in agreement and continued my way up the stairs. I don't think I can ever recall Arubrey giving me a compliment. Maybe he didn't realize his own words as he spoke them. Either way, it felt nice to hear. I made my way upstairs to my room, passing our library where Devin was occupied with his nose in a book. I did not bother to let him know what was decided of Pastor John. I would leave that for Leslie to discuss with him, among other things that were bound to come up in their conversation.

Once I was in my room, I made my rounds misting water onto the few flowers I kept in here, not bothering to shut the door behind me. These flowers were not for experiments. Instead, I kept them for my own personal enjoyment. Their beauty, fragrance, and longevity were comforting to me. I knew they could not last forever. Soon they would begin to wilt and die, no matter how much I tried to keep them alive. I felt like I was on the verge of losing myself sometimes. Maybe I too would wilt away into nothingness with my flowers.

I heard Devin's voice from down the hall. Leslie must have joined him in the library. I did not want to eavesdrop but shutting my door would do very little to keep me from hearing their conversation.

"So, you're going to let him live?" Devin asked.

"Yes. It has been decided. But he will take the fall for the murder of your family. I am truly sorry for your loss, Devin. But at least this way you can return back to your life as a free man."

"My life? What life is left? I have lost everything I ever cared for. You think I can just go back home and sleep soundlessly like nothing happened? Like none of this was all my fault?"

"Devin, none of this is your fault. You and your family were dragged into this because you were at the wrong place at the wrong time," Leslie tried convincing him.

"You're wrong. All of this is my fault. If I hadn't been an addict…"

"Stop. Just stop. You served our country honorably. I don't know what happened to you over there but I am sure it was horrible. And you needed a release from all the mental suffering it caused. I understand. And it's not your fault. Our country failed to give you the proper help you needed after your honorable discharge. Your family's death is no fault of yours to hold. Please, Devin, let your guilt go."

"My mind can't just forget the images of their lifeless bodies, Leslie! How can I let my guilt go if the memories are so vivid and horrifying?"

"Let me turn you," Leslie said with desperation in her voice. The words were surprising to hear. I wonder if she sounded like that when she asked Abraham to become one of us when he was on his deathbed.

I found myself standing in my bedroom doorway, eavesdropping. I knew I shouldn't but I was worried for my friend. And I was worried for Devin. I guess with everything that had happened, he had become more than just a human to me. He felt like a friend now too. Next time I talked to him, I would tell him that. Maybe he could find comfort in a new friendship.

"Turn me? Into what, a monster? Why the hell would I ever want to be the type of *creature* that can kill without care. Do vampires even feel emotions?"

Dead silence.

"Yes, Devin," Leslie's words came as a whisper now. "Vampires feel emotion. I was only suggesting it because overtime your human memories would fade, along with the pain they have caused you.

"Well, I am sorry to burst your fantasy bubble but like I said, I have no wish to be turned to forget the memories of my family. You know, immortality doesn't have to be the answer for all my problems. It's insulting that you would even suggest it."

"And what did drugs and vampire venom do? I'm sure you didn't run toward addiction because your family life was perfect!" Leslie snapped, finally losing her temper. I knew it was only a matter of time.

"You are absolutely right. My life was and still is far from perfect. I did what I did because it helped me forget the horrors which I suffered through to defend our country. You think my wife and child's corpses were the first I've ever seen? Do you know what it's like to have a child running toward you with bombs strapped to their chest? They use *children* for war. And there is no honor in having to kill a child to protect your own. Can you imagine what that's like?"

Leslie did not answer but I knew what she was thinking. It was our coven that hunted down and destroyed the immortal children within our own country. The children that were a domestic and international threat to humankind. They would have drained the world and not a drop of human blood would have been spared. That time period was the hardest for our coven. We hardly spoke to one another during those dark years. We were part of the Vampire Covenant with other covens from different countries within the world. Each of us in charge of implementing the law in our country to never allow children under the age of fifteen to be turned. And those that were already created had to be destroyed as well. Each of us, including Leslie, suffered every time we found one. It was a covenant we hated but knew was necessary. It was the reason why I did not try to stop Arubrey from destroying Jayden.

"No, Devin. I'm sorry, I am indelicate on the subject of children. I don't know what that would be like. And I don't know what having a child of my own is like either. That luxury was taken from me a long time ago," Leslie said nothing else, ending the conversation. I heard glass shattering moments later. I was not sure if it was Devin or Leslie who broke something.

I went back into my room, feeling guilty for eavesdropping. I would talk to each of them later after they had some time to cool off. For the time being, I decided to browse my closet to find something to wear. I loved hand to hand combat so I had a great variety of melee weapons to choose from. I picked up and put back down several different ones, examining them, trying to think of a way to incorporate them into my outfit. The smell of leather caught my attention and I looked to the wall where a leather bullwhip was hanging, almost identical to the one that was used on me when I was still human. This whip was intertwined with silver, braided along its length. I pulled my hair up and used the whip, wrapping it around, to hold my hair in its place. Just as I finished fixing my hair I was interrupted.

"Do you mind if I come in?" came Winona's voice from the hall.

"No, not at all. Is everything alright?"

"Yes, everything is fine. I just wanted to bring you this. I've been working on it for a while now." She handed me a white rectangular box.

I took the package from her, smiling. I was not expecting a gift. "What's the occasion?" I asked.

"Well, to be honest I have been worried about you."

"Worried? Why?"

"With everything that has been happening with Vincent now coming back into our lives, I have a bad feeling that something terrible is going to happen soon. And so, I wanted to make you this to help protect you, and the others." Winona nodded her head toward the box, instructing me to open it.

I removed its lid and underneath layers of red tissue paper was the most captivating craft I have ever laid eyes on. It was a dreamcatcher and its beauty left me speechless.

Winona started to explain the dreamcatcher piece by piece by pointing and touching each part of it as she talked. "Each of the three hoops are made from red willow and represent the circle of life, no beginning and no ending. I did a hoop for Arubrey, Leslie, and you, but the entire dreamcatcher is yours to keep. The webbing of each hoop will catch the bad dreams at night and they will be destroyed by the morning's sun. These feathers here represent a safe passage for the good dreams to float down to you while you sleep. Well, I know we don't sleep. But you understand the meaning behind it."

I was in awe. What she had made with her own hands was not done in the blink of an eye, even though she probably could make one that fast. I could tell my friend really took her time with this project, wanting every detail to be perfect. And it was. There was only one problem with it. "Wait a second," I said, "where is your hoop? You forgot a hoop for yourself."

Winona smiled and pointed to a single black arrow head that was attached to the center web of the dreamcatcher. "This arrowhead represents the spider that created the webs. And because I am the actual creator of the dreamcatcher, one could say I am the spider."

I set the dreamcatcher back down in its box and I hugged my friend tightly. "Thank you," was all I could say.

"You are very welcome, Sassandra. Just one other thing, would you be interested in learning how to Spirit Walk? I was hoping to teach the three of you together. I know it is traditionally only supposed to be kept within the tribe I was born to, but as you know they all passed on. This coven has been my tribe since Abraham brought us together."

I didn't know what to say. I was filled with happiness. "Yes, of course I would love to try and learn how to Spirit Walk. I already know you're an excellent teacher because you have already taught me so much!"

This time it was Winona who hugged me. "Passing along this tradition to my family means the world to me. Thank you for your willingness to learn. Now, if you'll excuse me. I am going to check back in on Pastor John. The smudging ceremony went well and he has been resting since." Winona left my room but not without looking back at me and smiling in the doorway. As she walked out of sight, I could hear someone else approaching. It had to be Devin. The others did not walk so loudly.

"Come in, Devin," I called before seeing him.

"Sorry to bother you. But I was hoping to speak with you before I left."

"Where are you going? Do you require something we do not have here for you?" I asked. I knew the mansion was fully stocked to house a human for several months. We had a storage room already full of toiletries and other various items humans require to live in comfort. "If you're hungry, we can have whatever you're craving delivered. Do you want new clothes? Let me grab my laptop, I was just actually just shopping for shoes earlier."

"No, that's not it. You all have already done too much for me, and I appreciate everything. But I'm afraid I cannot stay here any longer. I spoke with Leslie and I think it best if I try to get back to my own life. I'm sure after the pastor is arrested, I will have to make court appearances, amongst other arrangements, and I will need to meet with family and friends."

I was afraid of this. Devin wanted to leave. Was this because of the argument he had with Leslie? I am sure it was a cluster of multiple things all together. Leslie arguing with him did nothing to help the situation. I reached past him and shut my bedroom door. "She loves you, Devin," I whispered so only he would hear. He stared blankly at me. Did he not hear me? "You have to know that she loves you."

"If you're talking about Leslie then she has a funny way of showing it. Besides, my wife and daughter were just murdered. You can't expect me to just forget that I had a family literally *days* ago and move on so easily. Even if she is gorgeous and kind and immortal; it doesn't alter the fact that I have obligations to attend to."

I put my hand on his shoulder. "The only obligation you're obligated to is your own happiness. Please never forget that. And because Leslie is my friend and you are also my friend, I feel compelled to tell you a few things."

"What kind of things?" Devin asked me.

"Things that vampires should not tell humans. But it needs to be said. I do not know if it will change anything or not but I am going to say it anyway, in hopes that it does." I motioned for Devin to the chair that was sitting in the corner next to the bookshelf. He sat down and patiently wanted for me to continue. "I overheard your argument with Leslie earlier. I also have invaded your dreams, even before you met me when I was spying on you. I know of the horrors from your past in the military. I saw the children with bombs running toward you, I saw your convoy blow up with your comrades still stuck inside. I saw everything else that still haunts your dreams too."

Devin shifted in his chair, clearly uncomfortable talking about this horrible subject. "It is against the Vampire Covenant to turn a human who is younger than the age of fifteen into a vampire. This is a law that was created and implemented in the early 1900's, all agreed upon by multiple countries of our world. You see, vampire children were all the rave back then and many were created. However, none could be taught to control their thirst. They were savages. The immortal children were destroyed, even the ones that existed before the Covenant was created had to be destroyed and the ones who fought to protect their children were also destroyed. I will not betray my friend's trust by telling you the things she has overcome in her lifetime just as I have not betrayed your trust by telling her anything about your past. But I will tell you that there are horrors in the vampire community that we deal with so that humans do not have to witness. Yes, we thank you for your service, but please keep an open mind when it comes to our kind. Leslie has done honorable services to help protect our country as well. She's just very headstrong and is probably afraid of her own emotions of what she feels for you. It would devastate her if you left us."

Devin let his head drop into his chest. "I do not know how I feel about her. I feel like if I even think about my feelings toward Leslie, that I'd be betraying my wife."

"You do not have to have all the answers. You're allowed to have your emotions and whatever amount of time it takes for you to work through them. Trust me, Leslie has time to wait if she really feels the way I think she does. And if you choose to leave then you have the right to leave. We do not want you to feel trapped here with a bunch of vampires, although keeping a human or two around for warm refreshments does have its appeal," I said, turning the last part into a joke to lighten the mood back up.

"Ok, I'll stay for a little while longer. Besides, I'm not a free man yet," Devin said, standing back up.

"That's wonderful. And let me know if you want anything delivered. I don't think it's safe for you to go out alone. If you wouldn't mind waiting until sunset, one of us can accompany you."

"Speaking of the sun, will you come with me to the library? I would like to show you what I've been working on."

I followed Devin to the library down the hall, letting him lead the way. He took me to a desk that had papers scattered all over it. He was working on a plan. A plan that involved our coven defeating Vincent. He had started profiles on each of us, but he wanted more information such as our strengths and weaknesses and what we were most afraid of. He even had a paper on Vincent with information we had told him or he had overheard. There was even a blueprint of the plantation that was rebuilt that he obtained from the internet. Devin explained his plan that he had come up with, on his own, in full detail. It was an impressive plan, especially for a human to think of. It was also dangerous, and could go very wrong.

"You mentioned to me the other day that you've been working on a formula that involves moon flowers?" he asked me.

"Yes, that's correct."

Devin slid a paper across the table and I glanced over it, reading the information that was presented to me. I was impressed. "I see you've done your homework."

Devin walked around the desk, organizing papers and restacking them. "I have. Part of my military training, I guess. But I am afraid of one thing about this plan."

"And what's that?" I asked.

Devin swallowed before speaking his next words. "What if we fail? What if Vincent kills us all?"

CHAPTER   22
YEAR 1872: CHOICES

What did we do when our world came crumbling down and there was nothing we could had done to prevent it? We rebuilt it, one brick at a time. Luckily for New Orleans, the Civil War spared the destruction of the city unlike many others. New Orleans had become the second state within the country that held the highest per capita income, mostly which came from the port that brought in imported goods. Not only was the city booming but so was our coven. The years passed us by in the blink of an eye. We fixed up and rebuilt parts of our newly acquired mansion, even dedicating a room on the third floor to our lost friend, Abraham Lincoln. Arubrey's five-thousand-dollar investment on our home had started to pay off just months later after acquiring it. He kept his promise and all of our names were on the deed and he continued to invest money into other properties around New Orleans to fix and clean them up and then turn around and sell them for even more money. Fixing up our property, which included the most magnificent garden within the Garden District, took little time. The flowers grew perfectly and the others loved them so much they decided to surprise me by adding on a greenhouse addition, attached to the kitchen. The city of New Orleans and its patrons within it seemed to never sleep, and nor did we. We worked nonstop to turn our new house into a home.

We stuffed a human's pockets full of cash and had him acquire the three thrones, along with other memorabilia that once belonged to the late Abraham, at an auction for us just a year after the assassination. Arubrey was put off at spending money on what was already rightfully theirs, but nonetheless it all worked out and the thrones were safely delivered to New Orleans and no humans were hurt in the process. The three thrones now sit side by side within the grand entrance for tonight's Bloodfeast, where our coven would greet the vampiric guests that we had met throughout the years we lived in this city.

This would be our second Bloodfeast, the first being just the four of us running amuck within the city of D.C. just one decade ago. This time a small group of vampires within our growing community had been invited to our home to help celebrate this special occasion with us. Arubrey declared he would like to give a speech upon their arrival. None of us had any idea what he planned on saying, seeing how he was taciturn and somewhat abrupt compared to the rest of us. Winona prayed for him and made him promise to not scare our guest away.

We all were very busy, cleaning, rearranging furniture, or in my case, flowers. Leslie was polishing the black and white marbled floor within the entrance, yet again for the third time, insisting they were not clean enough.

"If you scrub any harder, you're going to crack the floor!" I warned my friend as I passed her carrying a vase of red roses and black violets, a thoughtful touch for a passionate homosexual couple that would be attending tonight's celebration.

She glared at me as I passed her by. "Is that not the third time you've changed that vase, Sass?"

I smiled at myself, sitting the white vase on a nearby table, adjusting a few of the roses. I just could not decide which vase to use. I had nearly a hundred to choose from.

Arubrey came down the staircase carrying a wooden crate. Was that one of the crates from the warehouse at the docks?

"What's in the crate?" I asked.

"Diamonds. Black diamonds to be exact, various sizes. I fetched them last night. They've just been imported from Brazil. Hopefully, the local jeweler across town has insurance." Arubrey gave me a half smirk. "I stole them," he admitted.

"And why do we need black diamonds?" asked Leslie, still scrubbing the same marbled tile.

"They're for the blood," he replied. "I will warm half the diamonds and chill the other half. That way they can help keep the temperature of the blood how each of our guests prefer it."

"Does that not seem a bit *extra*, Arubrey?" Winona chimed in, entering the room.

"We are vampires, Winona. Everything about us *is* extra," Arubrey answered her before entering the kitchen.

The day continued and as did the witty remarks we made toward one another, all in good fun of course. The sun finally took rest behind the horizon and I began to grow thirsty and decided to go hunting. Our guests for Bloodfeast would not start arriving until eleven later tonight and Arubrey would not let me have any blood from the kitchen, insisting it would be rude to start drinking without them. Leslie was proud to tell the tale of how she seduced thirty-three humans into willingly donating their blood for tonight's party.

"Oh, it was easy! I just dressed up as a nurse, wearing a simple white gown with matching boots. I wrapped one of our crimson curtains around my neck which made me look like I was higher up in rank. Then when I had them in bed, I would bat my eyes, telling them I was with the Red Cross and we were still in desperate need of blood."

I had to escape her story before she went into detail, ranking each human that she's ever laid down with, man and woman, which would take hours! I closed the door behind me, cutting Leslie's story off. The city was beautiful, basking in the remaining glow from the sunset. The clouds filtered an almost red glow over the surrounding mansions and buildings within the ever-changing city. The night's breeze of September flowed through my long hair as I ran down the darkening streets of New Orleans. I had plenty of time to spare before I had to return home so I decided to visit my favorite spot, City Park, which was located northeast in the heart of New Orleans and was surrounded by streams of water that ran into Lake Pontchartrain.

The park was new and still under development. After my first visit I had returned several times since, planting wildflowers seeds to help brighten the thirteen hundred acres of land. I walked along the path, taking my time, getting lost in thought as I cherished the views of the lake and flowers that I had planted and raised. The abundance of colors and scents from the various flowers calmed my mind as I walked amongst them. I took a deep breath through my nose, inhaling the smell of honey from some nearby Sweet Alyssums. The breeze picked up and with it delivered to my nose the scent of sweet lemon from the Four O'Clocks just across the other side of the path. I watched them closely as a large black and white moth with yellow spots crawled on top of one of the flowers, savoring its nectar. Vampires were not the only creatures that got thirsty at night.

Remembering my own thirst, I continued to walk along the path through City Park. As I was walking, making my way across the park and into the surrounding area on the other side, I passed a particular group of flowers which stopped me dead in my tracks. What stopped me was not the flower's scent nor their beauty, although they did hold a sweet cinnamon scent to them and their red petals seemed to be made of translucent wax paper almost too delicate to touch, even for a vampire. I recognized the flowers the moment I saw them and that is why I almost passed by without giving them a second glance. The reason I *did* was that these flowers were red poppies. Common as they were, they were uncommon in this setting because red poppies were native to France, not the United States. And on my last visit to the park, these red poppies, or known as coquelicot by the French, were not here. Nor were they planted by my hands.

What was even more intriguing was their meaning of eternal sleep and the only other time I had seen red poppies was from when I was still human, enslaved and brainwashed by the one who created me, Vincent. I thought back to the poppy field on the floral plantation, remembering Omari's spirit within my dream walking into the field of flowers after his death, where he would sleep for eternity. At the time the dream was comforting, but now that the flowers were here in New Orleans, right in front of my own eyes again, I found it quite unsettling. If I did not plant these flowers then who did?

I tried pushing the thoughts of Omari and the red flowers out of my mind while making my way back out of the park. City Park currently offered nothing for me to hunt and I was growing thirsty more and more.

Once out of the park, I made my way to the French Quarter, back to civilization. The streets were busy, as usual, flooded with humans going about their business, or in most of their cases, pleasure. Civilians of New Orleans needed no reason to celebrate, they just did so when they pleased. I watched many humans pass me by as I stood in the shadows of the night, carefully picking out my prey for the evening. Tonight was Bloodfeast, and so I wanted the most exquisite blood that Bourbon Street had to offer. I watched as the mortals passed me by one by one without any of them noticing my eyes upon them. The way they carried themselves was a contributing factor in the way their blood could taste. If a mortal carried themselves with confidence, then their blood usually tastes finer compared to the ones who walk with a slouch. The emotions of humans could slightly affect the taste of their blood when a vampire fed upon them. When a human was angry, the temperature of the blood would actually taste slightly warmer. The level of confidence a human has could make their blood taste stronger, like the level of alcohol in whiskey. The choices of prey to pick from were many but I took my time, wanting to make sure to pick the perfect neck to drink from!

I watched as a man with cropped blonde curls in his hair, dressed in a crisp blue business suit, passed me by. His scent lingered in the air and I knew I had found my prey for tonight's hunt. His brown dress shoes clanked on the sidewalk with every step he took, full of conviction. The days of only feeding off the guilty were long over. Everyone was guilty of something. I waited a few seconds after he passed me by before I started to follow him. My heels hit the sidewalk as I walked and fell into sync with his stride. The man crossed a street, stepping faster as he did to hurry across as a carriage was approaching the intersection. I came halfway across the road myself after the horse and carriage passed by before coming to a complete stop in the middle of it. I no longer had any desire to follow the mortal businessman to drink his blood, for something changed in an instant. It was a new scent that caught my attention; a familiar scent. It was the scent of danger.

A snarl ripped from my throat as I inhaled again, confirming what I feared. Vincent had crossed this very street. But something about his scent was different this time. It contained other properties as if something about him had changed. Was he traveling with another vampire and this was the change in his scent that I noticed? I knew how to recognize the difference between different scents of animals, humans, and vampires. Something about this seemed *different*. I knew I should go back home to alert the others but Bloodfeast was tonight and the three thrones had to be occupied for our guests to be given a proper greeting since Arubrey, Leslie, and Winona were the rulers of the vampiric community within this country. Was Vincent planning to attend Bloodfeast? He certainly was not invited. I would not let him spoil tonight's festivities. I had to stop him no matter the cost, even if it was with my own life. I changed direction in the street and began to follow the new scent, the scent that I knew might lead me to my own eternal sleep.

As I journeyed down the road I took my time, not wanting to rush into an ambush. The crowded street became almost isolated a few blocks later, only a handful of people walked past me, making their way to the festivities most likely. The wind was picking up and buildings seemed just as isolated as well, their structures getting taller and taller as I walked between them, following the scent. I passed a building with three single wooden doors, each of their colors different from one another. The first blue, the middle white, and the last red. It reminded me of the flag of the United States. The quietness of my surroundings left an eerie feeling within my stomach, as if I was being watched. I followed the scent up and down street after street. Turning right four times in a row but I did not realize I had gone in a complete circle until I passed the blue, white, and red doors again. I stopped, irritated by my mistake. Did I lose the scent? I turned around, looking at the three doors that reminded me of the flag. The blue door was still first, white in the middle, and the red was last. This confused me. When I approached the doors earlier, they were the same as they are now. But I had *passed* them, so the red door should be first and the blue should be last looking at them at this end of the sidewalk.

I approached the blue door and turned the knob. It was locked. I tried the white, locked as well. Same with the red door. All locked. Why was I messing with doors when Vincent was out there? Confused again, I turned back around and started to follow the scent again. This time it led me left instead of right. I continued to follow it, turning right and then left again, zigzagging my way through the streets before reaching the end. I came to a halt and actually took a step back, afraid of the scene I had stumbled upon. There at the end of the street, the way the scent was leading me, was a small field of red poppies and on the other side of the field was a colossal temple. This temple had been in the newspapers over the last two years. It was a new construction of New Orleans, another building to leave tourists and immigrants in awe when they would see it. Temple Sinai was due to open tomorrow at noon when they would strike the oversized golden bell twelve times that sat atop of the temple in the belltower. Temple Sinai looked the exact same as it did in the last photograph I saw of it, excluding the three sets of entrance doors which were painted in the same order of blue, white, and red. A crack of thunder rolled from behind me in the distance. A storm was heading my way.

It finally made sense. The red poppies and the sequence of colors the doors were in. The doors no longer made me think of the United States flag because of the order in which they appeared. Blue, white, and red were the colors of France's flag, the same place in which red poppies are native to. I knew New Orleans like the back of my hand, having explored the city many times, memorizing every detail of its magnificence. There were no poppies at City Park. There were no blue, white, and red doors. I was a mouse trapped within a maze of illusions.

The three sets of antique doors each creaked in agony as they opened simultaneously on their own from the inside. "Come, my child," a deep voice rang out from the temple, inviting me to enter.

I did not move. I did not recognize the voice but I knew the voice must have belonged to the one who tricked me into coming to this place. Was this the vampire that Vincent was traveling with? Had Vincent created a new vampire to take my place as his assassin? And if so, was he stronger than me?

I swallowed my fear. "I have no desire to kill you. I am seeking Vincent, the vampire in which you travel with. My quarrel is with him and him alone."

Identical triplets appeared out of thin air, standing in each doorway; all three were male and vampire. None of them had any hair on their head or face whatsoever, and all three were dressed in matching black suits with a gold chain around each of their necks. Their mouths did not open but their voice bellowed out into the night, "Behind each door is a gift. A gift I am willing to part with and bestow upon you. You cannot hold the weight of all three nor even two, but only one. You must make a choice of blue, white, or red." The three vampires stepped aside and gestured me to enter through each of their doors.

"What gift do the doors represent?" I asked the three vampires.

The sky began to change, getting brighter with each second. Was it almost sunrise? It couldn't be. What about the storm that was coming? How long had I been stuck in this illusion? It was a whisper in the breeze that answered my question.

"Blue will lead you to the one you seek. White will give you power no other vampire possesses. Red will answer questions you have never thought to ask. If you fail to make a choice soon then the sun will choose your fate for you."

I looked at each set of doors and then back up to the sky, contemplating my choices. A flash of lightning struck a nearby tree and it began to burn. Sunrise was coming and I had to make a choice. If I walked through the set of blue doors, they would lead me to the one I sought. That was obvious; Vincent. But what if I did find Vincent? Then what? Was I powerful enough to defeat him? It had only been one decade since our last encounter and I still was not confident in my skills to defeat him on my own, not yet at least. The set of white doors would give me power no other vampire possessed.

Power that could help me defeat Vincent once and for all. I desperately wanted that power. But if no other vampire possessed this power in which the voice speaks of, then how could he give it to me? The voice said I cannot hold the weight of all three nor even two, but only one. If that was true then how could he hold all three to offer me any choice at all? The answer was clear as day. This was another trick. I was not being offered three choices, but only one. One that would give me answers to the questions I had never thought to ask. The rain poured down upon me as the wind ripped through my hair, yet the sky was clear and still growing brighter with every second.

"What if I make my own choice by not entering any of the doors. What if I turn around and walk away?" I yelled through the storm.

The sky began to change again, the glow of the threatening sunrise began to sink and the sky turned back to darkness. The rain stopped just as quickly as it had started. The tree that was struck by lightning was no longer burning, and the thunder grew silent. The field of red poppies died and evaporated into thin air, revealing the road which continued on from where I was standing to Temple Sinai. The three triplets each smiled and made their way back into the temple, closing the blue, white, and red doors behind them. Once the doors were closed, they caught fire and the paint that covered them burned off, leaving three identical brown entrance doors in their spot, just as I remembered them from the newspaper articles.

"I must applaud you, Sassandra of the Ooljéé coven," came the voice of a woman. I looked around, trying to find where it was coming from. At the top of the temple, standing under the golden bell, was an older woman. Her skin was pale and her cropped hair was gray. Her eyes glowed red and she wore a black lace dress and a long golden necklace around her neck that drew the eye down to her bust.

"Who are you?" I asked the woman.

"I told you I would give you one gift, a gift which you must choose. If you want answers then you must walk through the door. If not then you are free to turn around and go. The decision is yours to make, and yours alone."

I took a step forward, followed by another, making my way toward the temple. I held the gaze of the old woman's red eyes until I was upon the steps and could no longer see her. I walked over to the right set of double doors, which were red moments ago, and pushed them open with ease. The temple was dark, with no sign or scent of the three bald triplets from earlier. They must have been part of the illusion as well. I stepped into Temple Sinai and closed the door behind me, all the while asking myself what am I getting myself into now?

CHAPTER 23
YEAR 1872: HURRICANE

As I entered the temple of Sinai, the doors creaked to a shut behind me, shutting me into the abyss of the unknown. I almost felt human, taking slow steps forward one at a time. I was trying to focus my senses on my surroundings, readying myself for a surprise attack. However, no attack came. My eyes adjusted to the dark and I saw that I was completely alone. I heard no sounds and the only scents I was picking up were those of humans, probably the ones that built the temple. The three bald vampires were nothing but a trick played on my mind. I found no proof of vampires within the room, with cathedral ceilings so high and beautiful even the god the humans would worship here would be impressed.

My guard stayed on high alert as I made my way toward the far wall where a staircase would lead me to the woman who was under the temple's bell; the staircase that would lead me to promised answers. As I approached the stairs, I stopped at a table that sat beside them, full of candles of all sorts and sizes. I removed a single match from the box and struck it, igniting a drop of light within an ocean of darkness that surrounded me. It felt as if I was underwater, drowning in my own insecurities and fear, but I also knew there was a way out of the murky waters that threatened to drown me. I knew I was meant for greatness and that I was still a flower who had not come to full bloom. I pushed the match to the wick of a candle and watched it burn for a few moments before turning my attention back to the staircase. I put my foot on the bottom step and started to climb the stairs that would lead me to a new me, because I knew once I reached the top, there was no going back down.

The staircase grew higher and higher with each step. I remembered being trapped in Vincent's illusion, climbing the stairs at the Ford's Theater the night Abraham was shot. My body wanted to turn back and run out of the temple. I pushed the bad memory out of my mind and refocused. The fear within me grew with each step I took but I continued to climb, my mind forcing my legs to move. I had to look at my fears and embrace them. I had to grab what I was afraid of by the throat and squeeze the life out of it because I was tired of being controlled by my fears.

Although climbing the stairs at a human's pace took longer than I anticipated, it was no illusion. I finally reached the top where a white door with a golden knob awaited me. I replayed the woman's words in my mind as I studied the door. If I wanted answers then I must walk through the door. If not then I was free to turn around and go. The choice was mine. I placed my hand on the golden doorknob and turned it, opening the door. The elder vampire woman, still wearing her black lace dress, stood with her back facing me, under the gigantic golden carillon. I walked through the doorway, into the bell tower.

"Close the door behind you," came the voice from the mysterious woman.

"And if I don't?" I asked her. She said nothing and continued to look out from the temple into the streets of New Orleans. The choice was mine. I closed the door and as soon as it clicked shut, I was standing in front of the mystifying woman. Her body stood straight, just over five foot tall and her build was slender. Her stance was relaxed with her hands clasped together in front of her and her eyes were closed. She stood motionless, waiting.

"Who are you?" I demanded.

The woman smiled before opening her eyes. What I saw in them was not what I expected to see. Earlier I saw them glowing red but now their color was hazel and filled with nothing but kindness.

"That is a very important question to ask, Sassandra. But I am afraid the timing is off. My name is Anne, but to understand the answer of who I am, you must first ask the correct questions in the correct sequence."

Anne. Such a fitting name for the remarkable woman who stood before me. Ask the correct questions in the correct sequence. It was easier said than done because I did not know what question to ask first! I pondered for a while, thinking of which question to ask. Hundreds flooded my mind as seconds passed us by. I thought back to when Vincent first changed me into what I am now; vampire. What did that even mean? He could not answer that question for me back then. And even if he could, would he have?

"Fifteen years ago, I asked Vincent what he had done to me. He told me he turned me into a vampire. That I was now immortal and would no longer age. I would have new strength, speed, and agility. That I would crave blood and need it in order to sustain my new powers. He answered my question of what he did to me but at the time, and up until now, I never thought to question how vampires came to be. I've only accepted the fact that we just... were. So now I will ask you. What is a vampire?"

Anne unclasped her hands and placed one on the bell. She ran the tips of her finger along the golden surface as she circled around the bell, coming to stand just behind me now. She did not whisper in my ear like Vincent used to but her words were soft spoken. "A vampire is a corpse which moves and thinks and has many desires but requires only one thing to thrive, which is to drink blood from a living being."

No more fear.

I reached out to the bell, placing my own hand on it and copied her movements, circling around the bell until I was now standing behind Anne. "I do not think you are the answer to my next question but I believe you know the answer. Who was the first vampire? The first of our kind?" I asked her, boldly placing my other hand on her shoulder and turning her around to face me again.

Anne tilted her head, letting her gray hair hang to one side of her head as she studied me before answering my question. "Everything about that man was absolute. There was no other perfect being besides him and there never will be another that comes close to everything that he once was. He was the first of our kind and he found me when I was human and he gifted me with thirteen children," Anne explained.

I looked into her hazel eyes and they were now filled with nothing more than truth and sadness. "How can a vampire have a child if the body is already dead?" I asked.

Anne clasped her hands together again in front of her stomach. "I was still mortal and he was the first vampire. He could do anything, including impregnating me. Our love was mutual and I was his first and he was mine. Our love was pure and absolute."

Anne turned to face the streets of New Orleans, not wanting to look me in the eyes any longer. She seemed burdened with a sadness that she could not escape. How long had she been carrying this sadness around inside of her? How old was she? I couldn't ask that; it would be too rude.

"When did he turn you into a vampire?" I asked, thinking this was a more polite way to ask.

"He changed me the day I gave birth to our thirteenth child. I gave him what he desired of me and in return he gave me immortality. I am the first vampire created by the first vampire, the first of the first, or so the others once called me." Anne did not seem happy about this. Something had happened. But she still did not give me the answer I was looking for. I was unsure if she was willing to continue to answer my questions.

I walked over to the ledge of the bell tower to stand beside her and looked down below. It was still night out and everything looked the same from before I entered the temple. "That was some display of power earlier. How did you do that? You can control the weather or something?"

Anne looked at me and started to laugh. "Oh child, I am not that powerful. I do not know of any vampire that can control the weather! Oh, what power that would be! Everything you experienced earlier tonight was all an illusion, placed by me within your mind."

I shook my head. "No. It couldn't have been. I felt my hair move within the wind. I could smell the smoke from the tree that was struck by lightning. I heard the thunder that came from the storm that was coming from behind me. How can all of that be an illusion if an illusion is just something you can see?"

"You're a cretin, Sassandra of the Ooljéé coven," Anne said. "You seek answers but there you stand, assuming you already obtain all the answers rather than asking questions."

I grew frustrated and started to pace. I was tired of Anne's games. And I still didn't even know who *Anne* was! I snapped my head up, looking directly into her eyes. "I don't know what to ask, damn you!" I yelled at the elderly vampire.

Anne turned to face me and her eyes started to roll within their sockets, moving faster and faster out of control. I watched in bewilderment as the hazelnut that once was full of kindness and sadness disappeared when she finally shut her eyes. "Damn me? I think not, my child. I have been damned for over five centuries. Yes, *centuries*, not decades like your adolescent coven. You think my power only affects what you can see?"

Anne opened her eyes and they now glowed red like before. Time had come to a complete halt. Nothing else mattered but this moment I was having with Anne. I was knocked off my feet and slammed into the wall as a blast of wind hit me. The rain poured down on us from all directions as the wind grew stronger and stronger. The strong winds peeled the roof of the temple off. The golden bell ripped free from the rope it was tied to and when it crashed, the floor crumbled beneath our feet and we plummeted to the ocean waters below us. We were now submerged within the waves of water that took over the streets of New Orleans from the hurricane. Anne was floating in front of me, eyes still red. I screamed in pain as lightning struck my body. The crack of thunder vibrated through my very soul. I could smell my flesh burning from the electricity that coursed through me, burning my arm just like Arubrey's. Yet, it seemed as if I had been drowning in this storm for days. When would this hurricane end? Surely Arubrey, Leslie, and Winona were out looking for me, even during a storm they would want to find and rescue me, wouldn't they? I could hear the old woman's laugh as she cackled at my misery. She was causing this. Anne's short gray hair transformed under the murky water, growing longer and thicker into rope. It intertwined itself around my neck and started choking me. There was no hope for me. This kind woman who offered me all the answers was now going to kill me. My eyes closed, accepting my fate, and darkness overtook me. I was dying, all because I mouthed off to this kind old lady.

I opened my eyes and everything was back as it was once before. I was standing back on my feet in the bell tower of Temple Sinai. The streets of New Orleans showed no evidence of being destroyed by tonight's hurricane. I looked at my arm and the blackened scars and burned flesh from being struck by lightning was no longer there. I was perfectly fine. The golden bell was still hanging from the rope, unmoved. Anne had done all of that to me, just by thinking about it. She was the hurricane of all vampires.

"That was three minutes of pain I gave to you," Anne said, softly speaking as she did earlier like nothing happened. "Now just imagine what I could do if you really pissed me off. Damn me, you say? No, Sassandra, I will damn you. From now on I expect nothing but respect from you. After all, I am your elder."

Three minutes? It felt like I was being tortured underwater for days! "Your power comes from your mind. As does Vincent's and even my own. Until now, I've never realized how powerful we could become."

"Sassandra, my confidant," Anne spoke as if we were now friends; as if she didn't just almost kill me. "The power of the mind is a universe in its own. My mind is what he loved about me. I can trance the mind's senses of sight, sound, smell, touch, and even time. It took centuries to learn what I can do. And I can even do it without making eye contact with my prey, as long as they're within my mind's range."

I worded what came out of my mouth next very carefully, not wanting to offend her again. "You said if I walked through the set of red doors, I would get answers to questions I never thought to ask. I did as you instructed. I walked through the doors to find answers; answers about Vincent and how I can defeat him. That is why I walked through those doors."

Anne stared at me with her hazel eyes. She looked me over, up and down. Her hand reached out and took a strand of my black hair between her fingertips. Anne ran her hands through my hair as her eyes looked into my own. "You are young, very young, compared to me. But I guess I am just as young, compared to the first of our kind."

"What does that even mean?" I asked.

"It means that even I can sometimes get lost in death."

I finally started to understand. She did not bring me here to help me. Anne brought me here so I could help *her*. If it was Vincent that I sought answers to and she was the one offering the answers then that means the two of them were somehow connected. That means… "How do you know Vincent?" I asked.

Anne put her hand out, inviting me to take it. "Walk with me and I shall tell you the answers which you seek."

I took her hand that she offered me into my own and our fingers intertwined. She gave my hand a gentle squeeze and with it we were transported to another place, another time, all within our minds. We were now standing in an ancient arena. Stone bowls of fire were balanced on top of pillars that were placed around the enclosed circle, lighting the dirt beneath our feet which was stained

312

with puddles of blood all around. The audience that surrounded us was grand in size and their cheers echoed off the walls. Two mortal guards, dressed in golden armor and carrying spears and swords attached to their hips were walking in our direction. They did not acknowledge us but walked right past and behind where we were standing.

Lying on the ground in another pool of blood were two other mortal men, both who were blindfolded. The two guards ignored the lifeless body of one and grabbed the arms of the other man and lifted him to his feet. Besides the blindfold, the man's body was naked, covered only by dirt, blood, and bruises. His lips were swollen and his nose was crooked, most likely broken more than once. I did not recognize the human, not at first. The guards supported the man's body and helped him walk to the center of the arena. The audience grew silent as a woman walked into the arena, joining the guards and the half dead human. It was Anne, wearing a white tunic. And there, around her neck was the golden amulet with an oval red stone, the same amulet Vincent now has; the same amulet I once held in my hands when I was human.

"Congratulations, Vincent," Anne's voice called out so the audience could hear her words as well. "You have fought bravely and you are now my champion. As promised, I shall grant you immortality for your victories." Anne lunged at Vincent, sinking her fangs into his throat. She sucked on his neck, draining what little blood he had left within his body. Vincent lost consciousness and his body had to be supported by the guards, who watched in awe as their queen savored the blood from her champion. The spectators erupted and their cheers vibrated the ground beneath me as I too watched Anne drain the blood from Vincent's body.

After Vincent was on the brink of death, Anne took a sword from one of the guards and slit her own wrist, bringing it to Vincent's lips, who was still unconscious. One of the guards opened Vincent's mouth and Anne's blood flowed freely down his throat. She leaned in toward his ear and spoke softly to him, "I knew your mind was the strongest out of all your siblings. You have made your mother proud, my son."

The sound of reality left a ringing in my ear as Anne's illusion ended. I released her hand and backed away from her. Could what she had just shown me be true? Could this woman standing in front of me be the vampire that created Vincent?

"You turned him into a vampire because he won some sort of battle? For what, your entertainment?"

I could see frustration grow in Anne's eyes. "You're not asking the correct questions, Sassandra. Try again, my child."

Now I felt frustration grow inside my own eyes. "I am not a child so stop calling me that! Now tell me what do you want from me, Anne? You did not bring me here to help me. You brought me here so I could help you. Tell me, how can I help you?"

"Very good, Sassandra. You have finally asked the correct question. Vincent was my last child that I gave birth to before I became a vampire. I gave birth to thirteen boys in total. Once my thirteenth son was born, I was changed by the vampire who fell in love with my mind. Once my youngest son was of age, they all competed against one another for many years. There could only be one champion, and that was Vincent. And so, he was gifted with immortality and on that night, he was no longer my son. Instead, he became my drudge."

My mouth opened but my words failed me. I could not speak because I could not believe what I was hearing. Vincent had called me his drudge, a slave to a vampire. That's all I was to him, was his property.

"You turned your son into a vampire just so he could become your slave?" I asked in disbelief. "My coven was right, the ones that don't know who their creators are wished they could know and the ones that do know who their creators are wished they could forget."

"Human slaves are weak. We tried it for a century before we realized we needed more of our kind in order to accomplish what we needed done," Anne said, as if turning humans into vampires to have stronger slaves was normal. I guess for her time period, it was.

"What could you possibly need vampire slaves for?"

Anne scoffed at my question. "How do you think France became so powerful? You think humans explored and conquered this world? You think human soldiers won our wars?"

After seeing Vincent bloodied, beaten up, and naked, I almost felt sorry for him. Almost. I can only imagine what he was put through, even after he was turned. No wonder he never spoke of his past to me. My mind was racing. I had a million new questions but none of them mattered. Not anymore, except one. "You never answered my question, Anne. How can I help you?"

"Vincent stole something from me and I need it back."

"The amulet," I said. Anne looked surprised that I knew of the object that was taken from her by her son, her *drudge*.

"You are familiar with my amulet?"

"Yes, I have seen it before," I admitted, leaving out the part where I've actually held it in my hands, twice. I did not want to anger her like I did Vincent when he first caught me with the amulet.

"The amulet was a gift from the only one I have ever loved. I want it back and Vincent must pay for his betrayal. My coven requires his death but I will not kill my son. I require you to kill him, Sassandra. Bring me his head and bring me my amulet."

"It will bring me great pleasure to destroy Vincent. But why doesn't a member of your coven kill him if you do not wish to?"

Seconds passed before Anne finally answered, "My coven has been in a web of lies for almost a century now. They have sent other drudges out to seek and destroy Vincent. The ones who never returned must have been killed by him. And the ones who did return were killed by us for failing. I had no choice but to volunteer in order to keep my coven in the dark."

"In the dark about what?" I asked.

"My secrets are of no concern to you."

"If you want me to be the one to kill Vincent then I'm making it my concern. Now answer my questions, just like you promised me you would."

Anne held my gaze for a moment, thinking. "The bald triplets you saw in the doorways earlier was an illusion, a version of myself that I push into the minds of my coven. I must keep my true identity a secret from them, for the safety of my life. What you see

316

now, my gray hair and wrinkles, is my true self. I killed the vampire in which I imitate and made his life as my own. I planted images in their minds, faking my own death. I have been deceiving my coven since then. They do not know who I really am. They do not know I am the first of the first. If they did, they would kill me. It was my coven that killed the first of our kind, my first and only love. They killed him because they wanted his powers. Vincent was part of the betrayal and he knows who I really am. The longer he continues to exist, the sooner my secret will come to light. My coven cannot find out my true identity. Now I am going to ask *you* a question, Sassandra. Will you please help me? Bring me my amulet so I can flee my coven and go into hiding. With my amulet I will no longer feel alone."

This was all too much. I should just walk away. No, not walk, run! I should run back to the safety of my own coven and away from Anne and Vincent. I should forget everything she told me and mind my own business. But I knew I could never forget her words she had told me tonight. I could relate to her feeling of loneliness. There was no turning back now. I made my choice by walking through the door.

No more fear.

"Yes, I will help you."

Everything around me turned to white. It was a brightness I had never experienced before. Blazing light so bright it must have burned my eyes. How long was I outside in the belltower with Anne? Had the sun come up and burned us both to death? Death was a pain in the neck. I could feel it, sucking the life out of me. Draining me into nothingness. Slowly the light that was everything started to dim and I was soon left in complete darkness. I was alone but I was no longer afraid. I thought of my coven, Arubrey, Leslie, and Winona. I longed to see my family again. I hoped they wouldn't grieve from my death. Maybe I shouldn't have followed the strange scent that led me to Anne. I should have drunk the blood from the man in the blue dress suit and gone back home. I still was extremely thirsty.

I could feel the frigid blood as it filled my mouth. Why was it so cold? I preferred my blood to be warm. It did not matter. Nothing else mattered except for this moment. I swallowed the blood and it left a chill in my throat as it went down. This blood was different from any human blood I had ever tasted. It tasted *powerful*. How could blood taste like power? Wait, wasn't I supposed to be dead? My hands wrapped around the wrist that was feeding me and I swallowed more of the frosty blood that was bringing me back to life. Am I turning into a vampire? It couldn't be because I was already a vampire!

"That's enough, Sassandra," came the soft voice of Anne as she pulled her wrist away from my lips. I wanted more of her. I wanted more of the hurricane of blood that I just consumed. A storm had never tasted so damn good.

"How do you feel?" Anne asked me.

I opened my eyes just in time to see the red glow of hers turn back to hazel. "What did you do to me?" I mumbled, dazed and a bit confused.

"I gave you answers and I gave you more power. Now you will be able to destroy Vincent. Bring me my amulet and bring me his head."

I took a moment to gather my thoughts and another moment to retain my courage. "I shall write to you once I acquire your amulet. But know this: I am not your drudge. You can come back here to retrieve the amulet from me, I will not be delivering it. And I will kill Vincent. He deserves nothing less than death. But his head belongs to me."

Anne placed her fingertips on the bell once again and walked around it. She looked at me and smiled before reaching for the rope to pull it down. The bell rang out, echoing off the surrounding buildings. Anne pulled the rope twelve times, making the bell ring out each time to let New Orleans know the hour of midnight had struck.

CHAPTER 24
PRESENT DAY: SUNRISE

The awkwardness between Leslie and Devin did not fade overnight. Neither was speaking to the other since their argument. I was relieved I would not be traveling with them, but at the same time I was worried their quarrel with one another would interfere with the plan. Would they be able to put their differences aside and work together? Devin approached Leslie's car, mouth hanging wide open as he admired the 1967 Alpha Romeo 33 Stradale. The paint was crimson red and had lean lines and seductive curves, much like Leslie herself. As he opened the passenger door to get inside, I wondered which body he enjoyed looking at more.

I helped Arubrey, Leslie, and Winona load two duffle bags and three large crates into an enclosed trailer, shutting its door and fastening a padlock to it. Even with as fast as Leslie's car could go, she would not be speeding with their haul. I gave my friend a goodbye hug, wishing her well and I waved goodbye to Devin. I hoped they would be okay. The garage opened and I watched the car drive away, hoping I would live to see my family again, until they disappeared around the corner and out of sight.

"They will be alright," Winona tried reassuring me. She rested her hand on my shoulder from behind as I continued watching the empty street, missing them already.

"Sassandra, Winona, we have a plane to catch," Arubrey reminded us, as he tossed a single suitcase in the trunk of my black SUV. Winona and I climbed in, me sitting in the back for the first time and Winona in the passenger seat. Arubrey pulled out of the garage, pushing the button at the gate to lock everything behind us. I looked down the street that Leslie and Devin turned on as we passed it by, heading toward the airport. There were many cars but no sign of Leslie's.

Arubrey got us to the airport in time and after we purchased three one-way tickets to Savanna, Georgia, I watched the security guard's eyebrows go up in bewilderment as he realized what single item was inside the briefcase. He wished us a safe flight as he handed me the briefcase back. We boarded the plane after a slight delay and pretended to be asleep for the duration of our flight; it was the easiest way for us to pretend to be human. Once our flight landed, we left the airport on foot, running in darkness toward the plantation.

As we ran in silence, I became lost in worrisome thoughts. I was afraid of what was to come. Would we be strong enough to defeat Vincent or was my obsession with revenge going to bring an end to the Ooljéé coven, including myself? My pace slowed and I watched Arubrey and Winona run in front of me. Were they running to their own deaths? I couldn't let them do this, not for me.

"Stop," I said, as I quit running.

Arubrey and Winona came to a halt and turned to look at me. "What's wrong?" they both asked together.

"We can't do this. I can't let you do this. Not for me. It's too dangerous. He's too strong."

Winona started to walk toward me, to comfort me and reassure me everything would be ok but Arubrey got to my side first.

"You're the one who needs to stop, Sassandra. How many decades is it going to take for you to realize your strength? How long will you keep second guessing your self-worth? You think we're doing this just for you? You have to remember that Vincent took Abraham from us too. You are not the only one he has done harm to. We've all wanted this for decades. And now is the time. Can you do this or not? Because *we* cannot do this without you. You're the strongest one here and you're the one who has to face him."

Arubrey's words were exactly what I needed to hear. No more fear. I gave him and Winona a nod and I started to run again, now leading the way. I was strong and I have come too far and waited too long to turn back now. Vincent was no longer my past, I was his. And I was running as hard and fast as I could. Tonight, Vincent's past would catch up with him.

We arrived just a mile outside of the plantation. The plantation that once held fields of flowers as far as the human eye could see was now just open fields of grass. It was dull, seeing so much greenery. I yearned for the vibrant colors that once occupied my past. But those days were over. I had to paint a new future for myself but I could not stroke my brush on the canvas of a new future until Vincent was destroyed.

"We've arrived," I informed Arubrey and Winona as we approached the green clearing in front of us. My vampire eyes could see the details of the white house from my past. The two-story house looked familiar but different at the same time. This was in part because the memory of the house was from when I was still human. Back then my brain could not process details like it does now since I became a vampire. I recalled what Anne told me about what vampires were and it gave me a new idea. I wish I had time to tell Arubrey and Winona about this new idea but something deep inside me warned me that we did not have time to spare.

The three of us started to walk forward in the veld of greenery that stood between us and the rebuilt plantation. I felt like Dorothy, walking through the poppy fields toward the Emerald City. But where we were going, I would meet no great wizard of Oz. Instead, what waited for me was a monster.

A singular door appeared in the middle of the field. A glowing red light appeared at the bottom of the door and erupted through its keyhole, inviting me in. I had no choice, I walked toward the familiar door as it beckoned me to it. I felt tipsy and out of control as I sank to my knees. I leaned forward, squinting one of my eyes to get a better look through the keyhole to see what waited for me on the other side of the door. Red consumed my mind, as I took a peep through the keyhole.

The field of grass started to shift, swaying in the wind. We all three came to an abrupt stop as something unexpected happened. Vincent now appeared one hundred yards just in front of us. "Welcome home, Sassandra."

My eyes glared at my creator and a growl erupted from inside me.

Vincent laughed out loud, a revolting sound I loathed. "Oh, how much I have missed you, my drudge!" he said, laughing again.

"I am not your property," I snapped back. "I'm going to enjoy killing you."

There's that damn laugh again. What was so funny? It was the three of us versus only him. Surely, we could beat him, couldn't we?

"Oh, my drudge, I feel sorry for you. I did not want it to come to this but you left me no choice. I would have been happy to let you live your own life, apart from me, but you insisted on trying to rule over our kind. How stupid are you, Sassandra? You think you can rule over me? Oh, please. I made you what you are. Without me, you are nothing!"

I clenched my fist, ready to attack. I went to rush him but my feet could not move. I looked down and the grass had grown around my ankles and was still moving up my legs, holding me in place. I looked back at Arubrey and Winona and they too had grass wrapped around their limbs as well. Arubrey was engulfed in a cloud of smoke as he teleported, escaping the clutches of the grass that had him bound to the earth. He appeared behind Vincent but he did not strike him. Arubrey stood motionless in fear.

"You think the three of you are more powerful than me?" Vincent asked us. "This is my plantation and here I am God."

Winona stopped struggling to break free from the grass and closed her eyes, embracing her surroundings. A white energy surged from her body, gliding toward Vincent. The brightness of her spirit threatened Vincent's power and I saw the fear in his glowing red eyes as Winona's Ka glided closer and closer toward him. Vincent laughed again, bringing Winona's spirit to a halt. Something had frightened her and the white Ka was now motionless, just like Arubrey was.

"I told you, Sassandra, on this plantation, I am God. My mind decides the laws here. I am untouchable and I have decided that you will watch as I kill your friends by making their worst nightmares into reality."

He was controlling us. I did not know how, but I knew he was controlling the three of us, separately, with his mind. His powers must have grown since 1865 and I was trapped once again in his illusion; we all were. I tried pulling my body free from the grass that kept growing, reaching my neck now. The weeds wrapped their way around my throat, strangling me, just like Anne's hair did once before.

As I was being strangled, the environment shifted around me. My arms moved on their own accord, hugging a large oak tree as the grass around my neck turned to rope and snaked its way down to my wrist. Moon flower vines were wrapped around the tree, growing up and around its thick trunk. I peered around the tree to see Arubrey and Winona, both still standing motionless. What was happening to them? I had to save them! I pulled as hard as I could but the ropes did not break. I was defenseless and I sensed Vincent standing right behind me.

The monster whispered in my ear, "Watch and learn, my drudge. I can teach your mind how to be powerful like mine, if you let me."

Vincent walked in front of the tree, now within my view, and he approached Winona's Ka. He reached his hand out toward the white energy, touching it. "Tell me, Winona," Vincent said. "Do you know what the opposite of a soul is? No? It's the flesh of the body." Vincent reached his hand out and touched Winona's Ka. The white energy began to vibrate, faster and faster the longer he held his touch. Winona started to scream and her Ka returned to her body, shifting the environment around me once again.

I was still bound to the oak tree but I was no longer at the floral plantation. I stretched my neck around the tree and saw Winona standing on a flatbed carriage, with four others, their hands tied behind their backs. There was a noose wrapped around each of their necks, all connected to a branch from the same tree to which I was bound to. They were all crying but I did not see tears of white feathers like I did before. This time Winona, and the others, were all blindfolded. Winona was mortal and she was about to be hanged.

"Tonight is a dreadful night." Vincent was speaking to the crowd of onlookers, "These witches have tormented our community long enough. Salem will not prosper until we hang each and every last one of these devils within our community! May they eternally pay for their sins in a fiery hell!" Vincent spoke to the crowd as they cheered him on, holding their pitchforks and torches. Winona began chanting in her native language as the others continued to sob uncontrollably. No one cared. The crowd looked at them with fear and hatred in their eyes. I watched in horror as someone threw a dead bird, its white feathers covered in its own blood, at Winona's face, leaving a smear of red across her cheek as it connected.

"Leave her alone!" I yelled. No one heard my pleas. The onlookers ignored me as Vincent looked directly into my eyes. His leather whip shot out from his hand, connecting with the backside of the horse. The animal cried out and took off, pulling the flatbed behind it. The women screamed out in horror as the wooden carriage beneath them was pulled away, causing the nooses to tighten around their necks, strangling them as they were hanged. I desperately tried pulling myself free from the oak tree to save my friend. I failed. I could not save her. Winona's body jerked as her neck snapped from the noose, along with the four others.

I cried out for my friend as I watched her energy fade. She was dying. Winona's body was the last to stop moving after fifteen minutes. The four others were no longer breathing and they no longer swayed back and forth from the branch above them. Winona was the last of the five to perish as black clouds now floated above me in the sky, blocking the moon from my sight.

"No!" I yelled again for my friend. She couldn't be dead. She was good. Winona was good. She didn't deserve death. "I can't do this without you, Winona. I need you. Please, wake up. I need you, please don't die!" I watched as Winona's body hung limp from the tree, unmoving and unable to answer. A crow cawed out from above me. I looked up, searching the branches for the bird but I could not find it.

"It's a pity about your friend," Vincent said, unapologetic.

"Damn you, Vincent. Damn you." I had no other words to say to the evil that stood before me.

Vincent laughed again, and the crowd vanished in the wind that blew around us. I was still tied to the oak tree and Winona was now the only one hanging from one of its branches. There was no saving her, she was gone.

Arubrey appeared in front of me, grasping at the ropes that were around my wrist, tied to the tree. "We have to get out of here," he urgently said as he was pulling at the ropes. "He's a lot stronger than the last time we encountered him. We cannot defeat him!"

"Hurry, Arubrey! He's coming!" I yelled as Vincent stalked closer and closer toward us.

"The smell of your smoke reminds me of many things," Vincent said to Arubrey as he drew in closer. "It reminds me of when my slaves revolted against me and burned my plantation down to nothing. But that scent of smoke was different from the scent of smoke you produce. That type of smoke takes me back to another time, another place."

The dark clouds above us started to thicken, making our environment almost pitch black. That is until the sky was lit up by a fire I had never witnessed before. Everything was burning.

Businesses, churches, and houses were engulfed in flames that the humans could not contain. Men, women, and children were all running to escape the uncontrollable fires that were spreading down the streets. Arubrey's eyes shined bright, lit by the wildfire that haunted his past. We were in London. And London was burning.

Arubrey stopped trying to rescue me and started backing away. "No, not again. Please, not again!" he whispered to himself. Arubrey fell to his knees and wrapped his arms around himself. I had never seen him look so vulnerable.

"Please, do not kill them. Let them go, kill me instead," Arubrey begged.

I could not see what was happening behind me but I heard a woman screaming and Arubrey sat there and watched, frozen in place. The Great Fire of London was spreading to our location. The out-of-control flames turned blue and were moving at a remarkable speed. Arubrey was still just sitting there, rocking back and forth as the fire circled around him, trapping him within. Why wasn't he teleporting away from the flames?

"Go, Arubrey!" I yelled at him. "Leave me, save yourself!"

The blue flames around Arubrey grew higher and higher. I could no longer see him and an emotion I had never felt before grew inside me. He was the one I could not lose. If he died, I wanted to die too. A horrific sound came from the circle of fire. A wail of agony, Arubrey was burning. There was nothing I could do to save him. I tried breaking free from my restraints that held me in place against this tree to no anvil. My efforts were useless. I could not save him, just like I could not save Winona. I had failed them both.

The flames that were burning London reached the heavens. They were so bright now I had to close my eyes, for I could not endure looking at them any longer. I heard Vincent's menacing laugh once again come from behind me.

"Their deaths were quick. Yours will not be. I have waited a long time for this moment and I intend to enjoy it. You betrayed your master and now you must suffer the consequences for your actions."

I opened my eyes to see my surroundings had changed once again. I was no longer in London. I was still tied to the large oak tree and we were back at the plantation. The white house I grew up in as a child was within walking distance from us. Arubrey's body laid just in front of me, his left arm was still burning with the blue flames. Arubrey no longer was screaming from the torture of the fire. His body lay motionless; dead. If it wasn't for the oak tree holding me up, I would have collapsed beside him and died with him. I wanted to. Just above Arubrey's body was Winona's, still hanging from the noose. A white feather fell loose from Winona's hair and floated down through the blue flames. I watched the feather turn black from being burned as it fell to my feet.

I felt disgusted as Vincent ran his nose from my shoulder up the side of my neck. "You smell delicious, my drudge. I am going to drain you dry. But do not worry, I promise to savor every last drop of your blood."

Shards of bark exploded beside my head as an arrow pierced the tree. Was someone attacking us? Vincent whipped around and started walking backwards, searching our surroundings to see where the attack had come from. Another two arrows flew past me, flying toward Vincent. He caught them both and snapped them in half with his fingers. We weren't being attacked; he was.

"Show yourself, if you dare!" Vincent yelled out into the night, searching.

"My pleasure, Sugar!" the attacker called back. I recognized the voice instantly. A gasp of relief and fear escaped my lips. Leslie.

Vincent's mouth curled into a wicked smile. "I was wondering what had happened to you."

"Tell me this, Vincent," Leslie called to him. "Are you brave enough to battle me in hand-to-hand combat, or are you too cowardly to fight without the power of your mind?"

"I would love nothing more than to kill you with my bare hands. How many arrows do you have? I do not think you have enough."

A plethora of arrows flew past me, directed at Vincent. He moved fast, easily avoiding each one, unphased and untouched by a single one. Leslie's fingertips brushed against my arm as she ran past me to attack Vincent. I could do nothing but watch as my friend took him on all by herself. Vincent's hand came down, narrowly missing her head. Leslie was the attacker but Vincent put her on the defense within seconds. Vincent's strikes had force behind them as his arms lashed out but Leslie was fast. She leaped into the air, avoiding the blows. Vincent grabbed her by the leg and yanked her back down, slamming her into the ground. He went to stomp her but she rolled backwards, avoiding the blow. Seven Chinese throwing stars soared through the air at Vincent. He flipped backwards to avoid the silver stars and caught the last one with his bare hand, burning his flesh. He pretended to whip it back at Leslie, faking her out. Leslie moved left and then Vincent chucked the star at her, piercing her chest, just above her right breast. Blood trickled down from the wound as it burned her skin and Leslie cursed, pulling the star out of her body and tossing it behind her.

Leslie drew her samurai sword out from its saya, taking a different stance, holding the blade high above her head. She closed her eyes, focusing. Vincent did not wait for her attack. He rushed her but she twirled out of the way, lashing out with her blade. The silver tip came very close to Vincent's neck but he jumped back, narrowly avoiding the silver blade as it whistled through the air. I am sure if the blade had struck him his head would be severed from his body. All she needed was one good hit and it would be over.

Leslie ran toward Vincent again, doing a no handed cartwheel with the sword whirling through the air pointed at him. Vincent dodged the blade again but he caught Leslie by the wrist, snapping her bones. Leslie cried out, dropping her sword. Vincent kicked the blade away, still holding onto Leslie's wrist. He turned her around and pulled her body in close against his.

"You're a decent fighter. Much better than Sassandra ever was." Vincent ran his finger across Leslie's cheek and down her neck. "Tell me, does your blood taste as sweet as your body looks?" he whispered to her.

"Now there's where you made your mistake, Sugar. There ain't nothin' sweet about little 'ol me."

Leslie started to reach her hand down in between her breasts. Vincent stumbled back, still holding on Leslie, as a bullet hit him between his glowing red eyes. His body quickly pushed the bullet out from the hole it made in his head, healing afterwards. Vincent started to yawn as Leslie withdrew her hand from her breast, holding Arubrey's dagger that was hidden between them.

Another three bullets all hit Vincent in the head and face. He hissed and tried hiding behind Leslie's body to shield himself, unaware of the dagger that Leslie now held in her left hand. She thrust the blade backwards, stabbing Vincent in his ribcage close to his heart. Vincent roared, releasing his hold on Leslie. He pulled the blade from his body, the wound already healing before the blade hit the ground by his feet. Vincent looked around, his eyes glazed over as he blinked and shook his head, feeling the effects of the attack.

Leslie picked up Arubrey's limp body, lifting him up over her shoulders, ignoring the blue flames that were still burning his flesh as if she could not feel the fire at all. She ran in the direction where the bullets had come from. Vincent stood there, staggering on his feet, unsure of what was happening. He looked at me and mumbled something, but I could not understand his words.

"You're looking tired, old man," I said to him. "Do not fight it. It is only a matter of time now."

Leslie returned a few seconds later, with the briefcase I brought. She walked to the front door of the white house and took out the item and hung it on the door before returning to the tree and cutting the noose from around Winona's neck. I looked at the door but nothing was there, only a door. Leslie paid little attention to

Vincent or myself. She held Winona in her arms and turned to face me. "You can do this, Sass," she said to me before running off again, leaving me tied to the tree. I looked at Vincent and he was still struggling to keep his eyes open.

I looked back to the front door, willing myself to see the truth. A red glow from the other side of the door began to peek its way from the bottom of the door, brighter and brighter with each passing second. Slowly but surely, the dreamcatcher that Winona made me appeared, hanging in the center of the door. My nightmare was almost over. I pulled the ropes that had my hands bound around this damn tree with all my might. Thread by thread, the rope snapped, freeing myself. I looked at Vincent and he did nothing to stop me. I walked to the door that held my dreamcatcher on it. I bent down to peer through the keyhole and let the glow of the redness fill my eyes.

No more fear.

I opened the door and walked through it. What I found on the other side of the door was not the inside of the house from my day as a slave. I had full control of my mind now and I also had control of Vincent's. I stepped through the door that led me back to the same oak tree where Vincent was waiting for me, his eyes no longer red. Vincent grabbed his whip and lashed it out toward me, but this time I was ready. This time, I was in control. I caught the end of his whip with my hand and I wrenched it toward me, ripping the whip from Vincent's hand. Shock ran across his face as I examined the leather bullwhip. This was the same whip he used on me all those years ago. I grabbed it with both hands and ripped the leather in half, tossing it behind me.

"You will never touch me with that whip again," I said to him.

Vincent charged at me but my mind was faster than his body. I did not need to search for what he feared most. I already knew what his worst nightmare was. I morphed my appearance into that of an old lady with short gray hair and wrinkles, wearing a black lace dress.

"Surprised to see me, my son?" I asked Vincent, changing my voice to sound like Anne's.

"It can't be. You're not her."

"Oh, my poor child. I have been tricking you for centuries now. You think you've been in charge all this time? You think you actually escaped me? You haven't even made it out of the arena yet. We've been entertaining our spectators for centuries now."

Vincent started to back away from me. I grew my hair out and it snaked its way on the ground toward Vincent, entangling around his legs and arms.

"You are nothing but a fly trapped in my web. I've enjoyed playing with you for over five centuries now but I have grown bored and our spectators want a new show!"

"Please, do not do this to me!" Vincent cried out. "I am your son!"

I pulled back on my hair, bringing Vincent closer to me. I grabbed him by his throat and pushed him up against the oak tree. "You're no son of mine. You're only a drudge I created for my own entertainment." I turned Vincent around and my hair transformed to rope, tying him to the tree. Vincent's body rebuked back, trying to escape. But he could not escape. My mind was stronger and his perception of reality had been tainted by poison.

"Tell me, drudge," I spoke softly to him. "Did you really think you escaped me? That you made it all the way across the world and took over a floral plantation and owned slaves?"

"I did. I must have. I remember everything," Vincent responded. "The wife and child I took from Omari. They were the first ones I tried turning. But I drank too much. I can remember ripping their bodies apart and burning them in the fireplace."

His response disgusted me. That's what he did to Omari's family? I could feel my blood boiling but I had to stay in control. A glimpse of Omari appeared before my eyes, tied opposite to Vincent on the other side of the tree. A flash of red came from behind Vincent's eyes. I was losing control. I knew I only had a short period of time left. I had to destroy Vincent before it was too late.

No. I suffered for years under his control. I wanted my revenge and I wanted him to suffer! A crow cawed out from a branch of the tree, grabbing my attention. I looked into the bird's black eyes and I felt a new power within me. The crow spread its wings and opened its beak, cawing out, over and over. One by one, smaller crows flew out of the bird's mouth, flying up to the black clouds in the sky above us. Hundreds of crows took to the sky, flying through the black clouds, tearing them apart. The brightness from the moon shone down on me. I was not alone. My entire existence the moon had been in the sky, watching over me. The moon flowers that grew around the oak tree began to come to life, blooming under the glow of the full moon.

I looked at the crow again, still sitting on the branch of the tree. I stared into its eyes and bowed my head to the beautiful creature. The Corvus spread its wings and took flight. The bird dove down, attacking Vincent's eyes with its beak and talons. Vincent yelled out but was unable to protect himself from the bird's attack. The crow ate one of his eyes and flew away with the second, leaving his eye sockets empty.

I turned to the grassland that surrounded us and using my mind I created a vast field of red poppy flowers. Vincent watched as Omari appeared in the field, along with all the other slaves he had me kill, and they began closing in on him. I repeated Vincent's words back, "You smell delicious, my drudge. They are going to drain you dry. But do not worry, I promise they'll savor every last drop of your blood."

Omari and the others surrounded Vincent and they each latched onto his body with their mouths, sucking the blood from his body. Vincent was powerless, bound to the tree. His legs gave out and the only thing holding him up was the gray rope that was once my hair, disguised as Anne's.

"Just kill me already. I beg of you," Vincent said.

Omari and the others vanished into thin air and Vincent's blood flowed freely now. I came to stand behind him, and spoke softly in his ear, "I already gave you the gift of immortality, my drudge. And now is the time I take it back from you. I now gift you the sun!"

As the moon began to fall, the shadows of the plantation moved with it until the sun began to peek over the horizon of the grassy field. I stood out of Vincent's view, leaving him to feel like he was going to die alone. The sun grew higher and brighter. I knew Vincent could smell the smoke as his flesh caught fire. He screamed as his body burned, tied to the tree, until he no longer had the energy within him to stay conscious. Vincent's charred body was limp against the tree and his screams faded away into nothingness.

"It's time to awake, Vincent. You aren't dead, you were only sleeping," I said to the vampire who created me.

Vincent still did not have eyes and I'm sure he was confused. Rightfully so. "What happened? Where's Anne?"

"You do not get to ask questions!" Arubrey yelled at him.

Vincent was sitting on the ground, his arms bound with silver around the trunk of the tree behind him. Needles and tubes were sticking out of various veins from within his body, slowly draining his blood into glass vials. I stood beside him, ready to change them out when they became full. Arubrey, Leslie, and Winona all sat across from Vincent, on their thrones that were hauled in crates from New Orleans. Leslie and Devin made it here exactly on time. I knew without them the rest of us would be dead.

"I present to you, Vincent, the vampire who orchestrated the assassination of President Abraham Lincoln. He also broke the Vampire Covenant by keeping his immortal child a secret," I said to my coven. "And he is also the vampire that created me."

"You cannot judge me," Vincent barked. "I am your elder!"

"We have discussed it at length already, even before we left New Orleans," Winona spoke. "The three of us will not be judging you."

This surprised me. What did she mean by that? "But you have to! He must be judged!" I yelled at them. What was wrong with them?

One by one, Arubrey, Leslie, and Winona stood from their thrones and walked toward the house, leaving me with Vincent. I did not understand this. What was happening? The door of the white house opened, the dreamcatcher bouncing against it as my friends entered the house and Devin closed the door behind him. Devin came down the steps, walked past the thrones and came to stand beside me and Vincent.

"I was instructed by the others that when this moment came that it would be you who would be conducting Vincent's trial. I will change his vials out for you when they become full."

I did not know what to say. My heart was touched.

"Have a seat, Sassandra," Devin said, pointing to the center throne.

I walked toward the throne, touching its wood for the first time in my existence. I took my seat and rested my arms on the dark wood. I looked down at Vincent. "I am Sassandra of the Ooljéé coven," I said to him. "And you're not going anywhere, ever again."

Vincent glared at me. "How did you beat me?" he asked.

"A long time ago I played opossum and I was able to scratch you. Do you remember? I figured if I could trick you as I did back then, then I could probably trick you again. You see, Vincent, we

339

knew your power was to make us live out our worst nightmares. Winona's biggest fear was the memory of being hanged in Salem, just before she was turned into a vampire. Arubrey's was being burned, just after he was turned into a vampire. And my worst nightmare is watching my friends die. But when I met Anne, she told me that not even her mind is strong enough to kill a vampire just by thinking it. I knew they weren't dead. I knew you liked playing games. What you didn't know is that Leslie would be able to convince you into fighting fair since she does not have an ability. Your ego has always been your greatest weakness. Once Leslie removed them from your range of illusions, they were able to break free from the spell you had them under. It was a human who came up with the plan to capture you. You taught me a lot about flowers when I worked on this plantation but not everything. I've had a long time to continue my research and I found some interesting things that you overlooked. There are certain types of flowers that have certain effects on vampires. Such as poppy flowers and moon flowers. A vampire and a human can look at these types of flowers and they would be two different colors to them. You only saw flowers after you became a vampire. You only knew them to have one color. I remember the moon flowers being white when I was human but turning blue in color after I was changed. Vampires are immune to everything. Or so you thought. Moon flowers can make any human hallucinate if consumed. For a vampire, you must extract the cells within the flower's stem and put them directly into the vampire's bloodstream. We soaked the bullets with poppy cells to make your mind drowsy and Arubrey's dagger was soaked with cells from a moon flower. The poison of the moon flower with the poppies warped and weakened your mind's ability. Once weakened, my mind was strong enough to overtake yours. I knew your greatest fear was Anne. So, I disguised myself as her."

Devin started working, changing out the glass vials of blood. Vincent did nothing because he was still weak from the silver around his wrist and from Winona.

"I can't control certain senses of the mind yet. Not like Anne, but I'm learning. Arubrey's teleportation smoke helped me set the scene when you thought your flesh had caught fire. And it was Winona who drained your energy when the sun was rising, making you think you were dying."

"Very good, Sassandra. But I am still your master. You wouldn't dare kill your master!"

I stood from the throne and with steady hands I unraveled the leather whip that I used to hold my hair in place, the silver momentarily burning my hand as I did. I snapped the whip at Vincent and the leather and silver wrapped tightly around his neck, his flesh now burning from the silver. "I have no master," I said, for the last time. And with one swift motion I jerked the whip back, ripping Vincent's head from his body.

I swayed, overcome with emotions as his head hit the earth. Devin came to me, taking my hand in his. "It's over, Sassandra. You did it."

Arubrey, Leslie, and Winona all came out of the house. They hugged me and they began to celebrate. I looked back to the oak tree and watched as another moon flower came to full bloom. I looked up to the sky to see the moon in all its glory. I thought of my parents and of Abraham. I hoped Omari was reunited with his family, and Jayden with his. I hugged all my friends again and thanked them for being part of my life. Leslie handed me the amulet that she retrieved from inside the house. It was still in perfect condition, "Esprit de la Mere", which Winona told me was French for, "Mind of the Mother" was still inscribed on the back of it. I put the golden chain around my neck and fastened it for the first time, letting the red stone rest against my chest, close to my heart.

Devin took hold of Leslie's hand and brought it to his lips, kissing it. "I want nothing more but your cold embrace," he said to her. Leslie beamed with happiness and pulled him in, kissing him on his lips. The kiss probably lasted too long for Devin but ended too quickly for Leslie, but they both seemed happy. I caught Leslie's eye and winked at my friend. I knew it was only a matter of time.

"Sass, you take a moment for yourself, ok? I'll collect Vincent's blood and I'll have Devin watch to make sure his body burns with the sunrise, which should be happening soon. Arubrey, Winona, can y'all pack up our belongings and take them inside the house? The sun's about to rise! Dev, sweety, can you stay out here and make sure Vincent's body and head burn? Just don't let his head get too close to his body, just in case."

I dreaded staying at this plantation but I knew I had to take shelter from the morning's sun. I walked up the steps and took the dreamcatcher off the door. I looked back at the oak tree to make sure Vincent was still dead. His body remained motionless and soon would burn in the morning sun. I put my hand on the doorknob, turned it, and pushed the door open. The nightmare was finally over.

ACKNOWLEDGMENTS

Writing my first book has been a rollercoaster of emotions. There have been several family members and friends who were right there with me during the twist and turns. When the ride went upside down and through dark tunnels, they still encouraged me to see it through until the very end.

My husband, James Skull, supported me when I wanted to leave my career to start a less demanding job in order for me to have more time and less stress so I could get back into writing. This book would not exist if I did not have his love and support.

My beta readers, Crystel Hamilton, Sylvia Darling, Tracy Miller, Vanessa Hoard, and Vanessa Parks, for letting me bug you nonstop about this story for well over a year.

All the graphic designers who competed for the cover design of this book. You all overwhelmed me (in a good way) with your talents. My editor, Casey Kaiser, for fixing my many, many, many, mistakes.

Dakota Parks for your graphic design skills and marketing ideas.

A sneak peek into the past…

Septenary Nights

The prequel of The Vampire's Drudge

EYE CONTACT

Sevin stood in the corner of the bedchamber, hidden within the flickering shadows from the candlelight. His chiseled body was motionless and could easily be overlooked by the eyes of mortals, or so he thought. The vampire could hear servants walking down the corridors of the castle, even though its walls were made of thick stone. That's one of the perks of being an immortal, heightened senses.

Prince Trevon entered his room and walked over to the high bed, getting ready to settle in for the night. The bed was large in size and Sevin watched in silence as the human climbed the stone steps up to his bed. He drew the purple curtains that enveloped the bed open and then stretched his arms wide, yawning from the strenuous day he had just endured. Being the Prince of New Spain did not come without responsibility; the same responsibilities Prince Trevon loathed. He wanted nothing more than to be free. Free from his duties and free from his family.

The vampire continued to watch the mortal prince with curiosity from the dark corner of the room. He had been watching him since the sun had set and found him quite intriguing. The human galaunt was remarkable at everything he did. He could tell that the king and queen were very proud of their son. They beamed as Prince Trevon put on a show to the Viceroyalty's guest of honor and even when he graciously let his younger brother win at both fencing and a game of chess. But as his mother cheered his younger brother on for winning and his father patted him on his back for letting the younger boy win, he seemed dissatisfied. His smile would quickly fade when his family quit watching him. Sevin wondered why Prince Trevon seemed so unhappy. This was the first human Sevin has encountered that captivated his attention. But Sevin pushed his lingering thoughts to the side and refocused on the mission he was hired for, which was to assassinate the prince. And that's exactly what Sevin was going to do. If the prince was so unhappy then the vampire would be doing him a favor by ending his life.

"Hola," the prince spoke. "I take you to be Fernando's replacement?"

This confused Sevin. Not because he did not understand

what the Prince of Spain was saying, but because there was no one else in the bedchamber with them. Was the prince speaking to himself? Surely, he had not noticed the vampire assassin lurking in the darkened corner. Sevin flashed his eyes over the room, double checking he wasn't talking to someone else he may have missed. No one else was in the room. They were alone, together.

Sevin took a step forward, out of the shadows. "Yes, Your Highness," the vampire said, bowing his head to the prince.

"I detest the formality. You may call me Trevon."

"I apologize Trevon, I hope I did not startle you standing in the shadows." Sevin responded, taking another step closer.

"Not in the least. You are immensely pale," Trevon said, starting to laugh as the word left his lips. "At first I thought you to be dead."

His laughter echoed throughout the bedchamber, bouncing off the stone walls. It was a sound that the assassin had never heard today until now, the sound of happiness. Sevin knew he would never forget the prince's laugh. And this saddened the vampire. Sevin also knew this would be the last time Prince Trevon ever laughed again.

"The jug and towels are over there," the prince said, pointing.

Sevin looked to where his outreached finger was pointing and automatically took a few steps toward the table where the jug had been placed before stopping in his tracks. What was he doing? He wasn't a servant. But this would allow him to get closer to the prince and make it easier, and less scary for the prince, to kill him. He wouldn't see it coming.

Sevin grabbed the two towels and the red painted glass container that was already full of water, and returned to kneel at the prince's bed. Prince Trevon had removed his outer garments and was now sitting on the steps with his dirty feet in the stone basin. Sevin looked down at the prince's feet, ready to strike.

"After you sponge my body, you may blow the candles out." the prince ordered the vampire.

Sevin looked up into Prince Trevon's brown eyes, forgetting everything as they made eye contact for the first time. A wave of emotion came over Sevin as he stared into Prince Trevon's eyes, not wanting to ever look away. The only thing he was sure of was that he would be willing to do whatever the prince asked of him tonight.

Maybe the vampire could let the prince live, just one more night...

www.ingramcontent.com/pod-product-compliance
Lightning Source LLC
Chambersburg PA
CBHW060225030726
47499CB00004B/1196